LOVE UNEARTHED

LOVE UNEARTHED

MICHAEL HARTWIG

Herring Cove Press

Contents

Prologue

Several years ago, I began to work on a historical novel about Rome in the 1500s. I wanted to find a more interesting way to inspire my college students to explore other religions, to ponder interfaith questions, and to examine the relationship between religion, philosophy, art, and archaeology. The story involved Cardinal Giovanni Salviati (a Medici) and an artist he brought to Rome, Francesco de' Rossi. Francesco gradually became known as Francesco Salviati, and I always thought there must be a love story there. I imagined a third principal character, Lucia Ruiz. Her parents were Iberian Jewish immigrants who died of the plague after several years in Rome. Lucia shared her father's facility for languages and became Salviati's in-house scholar and translator. She inherited a grimoire (a book of magic) and came to realize she was a sorcerer.

During the pandemic of 2020-2022, I began to write gay fiction. One of the early books I wrote, Oliver and Henry, involved the story of a college student raised by two women in Boston. Oliver goes to Rome to find his biological father, who he located through DNA tests and ancestry work. He discovers that Henry is a Roman Catholic priest, conservative, and engaged in work to thwart the Catholic Church's embrace of gay people. Their relationship unfolds in the shadows of the Vatican and involves a clash of very different worlds and ideological views. Despite their antipathy, Henry names Oliver heir to his sizable estate. Oliver meets Henry's financial advisor, Giancarlo, and they both fall in love. This helps Oliver resolve his own internal struggles about his sexual orientation. Their relationship intensifies, and Oliver discovers the wonders of Roman archaeology, art, and culture. Together, they face intrigue and tragedy involving Henry. Eventually, Oliver moves to Rome to live with Giancarlo and becomes an archaeologist.

I wrote a sequel to Oliver and Henry. A Roman Spell picks up five years later. Oliver and Giancarlo have a son, Luca, and they discover he has abilities, magical ones. I kept gravitating back to the unfinished historical novel and felt like Luca was speaking to me, wanting me to tell Lucia's story. Through a series of serendipitous twists and turns, Luca inherits Lucia's grimoire. Oliver and Giancarlo struggle with parenting a young wizard. When they have a second son, Francesco, they discover uncanny connections between their two boys, culminating in Luca donating marrow to save Francesco from a rare blood disease. The book recounts not only the magical story of Luca, Francesco, Oliver, and Giancarlo, but describes the enchantments of life in Rome.

Love Unearthed is the third book in the trilogy, Roman Bonds. Luca is now twenty-one and Francesco, sixteen. Luca has discovered he is gay. He meets an aristocratic contemporary, Donato, in front of a sarcophagus in the Vatican Museums – one that depicts Jesus as a magician. Their mercurial and passionate relationship unfolds against a clash of ideologies – the progressive one of Luca's family and the conservative one of Donato's. The plot thickens as Oliver and Giancarlo face a crisis in their own relationship and travel to Provincetown to celebrate Oliver's mothers' fiftieth anniversary. Can Donato break free from the controls of his father? Can Oliver and Giancarlo heal their differences? Can Luca find a lover who will not only embrace him as a gay man but as a wizard? Anna and Rita welcome everyone into their home and hope that Provincetown will work its magic.

The magical sarcophagus in this book actually exists and is part of the Vatican collection. There are several early Christian sarcophagi that depict Jesus using a wand-like instrument to perform miracles. Here's a link to the one that inspires this story:

http://www.rome101.com/Christian/Magician/pages/Vat31532_0000.htm

The sarcophagus of the two brothers also exists in the Vatican. Here's a link to that sarcophagus:

https://www.museivaticani.va/content/museivaticani/en/collezioni/musei/museo-pio-cristiano/sarcofagi-_a-doppio-registro/sarcofago-_dei-due-fratelli.html

In chapter thirteen, Praiano, the characters Patrizio, Pepe, Nunzia, and Zeno are characters from another one of my books, Old Vines. Without giving too much away in this prologue, Giancarlo crosses paths with them in Nunzia's pensione, the Belvedere, on the Amalfi Coast.

I want to thank those who have read the original draft and provided helpful feedback and suggestions.

A special thanks to Flavia Vitucci, a Roman guide and friend, who made edits to the Italian and whose academic and professional work on the Christian sarcophagi of Rome has been the subject of many fun and insightful conversations during visits to Rome over the years.

I

Chapter One – A Magical Sarcophagus

Luca felt a rush of air across the back of his neck and a sensation of warmth fill his chest. He had a gift for picking up energy and impressions that resided in ancient monuments, archaeological sites, and historic buildings. At first it was startling and unnerving but with some coaching when he was a child, he had learned to recognize what was happening and embrace it as a gift.

He looked up at the group of students standing in front of his father in the middle of the Pio-Christian section of the Vatican Museums. It was a modern exhibit hall built to showcase the world's largest collection of early Christian art – an assembly of funerary fragments and sarcophagi from as early as the third century. His father, an archaeologist, was leading a tour, and the group was standing in front of the magnificent Jonah sarcophagus – a tomb depicting the prophet Jonah being tossed overboard, swallowed by a sea monster, and spit out onto the shore where he reclined under rich foliage. The owners must have been wealthy to commission such a splendid piece, and they must have wanted to keep some of their neighbors in the dark as to their religious affiliation since the figure of Jonah looked very much like Endymion, a figure from Greek and Roman mythology who had been cast into a perpetual sleep by Zeus to preserve his youth and beauty.

Luca wondered if there was something about the sarcophagus he was sensing or if he had felt something from one of the students. He scrutinized the group of Americans who seemed only minimally interested in the exhibit. He imagined they couldn't wait to be outside again, eating gelato, sipping espresso, or meeting other young people from around the world in the Piazza Navona or at the Trevi Fountain.

No one seemed to be the source of his sensations, and he didn't feel any particular resonance with the sarcophagus. He pivoted and glanced up and down the line of tombs artfully placed on staggered risers and illuminated by large overhead windows. Just down the row, a young man stood in front of a large sarcophagus, one Luca was all too familiar with.

The minute Luca spotted him, the man looked up and Luca felt a pulse of energy graze the surface of his skin. Luca turned back toward his father to get his attention. He raised his brows, nodded, and left the group of students, walking toward the man who was crouching in front of the intricately carved marble surface.

The images were especially meaningful for Luca as they depicted Jesus as a magician, using a wand to change water into wine, multiply loaves, and raise Lazarus. During childhood, Luca came to realize he was a sorcerer, and the depiction of Jesus as a magician helped him embrace his identity more positively.

Luca walked nonchalantly toward the piece, gaining a closer view of the man. He looked roughly his own age – about 20 or 21.

He was tall, thin, aristocratic – wearing a white pressed shirt, vest, and gray slacks. He had a long neck and a graceful face with a prominent forehead, slender nose, and dirty blond hair. He looked like he might be northern Italian.

The man glanced at Luca, and their eyes connected. The man nodded and smiled as he proceeded to a large funerary fragment farther down the row. With some effort, Luca had learned to distinguish erotic chemistry from something deeper, more complex, something perhaps from another time or past life. The fellow was clearly handsome and appealing. He had an exotic and sophisticated aura that drew Luca in. But Luca felt his body become warm and calm and knew that meant they had been connected in another age. He sensed they had been friends, perhaps more. There also seemed to be a connection with the sarcophagus, as if perhaps they had stood before it in the past.

Luca pretended fascination with the artwork of the first sarcophagus the guy had been observing, leaning over it, and scrutinizing its etchings. When he looked back up, the man had wandered deeper into the hall, stopping at another piece, running his hands over the marble figures. He glanced toward Luca, who quickly pivoted, pretending to study what was in front of him when, in fact, he remained fascinated with this enigmatic man perusing the museum.

When Luca stood back up and glanced around, he saw no one. Suddenly, the man approached from behind the adjacent sarcophagus, and they stood facing each other. Startled, Luca nodded nervously and walked past him. As he did, he could feel intense heat and fought the urge to say something.

Luca returned to his father's tour group and watched the individual leave the gallery, disappearing almost as mysteriously as he had appeared. The students had become more engaged, chuckling as Oliver told anecdotes about the history of the collection. He smiled as he observed them swoon over his father's tan caramel skin, his blond hair, blue eyes, and trim athletic body. Even at 43, Oliver looked like a surfer from California but was, in fact, an academic nerd, always reading books and writing papers.

Once Oliver finished the tour, he and Luca left the museum and walked toward the nearby Borgo Pio for lunch. Warm spring sunshine bathed the Vatican walls. They passed countless tourists lining up to enter the museum, and walked into the adjacent medieval streets where, over the centuries, artisans and shopkeepers made a living serving pilgrims.

They entered one of their favorite restaurants, a modest establishment with stone walls, dark green shutters, and weathered wooden floors. Martino greeted them. *"Buon giorno! Professore! Luca! Tutte e due. Che piacere!"*

"The pleasure is all ours, Martino. How are you?"

"Benino," he replied with a jovial smile.

Oliver never tired of the enchantments of Rome. He treasured the intimacy of knowing the wait-staff by name and recognizing locals with whom he had eaten for two decades. Several nodded his direction – some older neighbors and others who worked in the Vatican – priests, librarians, and secretaries. The eternal city existed on two levels. There was the harried one filled with millions of tourists who fought each other for access to the great monuments of history — the Vatican, the Forum, the Colosseum, and countless museums, squares, fountains, and archaeological sites. The other comprised cozy neighborhoods, where locals strolled to the corner café to grab a croissant, espresso, and catch up with neighbors. Oliver spanned the two worlds, serving as a guide in one, and with his husband Giancarlo, raising two boys in the other.

Martino's hunched back and labored walk betrayed years of serving tables and keeping weighty secrets, confidences shared with him, or bits of information gleaned as he brought food to diplomats, cardinals, and politicians who dined at his restaurant.

He showed Oliver and Luca a table and they quickly ordered. "Can we get a nice mixed green salad and two bowls of carbonara?" Oliver asked as he glanced at Luca to see if he was of the same mind. Luca nodded.

"*Subito*," Martino said, rubbing his hand over Luca's shoulder and adding, "Your son is so grown up!"

"Hmm," Oliver said, glancing at his son apprehensively. He was proud of Luca, but lamented his passing childhood innocence. It seemed like just a short while ago he was five and they walked hand-in-hand through their old neighborhood of Trastevere. Now his son was a university student and had developed a mind of his own, increasingly more independent and inscrutable. As Martino retreated to the kitchen, Oliver looked over at his son and asked, "So, who was the guy at the museum?"

"You noticed him? He wasn't a figment of my imagination?"

Oliver nodded, chuckling.

"I don't know. I've never seen him before."

"And?"

"Well, I felt a connection."

"What kind?"

"Dad!"

"I'm just curious."

"I felt both a past life connection and some chemistry, as you and papa refer to it."

"He seemed interested in the sarcophagi. Not typical of someone your age."

"I know. That was odd to me. I first felt the connection when he was standing in front of the Abraham, Moses, and Jesus sarcophagus."

"Ah yes, Jesus the magician."

"I know the wands may have been inserted during restorations, but I still find the images comforting. Jesus is clearly a wonderworker and someone at some point in history didn't find anything discordant about portraying him as a sorcerer."

"So, you think there might be a connection from another time with this guy?"

Oliver chuckled to himself at how nonchalant it had become to refer to past lives or psychic phenomena with Luca. It was as if they were discussing everyday topics – weather, sports, or dinner plans. When they first noticed Luca's gifts, Oliver and Giancarlo were startled, bewildered, and concerned. Neither had grown up knowing people with such abilities and had always imagined raising boys who talked about sports, dates, vacations, and careers in finance, education, law, or medicine.

"Perhaps there was a connection. But he just disappeared. I'm not sure what that means."

Martino returned with salad, a carafe of wine, and some oil and vinegar. Oliver dressed the lettuce and Luca poured them both a glass of the local, crisp Frascati wine. "Cheers," he said as he lifted his glass to his father's.

"You still have the family gathering on your calendar for this weekend, right? Carlo and Maria have made reservations at the restaurant they love so much. It will be all of us together before everyone gets busy with summer activities."

"Yes. I'm free. The one you should be concerned with, though, is Francesco. He's always out with his friends."

Oliver glanced off into the distance. His younger son was entering the tough teenage years. He was sixteen going on twenty. He was always surrounded by attractive girls who hung on him as if he were a rock star. He had a busy social life with parties each weekend and soccer during the school week.

Francesco had inherited a blood disease that was under control after Luca donated bone marrow when they were both younger. During early childhood, Francesco was frail and thin but had developed into an athletic teen with wavy dark hair, expressive eyes, a prominent nose, and a luscious mouth.

The affectionate bond that had developed between Luca and Francesco in childhood gave way to a more distant but respectful camaraderie as they grew older. Francesco spent considerable effort differentiating himself from his fathers' and brother's sexual orientation even if, deep down, he admired and loved them. He was a head turner and had developed strategies for averting male attention, which he received often. This unnerved Luca from time to time as his tactics were sometimes misinterpreted as homophobic.

"Francesco assures me he'll be there. I told him how much it means to Maria and Carlo," Oliver noted.

"Is he coming with us this summer?" Luca inquired.

"He says yes, although I don't think he's too excited. He says there's nothing for him to do in Provincetown – no women to meet and no friends to hang out with."

"He'll make friends right away. He always does," Luca noted as he took a bite of salad.

"I know, but he's still apprehensive. So, back to the guy at the museum. Is he your type?"

"Dad!"

"Don't pretend you don't have a type. We all do."

"Well," Luca began tentatively. "There was something exotic about him. He had a noble appearance to him – tall, thin, long neck, prominent forehead. The blonde hair was striking – as I'm sure others have told you!"

Oliver blushed.

"Again, it's probably nothing. Another passing phantom amongst the ruins and monuments of Rome."

Oliver leaned his chin on the back of his hand, braced on the edge of the table. He was intrigued and wanted his son to continue.

"Don't look at me like that," Luca stated emphatically and playfully.

"I'm happy for you. I'm glad you're open to meeting someone again. You know, I was your age when I met your papa. We Monte-Fitzpatricks start young. Your grandmothers did, too."

"I'm in no hurry. I have my studies to finish and a practice to launch."

"I know I don't have to tell you this – but things will happen when they are supposed to."

"Yes, I know. Synchronicity or something like that."

"Precisely."

Martino returned to their table with two steaming bowls of carbonara. The creamy egg and cheese sauce coated the spaghetti and was peppered with crispy pieces of guanciale. Both dug into their dishes and, in unison, said, "Hmm! Delicious."

"So, when are exams?" Oliver interjected between forks of spaghetti.

"In two weeks."

"Are you ready?"

Luca nodded.

"And next year?"

"I have classes picked out."

"Are you going to study with Doctor Moretti?"

"Yes. In fact, he's agreed to work with me on my senior project. He's amazing."

"It is so fortunate you both connected. It's not often that a classically trained psychologist is open to psychic phenomena."

"I think he's one of us."

"You mean one of you?"

Luca nodded. "He's hinted at things – like sorcery, imagination, intuition, and even past lives. But he has to be careful. Even though he has academic tenure, he could be marginalized."

"And graduate school?"

"I want to get certified to do counseling so that I can combine the psychic work and hypnotism with classic psychotherapy."

"I'm so proud of you! Both of us are, even though Giancarlo isn't into this as much as I am."

"He's come a long way!"

"Indeed, he has!"

Martino came and removed their plates and offered them a bit of desert. Both shook their heads, striving to stay trim and fit.

"Well, I have another tour later this afternoon. What are you going to do?"

"I guess I'd better study. See you later for dinner?"

"Sounds good," Oliver replied.

"*Allora. Ciao.*"

"*A dopo.*"

They embraced, and each walked in opposite directions down the Borgo Pio.

2

Chapter Two – Introductions

Later that weekend, the family gathered for dinner at a local trattoria – a classic Roman establishment that served simple but delicious food on a large terrace where people ate *al fresco* enjoying the sensuous night air of Rome.

Giancarlo passed a plate of grilled meat to his sister and said, "Maria, why don't you and Carlo come to Ptown this summer? Anna and Rita have plenty of room."

Maria was a beautiful woman. She had aged well. She had silky brunette hair with blond highlights. Her skin was luminous. She had large expressive eyes framed with playful red glasses. Since she met Carlo, she shed much of her conservative lawyer image and had become more whimsical in how she dressed, using colorful scarves and accessories to project a more spirited personality.

She and Carlo moved from Milan to Rome to be with Luca and Francesco. Maria had served as the biological and surrogate mother for them both. With Francesco's health crisis, she wanted to play a more active parenting role than she had with Luca. Luca still called her *madrina* – godmother, but Francesco called her *ma*. Carlo was *Zio Carlo*, although he really served as their third father.

"That's very kind of you, Giancarlo, but we're going to Ischia with friends in August," she replied, passing the platter of food down to Oliver and the boys.

"We'll all miss you. Anna and Rita are planning a big celebration for their fiftieth anniversary," Oliver added.

"They've been together that long?" Carlo asked, furrowing his forehead.

Oliver nodded, glancing over at Francesco, who seemed bored with the conversation and was busy cutting into a juicy veal chop. Oliver gave Giancarlo a look. He got the message and asked, "Francesco, how did exams go?"

"*Tutto bene, papa*," he said, assuring him things had gone well. He avoided looking at him in the eyes.

"And this summer?" Giancarlo continued, trying to engage his younger son.

"I'm hanging out with my friends," he said casually.

"I can get you an internship at the bank if you like."

"I'm okay. Thanks."

Oliver and Giancarlo looked at each other and then gave Maria a look. She shrugged her shoulders. She looked over at Luca and noticed he was gazing off toward the other side of the terrace.

"Luca. What will you be doing this summer?" she asked, wanting to get his attention.

To Luca's great surprise, the guy he had spotted at the Vatican Museums was sitting a few tables away. He was with an older couple, probably his parents. There was a resemblance amongst them. Maria's question jolted him out of his daze. He turned back to his family and said, "Oh. I'm doing some research for school and some coaching with Rahel."

"Cool," she said. She poured herself and her husband, Carlo, more wine. "Are you going to spend any time in San Felice Circeo this summer?" she asked, turning toward her brother.

"I'm sure we'll go down at some point. And you?"

"Yes. We should coordinate our visits."

Oliver took a deep breath and scanned the table. It was one of those magical Roman nights when the air was pleasant and people were enjoying delicious food. Patio lights strung between several poles gave the area a festive atmosphere, and servers dashed back and forth from the kitchen carrying platters of grilled vegetables, meat, salads, risotto, and lots of wine.

Luca glanced back across the terrace, and Giancarlo followed his gaze. He raised his eyebrows and leaned quietly over to Oliver. "That's Signor Bianchi over there. He's one of the ministers of finance. Why is Luca looking at him?"

Oliver didn't have a direct view of the Bianchis. He casually stood and walked behind Maria, placed his hand on her shoulder and said to her, "What a wonderful evening. Thank you and Carlo for getting everyone together."

He nonchalantly gazed across the adjoining tables and noticed the focus of Luca's attention. He walked back to his chair, sat down, and whispered in Giancarlo's ear, "Luca and the Bianchis' son spotted each other at the Vatican Museums the other day. Luca seems intrigued by him."

Giancarlo looked alarmed. "Have they met?"

"No. They just noticed each other. Why?"

He leaned toward Oliver and said quietly, "Gerardo Bianchi is very conservative. I doubt he would be happy if his son became friendly with Luca. He only tolerates me because he must."

"Hmm," Oliver murmured to himself, glancing over at Luca. He sensed a bit of Italian theater would unfold before long. He hoped his son wouldn't be hurt.

Francesco perked up when a young woman sat at a nearby table. He sat more erect, held his shoulders back, and cocked his head slightly back. Predictably, she noticed him and winked. Francesco excused himself and went to the bathroom, returning past the young lady's table, giving her an intense look. Her parents noticed and looked over at Francesco's family, not sure what to make of them all.

As people finished their meals, servers came to remove plates and take dessert and coffee orders. The restaurant was known for its torta di ricotta – a rich cheesecake with soft raisins and a crumbly crust. Maria ordered a few pieces for the table, and everyone had an espresso. When they finished, Giancarlo rose and walked toward Signor Bianchi's table. Oliver followed behind.

"*Gerardo. Che sorpresa.*"

Gerardo stood and shook Giancarlo's hand warmly. Gerardo was tall and slim, with a long, slender nose and graying hair. He had an intense and wiry demeanor.

"Let me introduce my wife, Laura," he said as he placed his hand on the small of her back.

"*Piacere,*" Giancarlo said. "And this is Oliver," he added with a warm smile.

"*Piacere,*" both Gerardo and Laura said. Giancarlo always introduced Oliver as Oliver, never as partner or husband. He worked in the conservative banking environment. By now, everyone knew Giancarlo was gay and had a family with children, but it helped if he avoided the jarring word, husband.

"And these are our sons, Francesco and Luca."

"*Piacere,*" everyone said as they shook hands. Laura gave Oliver and Giancarlo a scrutinizing and curious look.

Gerardo then said, "And this is our son, Donato."

"*Piacere*," everyone repeated, as Oliver and Giancarlo extended their hands to him.

Luca and Donato stood facing each other, unsure whether to say something to one another. Donato was more casually dressed than he had been at the museum, and Luca had a difficult time not gazing mouth agape at him. His hazel eyes were dreamy, surrounded by pronounced brows. A few locks of his dirty blond hair fell playfully over his forehead. He wore a tight-fitting pullover, and his classy jeans partially concealed tan leather loafers. He seemed nervous, his eyes darting back and forth evasively. Luca stared, hoping Donato might finally return his regard.

He did. Their eyes connected, and Luca felt Donato's curiosity. He noticed Donato furtively glancing at his chest. Luca was glad he had worn a slim tailored shirt. Donato continued scrutinizing Luca's body, noticing his upper legs pressed against the fabric of his jeans and the hint of round, firm buttocks behind.

Luca smiled self-consciously as their gaze became awkwardly protracted. He took a deep breath and pierced the silence, saying, "I saw you the other day at the Vatican Museums when my father was giving a tour. Are you an archaeology student?"

Donato blushed, then chuckled nervously, saying, "No, but I like history. And you?"

"I was just there accompanying my dad, who is an archaeologist."

"Wow. I didn't realize," he replied as he scrutinized Luca's father standing just behind Giancarlo.

Laura walked toward the street, accustomed to giving her husband time to speak with clients.

Donato continued to stand near Oliver and Luca. As he stood poised and quiet, most would have thought him aloof, but Luca was quick to pick up on his shyness and attempted to engage him. Luca asked his dad, "Maybe Donato could join one of your upcoming tours? Do you have anything interesting coming up?"

Oliver rubbed his chin thoughtfully and said, "Next Thursday we are visiting an underground site that was recently opened. Would you like to come?"

Donato smiled and nodded. "That's very gracious of you."

Luca had been scribbling something on a small card. He reached over and gave it to Donato and said, "Here's my father's card and my contact information. Let us know how to be in touch with you, and we will send you details."

Donato glanced at the card and blushed. He looked up at Luca and nodded warmly. Maria and Carlo were already standing along the street, waiting for everyone else. Giancarlo finished his conversation with Gerardo. They all nodded to each other in making their exit. Luca glanced back at Donato as he stepped out onto the street with his parents, giving him a protracted, intense look.

Back at home, Francesco went to his room, where he buried himself in social media.

Giancarlo and Oliver sat in the living room and clicked on a movie. Giancarlo was nervous about Luca having met Gerardo's son. Gerardo Bianchi was not only a conservative banker and politician, but he was also active in several organizations that lobbied against gay rights. "I hope Luca doesn't get his hopes up about this Donato guy. I don't think there's a future in it. His father will never tolerate their friendship."

"He seems like a nice boy — handsome and smart. Luca seems attracted to him. You could see the excitement in his face. If we say something to discourage him, it will only make him more determined to pursue him."

"Do you think he's gay?" Giancarlo asked.

"There wasn't any protracted eye contact, but since I'm increasingly invisible, that's not much of a sign."

"You're hardly invisible!"

"But he seemed to have that gay boy infatuated look on his face when he and Luca faced each other. He has impeccable taste in clothes and had a special way of standing – a kind of regal look. Although, you know, all you handsome Italian men look gay to me. It's hard to tell."

Giancarlo gave Oliver a playful glare. Then he said, "Hmm. Let's keep an eye on Luca. If need be, I can always run some interference through work connections."

Luca finished sorting some things in the kitchen. He grabbed a glass of water and passed through the living room toward the stairs leading to the study and his room.

"Good night," he said to his fathers. "It was a nice evening."

"Yes," Oliver said.

"Tell me more about this Donato guy," Giancarlo interjected. "Where did you meet him?"

"At the Vatican Museums, just in passing. He seems like a nice guy."

"Yes. He does," Giancarlo nodded. "His father is quite well known. Unfortunately, he's active in lobbying against gay marriage, gay rights, and other progressive social issues."

"Hmm," Luca said. "I didn't realize that. And you are friends?"

"Not exactly. We cross paths because of his work as a minister of finance and my work at the bank. He puts on a good face."

"Maybe his son is different," Luca suggested.

Giancarlo nodded. "Yes. One would hope."

"Well, good night."

"See you in the morning," Oliver added.

Luca went to the study and sat in one of the easy chairs. He searched on the internet for information about Gerardo Bianchi and, sure enough, he was quite the conservative. He still hoped he might hear from Donato, and finally, a text appeared on his phone.

"Luca. This is Donato. Nice to meet you at the restaurant. You have a nice family."

Luca was surprised Donato mentioned his family. He replied in a text, "Nice to meet you and your family, too. Amazing that our fathers know each other."

Donato was used to meeting people his father knew, since his father was such a public figure in the government. What had surprised Donato was that Luca's family was gay – that he had two fathers. He had scrutinized his father's reaction when he met Oliver. His father had bristled but concealed his discomfort carefully. He was always the diplomat.

"When is your father's tour?" Donato texted, trying to extend the conversation.

"Next Thursday. 10 in the morning. We meet at Santa Maria in Cosmedin. Hope you can come."

"I'll be there," Donato replied. He feared the conversation would end. He tried to find another thread of common interest and asked, "Are you at the university?"

"Yes, and you?"

"Yes. I'm studying finance, as you might imagine."

"Me, psychology."

"Do you have exams soon?"

"In two weeks. You?"

"Same."

"Well, I better get back to studying," Luca noted, not sure where to take the conversation.

"Me, too. See you next Thursday?"

"*Si. Ci vediamo.*"

3

Chapter Three – A Face From the Past

Luca stood outside Santa Maria in Cosmedin, a venerable church at the edge of one of the more historic areas of Rome. The current structure had been built on top of an earlier one that had been a *diaconia*, a place where early Christians provided charity for poor Romans. The basilica was known for the large piece of ancient Roman marble called the *Bocca della Verita* – the mouth of truth – affixed to the wall under the portico. It was made famous in the movie Roman Holiday when Gregory Peck put his hand in the marble mouth as Audrey Hepburn looked on.

He noticed Donato's lanky yet graceful body walking toward him on the sidewalk lining the busy street. As he caught sight of him, he felt his heart race and his pulse quicken. He seemed even more handsome than he recalled from their brief encounters. Donato smiled and waved when he saw Luca.

Donato crossed the street and approached Luca. Both felt

awkward, unsure whether to embrace or shake hands. Donato extended his hand, which Luca shook warmly. Then Luca affectionately took Donato's upper arm and led him across the street to where Oliver was preparing to lead the group of guides into the new excavations. "Come. Everyone is gathered inside."

"Thanks for inviting me," Donato said as they darted between cars.

"I'm so glad you could join us. My father has been waiting for this for some time. Archaeologists are excited about the structures from ancient Rome that were uncovered. The group comprises guides who hope to include this in future tours."

They walked inside just as the tour was about to begin. A local archaeologist made introductions and then Oliver led everyone down an iron staircase to a surface about 10 meters below the current building's foundations. Lights had been strung along ancient brick walls covered in decorative plaster. The floor was uneven but covered in ornate black and white mosaic tile. They walked through what was described as a home dating from imperial Roman times.

Luca's interest in Donato distracted his heightened intuition. In similar settings, he usually picked up impressions or feelings from former ages. His psychic coaches had concluded that Luca had a gift for time travel, not in the science fiction sort of way, but in the sense that he moved back and forth in consciousness – tapping into his self as it existed in other ages or was unfolding in the future. He also was adept at scanning time at historical sites, picking up on events, people, and conversations that had taken place in them. But today, trailing just behind Donato, all he could think about was holding Donato's hand, embracing him, rubbing his nose in the blond hair on the back of his neck, and whispering in his ear. It was an unusual sensation; one he hadn't felt for some time.

He still wasn't sure Donato was gay. If not, he hoped Donato didn't see through him, see him undressing him with his eyes. But the fact that Donato came to the tour and seemed excited, even a bit giddy, was encouraging.

The group stopped in a room where rich frescos decorated a dining room wall. The lead archaeologist provided detailed commentary. Luca noticed how captivated his father was and how he provided additional context and information to participants. He glanced over at Donato, who was equally absorbed in the presentation. The dim lighting cast a curious glow on Donato's face, and as had happened to Luca in similar settings, Donato's face began to change shape. Luca's teachers had explained how another level of consciousness takes over when traditional senses blur. If one lets go of one's attachment to the present, other dimensions of the self, particularly those rooted in other times, can emerge.

Donato's face became rounder. His eyes darkened, his hair became coarser, and his lips pressed closed. Donato turned toward Luca, and Luca gasped for air as Donato's eyes, actually eyes within his eyes, gazed at him. His stare was friendly, tender, and warm. Donato was clearly a dear friend from another age, and they recognized each other.

The intensity of their regard startled Luca. He looked off into the distance to dispel the impression and return to the current moment. When he glanced back at Donato, he saw the long angular fair face of his new friend who smiled innocently at him, Donato apparently oblivious to their momentary flashback. Luca's heart raced. He took several deep breaths to calm himself down and focused his attention on his father's lecture.

The tour continued for another half an hour and ended with a small reception in the building under which the excavations had taken place. Oliver was engrossed in conversation with his colleagues, and Luca was eager to uncover more about his new chum.

He led Donato outside. It was a beautiful day. The sun was warm, and a gentle breeze blew through the majestic umbrella pines hanging over the roadway.

"What did you think?" Luca asked.

"It's amazing, and your dad is very knowledgeable. I can't believe the structure is so well-preserved."

"I know. It's like a window to another time," Luca added.

"Hmm," Donato murmured. "The more things change, the more they stay the same," he added.

"I could see myself in that house with the tile floors, the frescoed walls, and the courtyard with a fountain."

Donato raised his brows but struggled to say more.

Luca sensed an awkward pause and interjected, "I have an idea. Do you have any plans this afternoon?"

Donato was taken aback by Luca's enthusiastic and quick shift of subject, and nodded no.

"Do you want to go to the beach?" Luca asked, surprised at his own forwardness and spontaneity.

He had clearly stepped beyond his comfort zone. He had only dated once, at the *liceo*, Italy's version of high school. There was a guy on the swim team he liked. Gino was handsome and had an affable personality. People loved to be with him, and he liked being with Luca. They got close, even to the point that Luca invited Gino to Courmayeur when the family went skiing. They shared interests in sports, but not much else. Gino wanted to study law and, when he found out that Luca wanted to study psychology since he was a psychic, he freaked out and broke up with him.

Since then, Luca had buried himself in his studies. He hung out with his swimming buddies, but never pursued anyone again. He knew he had to get past his hurt and reticence, but no one had ever interested him enough to pursue things – until he met Donato.

Donato stared at Luca, waiting for more explanation. He was eager to get to know Luca, too, and wondered what Luca had in mind.

"My family has a house at San Felice Circeo. It's a beautiful day, and I don't feel like studying. We could spend the afternoon there and come back later."

Donato nodded. "Sure. Sounds like fun. But I'm hardly dressed for the beach."

"Not a problem. I have extra shorts and swimsuits there. We can change, walk along the beach, or take a swim in the pool."

Donato's eyes widened. Then he asked, "How do we get there?"

Luca stared at a car parked just outside the archaeological site. "My dad's car!"

"He won't mind?"

"No," Luca said, certain that his dad would be delighted if he knew his son was pursuing someone. "*Andiamo?*"

"*Sì.*"

Luca went inside, got keys from Oliver, and returned, inviting Donato to take a seat on the passenger side. They quickly sped off into Roman traffic, passing the Circus Maximus, the Baths of Caracalla, and finally through the Roman walls toward the coast.

The proximity of their bodies in the close quarters of the front seat forced a level of intimacy that was anxiety producing for both. Luca felt heat emanate from Donato's body and could almost hear his heartbeat. When he shifted gears, he couldn't help noticing Donato's muscular thighs pressing against his jeans. Luca turned up the AC fan and clicked on some music to fill the tense space between them.

Donato leaned against the door to gain some distance himself. He was used to driving in close quarters with teammates to meet up with friends, but he didn't know how to handle this novel situation.

Luca was a new acquaintance; someone he barely knew. Yet he sensed there was an implied familiarity, almost as if he and Luca were old friends reconnecting.

The music relaxed them both. "So, you like Eros?" Donato asked, surprised that Luca was playing one of his favorite musicians.

"Yeah, and you?"

"Him and Laura Pausini," Donato replied.

"A romantic, huh?"

Donato blushed and rocked his upper torso to the beat of the music. "British? American?" Donato asked casually.

"Gaga, Sting, Elton, and a new group, Chvrches, from Scotland."

"Did you see the Netflix series, Heartstopper? They have a song in the soundtrack," Donato inquired excitedly.

Luca took a deep breath and griped the steering wheel. Donato may have looked like he was cut from the same conservative cloth as his father, but if he had been watching Heartstopper – a series about two British high school boys who fall in love – he was on Luca's team. Luca fought every urge to reach over and take Donato's hand, affirming their affinity, but he checked himself and simply turned toward him and smiled warmly, nodding.

Donato's body relaxed. He pulled himself away from the door, settling into the middle of the passenger seat. He leaned his head back and savored the serenity of being with someone who seemed to resonate deeply with him. He wasn't sure Luca was gay, but his fathers were, and each time Luca looked at him, there was warmth and affection.

Luca shifted the car into a higher gear as they merged onto a back road with no traffic. As he did, he let his right hand graze the edge of Donato's leg, and they both felt the sensation. Neither said a word, both settling into a realization of their growing attraction for each other.

Soon, they approached San Felice Circeo, an upscale seaside resort built at the edge of a national park along the Mediterranean. Luca made his way through the village and up an incline, passing posh villas lining the road. He pulled up to an entrance, punched in a code, and then drove inside the compound as the double gate opened.

Luca's great grandfather had built a villa on a hill overlooking the sea. Giancarlo and his cousins each had a suite with unobstructed views of the town and coastline. A large kitchen and living room filled the ground level, where a stone deck led to a large pool. "This is amazing," Donato exclaimed as they pulled up to the front of the house.

Luca was surprised at Donato's reaction, since he assumed his affluent and well-connected family must have had something even more impressive. Luca responded, "It's nice. We enjoy coming here and spending time with extended family. I'm sure you all must have something like this, too."

Donato shook his head. "We have an apartment in Courmayeur, in the Alps, but nothing along the sea. My parents are not beach people. We get invited to others' homes, but we tend to go to the mountains in the summer.

"Hmm," Luca murmured, the wheels in his head turning now that he knew Donato must be a skier, like him. He continued, "Come on. Let's change."

Luca unlocked the door and led Donato up to his family's suite. He searched through the dresser and found swim trunks for them both. He threw one at Donato, who caught it midair. Donato retreated to the bathroom and changed. When he came out, Luca had already put on his suit. They both stared at each other with intense curiosity.

Luca was a swimmer and had a broad chest, well-defined pecs, and a soft coat of dark hair that covered his torso. Donato's eyes widened as he noticed the contours of Luca's sex pressed against the soft fabric of his suit.

Luca was surprised by Donato's lean body and the muscular thighs pressing against the legs of his suit. It had been two years since he felt such a strong stirring for someone, and he wasn't sure how to proceed.

"*Vuoi andare alla spiaggia o in piscina?*" he asked Donato, wondering if he preferred the beach or the pool.

"Don't you think the ocean will be too cold this time of the year? The pool is heated, right?" Donato responded.

Luca nodded. "*Allora, la piscina*," Luca said as he walked downstairs and out onto the deck, diving into the pool.

Donato followed, enthusiastically leaping from the edge and plunging into the turquoise blue water. He swam up to Luca and splashed him playfully. Luca reciprocated, placing his hand on top of Donato's head, and pressing him under water.

Donato pushed back against Luca's chest, taking delight in the well-formed pecs he felt under his hands. He felt himself become aroused as their bodies thrashed back and forth in the playful exchange, Luca clearly formidable.

Donato swam toward the other edge of the pool, and Luca followed. They rested their heads on the lip of the pool and relished the warm sunshine beating down on their faces. Luca observed their bodies floating before them – his dark and tan, Donato's light and golden.

"It's beautiful," Donato mused as he looked up at the deep blue sky.

"I feel very fortunate being able to come here. I love the view of the coastline, the scrubby pine trees of the nearby park, and the soft sand lining the beach. My brother, cousins, aunts, and uncles all gather here for holidays and birthdays. It's a happy place for me!"

Donato turned toward Luca and smiled tenderly. Donato's hazel eyes glistened, and the blond tufts of his hair had already begun to bounce back as the water dripped from them. Luca wanted to reach over and twirl his finger in one of them, but held back.

Donato found it difficult to keep from staring at Luca's face – round, boyish, and playful as dimples formed when he smiled – and, at the same time, intense and manly as a thin dark beard lined his jaw and circled his luscious mouth. Then Donato was struck by a fascinating oddity amongst southern Italians and asked, "*Come mai?*"

"*Cosa?*"

"*I tuoi occhi azzurri!*"

"I got them from my dad, Oliver. He's got blue eyes, too," Luca said matter-of-factly, trying to defuse an intensifying allure that was developing between them.

Donato pushed off the wall and swam toward the other side. His body glided smoothly along the surface and his arms moved gracefully from one stroke to the other. Luca surmised he was a fellow swimmer and followed him.

When they got to the other side, Luca asked, "So, you must be a competitive swimmer?"

"Yea. How did you know?"

"Recreational swimmers don't stroke like that."

"You?"

Luca nodded. "Breast and freestyle."

"Backstroke and freestyle," Donato responded.

"How did we never cross paths at swim meets here in Rome?" Luca inquired.

"We lived in Milan. My father had an apartment in Rome, but my mother and I remained in Milan where I went to school. We moved here just two years ago."

With new information about his athletic past, Luca scrutinized Donato's body as he stood in the shallow end. He had slim hips and a muscular abdomen, evidence of his backstroke specialty. His shoulders were broad and his back well-developed. He glanced down and tried to imagine him in a Speedo and felt his pulse accelerate. "*Vuoi fare una gara – quattro giri?*" Luca asked, daring him to a race.

Donato nodded. He bent over and took off his trunks, tossing them on the deck.

Luca's eyes widened. "You're taking this seriously! Are you sure you can handle the competition?" Luca pulled off his trunks and tossed them near Donato's.

They both leaned against the wall and crouched forward. "Four laps. Ready, set, go!" Luca shouted.

Both pushed off the wall and stroked vigorously across the pool. They arrived at the other side at roughly the same time. Luca made a quicker flip turn and pushed ahead of Donato. Donato tightened his muscles and pressed his palms firmly against the water, catching up to Luca. They both were neck to neck in the third lap and, after the last turn, Donato pulled ahead. He beat Luca by a few centimeters and stood up jubilantly.

Luca recovered his breath and extended his hand to Donato in congratulations. Donato pulled him close in an embrace, and their cocks grazed each other just under the surface of the water. Both stared at each other, their regards filled with both longing and trepidation, neither certain of the next move.

"You're fast!" Luca said.

"And you're a formidable rival."

They both chuckled. Then Luca interjected, gazing into Donato's eyes, "*Vuoi un café o qualcosa da mangiare?*"

Donato was relieved their afternoon together might be extended, but he wanted to give the impression that he was simply hanging out, without an agenda. He said, "Don't make a fuss. I'm not that hungry."

"It's nothing. We could have a plate of pasta and some wine."

"*Allora. Andiamo?*"

They leaped out of the pool. Luca bent over and grabbed both suits. Donato gazed at Luca's back and buttocks, glistening in the sun. He felt himself stir. Luca pivoted and tossed Donato's suit to him, looking at his ample veinous cock, slightly darker than his golden skin. Donato stepped into his suit, raising his brows as Luca continued to watch. Luca quickly turned sideways, slipped on his suit, and then went inside to get towels.

As they dried, Luca searched the kitchen for wine, coffee, and some sauce for pasta. "*Ecco,* here's some meat sauce my dad makes," he said as he pulled a container out of the freezer.

"Is there a place for me to change?" Donato asked.

"Upstairs. If you need any shorts or shirt, help yourself."

Donato went upstairs while Luca began to prepare the food. Donato rummaged through Luca's drawers and found a cute pair of shorts and a tee-shirt. He sniffed them, hoping to capture Luca's distinctive scent. He put them on and returned downstairs.

Luca's eyes widened as he saw Donato in his shorts. "They look better on you than on me!"

Donato blushed. "Anything I can do to help?"

"Can you stir this while I go upstairs and change?"

Donato nodded, and Luca ran quickly upstairs to change. He returned in a pair of jeans and a sweatshirt from Boston.

Luca poured them each a glass of wine and said, "*Salute!*"

Donato raised his glass and nodded. "I can't believe our fathers know each other."

"It's a small world."

"I guess they're in the same world of finance," Donato observed. "It was nice to meet your family the other night."

"Hmm," Luca replied. "And yours, too."

"So, what's it like?" Donato asked.

"What?" Luca replied.

"How is it having two dads?"

At first, Luca was taken aback by Donato's blunt question and feared he might share his father's antipathy. Luca was used to the question and gave his standard answer. "I don't even think about it. It's always been my life. My fathers love me. I love them. *Basta.*"

"Did you ever have trouble in school or with neighbors?"

Luca thought back to elementary school when his classmates made fun of his drawing two fathers in art class and shouted *frocio* - faggot - at him. At the time, it was traumatic, but over the years, those incidents were less frequent, and the naturalness of his family dominated his own sense of self. He shook his head no.

"And you?" Luca asked.

Luca's question startled Donato, and he feared he was being coaxed into coming out. Evasively, hoping to distract Luca, he answered, "Having a father who is in politics is a challenge, as you can imagine."

Luca nodded, realizing Donato was avoiding other questions.

"There were clear expectations laid out about my comportment in public," Donato continued. "I've always been on a short leash and under intense scrutiny."

Luca took note of Donato. He was just like his father — elegant, refined, and privileged. Luca was typically attracted to guys who were more athletic, casual, and unpretentious. But there was something about Donato that drew him in. He gazed into his eyes – hazel, expressive, fiery. There was a certain heat that emanated from him. He could feel it – an energy or intensity rising from a furnace deep within. On the outside, he appeared calm, cool, collected. But it was only a façade, and he was eager to find out more.

"Where are you from?" Luca pressed to find out more.

"Milan, of course."

"Why, of course?"

"Banking. Finance. Fair skin."

"I hadn't noticed," Luca said playfully.

Donato raised his eyebrow and followed with, "And you?"

"Here. Roma."

Donato squinted in disbelief.

"Well, it's a bit more complicated."

"I thought so," Donato noted.

"My dad is American, and my father is Roman."

"You use two different words for your fathers."

"Yes. I grew up calling one dad and the other father or, I should say, papa."

"And mother?" Donato asked hesitatingly.

"My papa's sister, Maria. My parents did artificial insemination using Oliver's sperm. Maria wanted children but didn't want to be a full-time mother, so she served as a surrogate for my fathers."

"And how did all of that turn out?"

"It's been wonderful. My brother had a blood disease, so Maria moved to Rome to be more involved. Since he was young, I have had two fathers, a mother, and Carlo, who we call *zio*."

"It isn't confusing?"

"No. In fact, it's more like historic households that included cousins, aunts, uncles, parents, and grandparents. Kids used to be raised by multiple adult figures."

Donato fussed nervously with his glass. Without looking at Luca, he timidly asked, "And you?" He cleared his throat. "Are you?" He left the end of the question unspecified, but it was clear he wanted to know if Luca was gay.

Luca was used to the question and replied without hesitation, "Yes. I'm gay."

Donato took a deep breath, almost as if Luca's answer made sense to him. He assumed a kid raised by two fathers would end up being gay.

Luca then added pointedly, "My brother, Francesco, is straight."

Donato's face twitched, and Luca noticed. Luca added, "Kids turn out like they do in straight families. Straight parents produce gay and straight kids. Gay parents produce gay and straight kids. Sexual orientation is a given. It's not something you learn or pick up from your parents."

"Yes. I know," Donato said, trying to convey to Luca he was more enlightened than his questions made him seem.

Luca was dying to ask Donato about his sexual orientation. The more they sat together, the more he could feel Donato's internal struggle. He sensed their coming together was, in fact, significant. He believed he was there to help Donato come out, to embrace his sexuality. He also sensed it would be a tortuous process. For the moment, he just wanted to enjoy the afternoon and not force things. In fact, if Donato was to come out, it would only be once he had become comfortable with him and with other gay people, and Luca would need to make it look unremarkable.

Luca gave the sauce another stir and dropped some pasta into the boiling water. He glanced out through the large windows at the sea and shifted subjects. "It's so magical here. I love the views."

"Hmm," Donato replied. "It's amazing. Thanks for inviting me. I'm so glad we met." He smiled warmly at Luca.

Luca was taken aback and yet encouraged by Donato's sentiments. He smiled and said, "So, what were you doing in the Pio-Christian section of the Vatican museums? Not too many people our age stroll through there."

Donato blushed. "I like archaeology."

"But you're studying finance."

"I must. It's my parents' dream for me."

"But don't you get to pursue your own dreams?"

"It's complicated."

"Hmm," Luca murmured.

"I like to visit the museums in Rome. It's a pleasant break from studies."

"Me, too. Although it's always been a part of my life since my dad is an archaeologist."

"And you're studying psychology to be a therapist?"

"Of sorts."

Donato raised his brows. Luca didn't elaborate.

"Do you have a favorite museum?" Luca asked.

"I love the Palazzo Massimo and the Capitoline Museums."

"Me, too," Luca blurted out enthusiastically. "Why the Pio-Christian section of the Vatican Museums the other day?"

"Someone mentioned the early Christian sarcophagi to me. I decided to check them out."

"And?"

"They are amazing. The art is impressive for so early in Christian history."

"Any memorable pieces?"

Donato looked off into the distance. He turned back toward Luca and said, "Two of them."

"Which?"

"There was the one of the two brothers. It was a beautiful piece, but I thought it fascinating that in the center where one would normally find carvings of a husband and wife, there were two men. The museum plaque says it's two brothers, but what brothers would represent themselves that way or even be buried together? Wouldn't one or both of them have had wives? I'm thinking it must have been two male lovers."

The ease at which the words 'two male lovers' flowed off Donato's tongue was encouraging to Luca. Perhaps Donato was so inclined.

"And the other?" Luca asked, intending to return to the two brothers later.

"The one where you noticed me."

Luca swallowed and felt his heart pounded rapidly. If Donato could recall the very place they had first noticed each other, things were promising. He took another look at Donato, at his angular face, his long neck, and his full lips. What would it be like to kiss him?

"You mean the Abraham, Moses, and Jesus piece?"

"You know the name of it?"

"It really doesn't have a name, but it's well known and features prominently in a lot of studies."

"Tell me more."

"It's boring and terribly academic. Let's save it for another time," Luca said, wanting to avoid the inevitable discussion of Jesus the magician.

The pasta was ready. Luca drained it and tossed it in the sauce, sprinkling some parmesan cheese on top and handing Donato a steaming bowl.

Donato inserted a fork into the pile of spaghetti, twirled it, and then lifted it to his mouth.

"Hmm. Delicious!"

"*Grazie*," Luca replied. Then he asked casually, "*Fidanzata?*"

Donato nodded no, avoiding a protracted explanation of his dating history. He didn't have a girlfriend, nor did he have a boyfriend. His parents had introduced him to many of their well-connected friends' daughters, but he never pursued anyone, male or female.

"And you?"

"*Nessuno.* No one."

"*Mai?* Never?"

"There was someone earlier, but it was a short thing. It didn't go anywhere."

"You? Before? You must have had the girls chasing you."

Donato blushed. He evasively took a long sip of wine and shook his head no. "I've been too busy with school."

Luca stared at him, his hand holding up his fork in anticipation of an elaboration. Donato felt the implied curiosity and sighed heavily. "Plus, I've been trying to sort things out."

"What kind of things?" Luca asked, already knowing the answer.

"Preferences."

"Ah," Luca said without making Donato any more uncomfortable than he already was. But he knew Donato wanted to come out, that he needed to come out, so he decided to help him. "Do you think you are gay?" he asked without softening the bluntness of the question.

Donato's eyes turned red. He nodded timidly, choked with emotion.

"*Bravo. Un primo passo.*" Luca recognized that first steps were always difficult. As a teenager, even with gay dads, he struggled to declare his orientation. "If it's any consolation, it was difficult for me, too."

"How? You have a gay family," Donato said, wiping a tear from the corner of his eye.

"It's never easy. Although I imagine in your family, it might be a bit more challenging."

Donato chuckled nervously. "Precisely. My parents expect me to walk in their footsteps – degree in finance, career in banking, wife and kids, then politics."

"What do you want?"

"It doesn't matter."

"Of course it does."

"No. You don't understand. It's impossible to deviate from the script."

"It might be difficult, but you can do it."

Donato shook his head. He took a sip of wine, sighed deeply, and slouched back in his chair. "*Mi dispiace.* I didn't want to unload all of this on you."

"Don't apologize. I'm honored that you feel like you could trust me."

"I've never admitted things to anyone before."

"Why me? You hardly know me."

"I don't know. Maybe it's because I don't know you that it's easier. But," Donato paused. He struggled to formulate the words. Then he said, "When I saw you in the museum the other day, I felt an odd connection. Then when I saw you at the restaurant yesterday, the sensation was even stronger. It's as if I already knew you."

Now, more than ever, Luca was convinced they had a connection in another life. But he didn't want to frighten Donato any more than he already was. He just nodded and smiled warmly.

"That's weird, isn't it?" Donato elaborated.

"No. It's not."

"Maybe we met at the university?" Donato asked.

"No. I think I would have remembered," Luca said warmly.

Donato blushed and lifted his wineglass to take a long sip, trying to avoid Luca's mesmerizing eyes.

They finished their pasta and wine. Luca rose to clear dishes. He went to the sink, and Donato followed. As Luca rinsed dishes, Donato took a dishtowel and dried them. At one point, Donato reached for a dish in Luca's hand and placed his hand on top of Luca's, gazing into Luca's eyes.

Luca wanted to kiss Donato's luscious mouth, but held back, not wanting to force things or make Donato uncomfortable. Donato, without hesitation, leaned toward Luca and gave him a warm kiss. "I've been wanting to do that all afternoon."

Luca set the dish in his hand down and placed his hands on Donato's shoulders, squeezing them affectionately. "You have such beautiful eyes," Luca said.

"Yours are piercing and haunting," Donato replied.

"No straight man says that," Luca observed. Donato blushed and chuckled.

Donato rubbed his hands over Luca's chest. Luca closed his eyes and savored the feel of Donato's warm, strong hands gliding over his body. It had been years since he had come out, but there had been only limited exchanges with guys. He felt his body spring to life, his skin vibrating intensely.

Luca leaned toward Donato and pressed his mouth around Donato's luscious lips, feeling the warm, wet contours of his mouth. Donato rubbed his hands along Luca's back and pulled him close.

Luca melted in Donato's embrace. He opened his eyes. They gazed at each other for a protracted period until both became nervous about the intensifying longing between them. Donato was hesitant to do more, and Luca didn't want to push things.

"What a nice surprise," Donato said warmly.

Luca nodded and said, "*E allora?*" He hoped Donato might want to do more, but resigned himself to a simple exchange.

"Should we get going soon?" Donato asked awkwardly, nervously.

Luca stared deeply into Donato's eyes. He nodded stoically. "I'll finish the dishes if you want to get your things."

Donato went upstairs, folded his pants and shirt, but kept wearing Luca's shorts and tee-shirt. When he returned, Luca noticed and beamed.

"Do you need any help here?" Donato asked, looking at the counter.

"No. All set. Let me go upstairs and use the bathroom, and then we can head back to town."

Donato looked at him sadly. "I know," Luca remarked. "I had a good time."

"Me, too. I hope we can do it again."

"*Senz'altro.*"

Luca went upstairs and returned with his things. They got into the car and drove to the city where Luca left Donato at his parents' house in the Prati neighborhood.

4

Chapter Four – First Date

A few weeks later, Luca texted Donato. "*Ciao. Come stai?* Did you finish exams? Do you want to celebrate?"

He had been eager to see Donato after their first outing, but had been busy with schoolwork and didn't want to appear too enthusiastic about their seeing each other again, fearing he might frighten Donato away. In the interim, they had exchanged texts and had befriended each other on social media.

Luca spent an inordinate amount of time searching through Donato's photos on various media platforms. At first, he had been discouraged by the number of affectionate selfies Donato had taken with women, but then concluded that at least there weren't any with men. The competition was nonexistent. Luca increased his workout time, fussed over his hair, and read up on gay relationships. Although his dads had shared information about sex when he was younger, the questions now were more personal, particular, and embarrassing. He would get his information online.

Donato had had a difficult time concentrating on his studies.

He daydreamed of Luca, fantasizing about their first kiss, his first kiss of a man. He, too, had downloaded photos onto his phone. He mused on their fun afternoon - how natural it felt being with Luca, how easy it was to talk with him, and how alive he felt in his presence. He craved Luca's body and longed for a reunion.

When Luca suggested they get together to celebrate, Donato replied enthusiastically, "Yes. Would love to."

"How about the Vinoteca, near Piazza Cavour?"

"*Perfetto. Oggi? Alle quattro?*"

"Yes. I'll see you later," Luca concluded.

Luca spent much of the afternoon obsessing over what to wear for his date with Donato – at least he considered it a date, even if it hadn't been identified as such. The weather was spring-like – cool and sunny. He selected a light shirt and a blue cotton sweater that showcased his muscular chest. He slipped on his favorite jeans and a pair of sneakers his grandmothers had sent from the States.

Francesco pretended to be uninterested, but was secretly curious about Luca's new buddy. He loved his brother, and he wanted him to be happy. While he grew up in a welcoming family where being gay wasn't an issue, he knew it was still difficult for his fathers and brother. While he had countless dating opportunities, he knew Luca had few. And, when Francesco thought about the openly gay people he knew at school, he wasn't surprised at how difficult it still was to be a gay teen. There just weren't very many promising romantic options.

Francesco sat intentionally in the living room, where he would see Luca before he left. Luca walked through the room, and Francesco furtively scrutinized his attire. "*Bello!*" he exclaimed as Luca passed.

Luca was caught by surprise as his brother had been lying deep in the cushions of the sofa. He blushed. "Just going out for a drink."

"It looks like you spent a lot of time picking out clothes for a simple drink."

"You never know who you will run into."

"Come on, *fratello*! I know you. You have the hots for this guy. I saw you looking at him the other night."

Luca was both surprised and not. Francesco was a pro at pretending to be indifferent to the world around him while gathering detailed information about what was going on.

Francesco added, "He's cute. A bit nerdy, but cute."

"*Vediamo.*"

"I'll be waiting for a report when you come back."

Luca's heart skipped a beat. Francesco's question underscored the uncertainty of the meeting. It felt like he was going unprepared for one of his school exams. He went out the door, raced down the stairs, and exited the courtyard onto the street. It was a 20-minute walk to the Vinoteca.

Donato trembled as he buttoned his shirt and adjusted his jeans. It had been one thing to incidentally run into Luca at the museum, another to have an unplanned outing by the sea, but this was a more intentional decision to pursue a man. He stood in front of the mirror and turned to the side, observing how the shirt fell on his hips, how his pants hung, and whether his hair was in place. He had been on plenty of dates with women, but never with a man. He was apprehensive about their eventual conversation. What would they talk about? How would he express his emotions? Would there be some presumed intimacy at the conclusion? He took a deep breath, stared into the mirror one more time, and then headed out of his room, downstairs, and out onto the street.

Luca walked into the cozy wine bar where a sophisticated and hip crowd gathered for creative appetizers and select wines from around Italy. After his eyes adjusted to the darkness inside, he spotted Donato sitting at the bar. He was bent over, scrolling through his phone. Donato glanced up.

"*Ciao*," they both said. Luca leaned forward to embrace Donato, who reciprocated warmly, exchanging cheek kisses.

"I like this place," Luca began. "Not too many people know about it."

"Oddly, my father introduced me to it. It's got a great vibe."

A cute male server pointed to a table, and they sat. He winked at Donato and asked, "What can I get for you?"

Donato was oblivious to the waiter's flirt. He couldn't extract himself from Luca's eyes. They seemed particularly piercing – the bright blue orbs glistening in a narrow beam of light streaming through the wooden blinds.

Luca glanced at the menu and quickly ordered a glass of Sicilian red and a plate of mixed bruschetta. Donato finally glanced up at the waiter, their eyes finally connecting, and said, "I'll have the same."

The waiter left unceremoniously, perhaps disappointed with Donato's focus of attention. Donato wrung his hands nervously and said, "So, how did exams go?"

"Good. And yours?" Luca replied.

His legs were shaking with adrenaline coursing through his body. Sitting across from Donato was intoxicating. He took time to scrutinize his tall, elegant face again – his long, sensuous nose, his full luscious lips, his dirty blond hair, and his hazel eyes. Donato had on a light blue oxford cotton shirt with the sleeves rolled up. His forearms were stretched across the table toward Luca as if he were ready to take hold of his hands. Luca felt like his heart would leap out of his chest.

"The same. And what are you doing this summer?"

"I have some internships, then I'm going to the States to see my grandmothers."

"Both live there?" Donato asked.

Luca nodded. "But I never knew my papa's mother. These are my grandmothers on my dad's side. They are Oliver's mothers."

"Oh," Donato said, clearly confused. "I'm sorry for being so dense."

"Don't apologize. It's a unique situation!"

"Where do they live?"

"Provincetown."

Donato had a blank expression on his face.

"It's a small village on Cape Cod, on the ocean. Not far from Boston. We go every summer. And you? Where will you go this summer?"

"We'll go to the mountains in August. I have a job in a bank until then."

Neither knew where to take the conversation next. Both had been eager to see each other again. Luca detected Donato's conflicted feelings of excitement and anxiety, longing and dread. His eyes were restless, darting back and forth, but his body was stationary, solid, and leaning toward Luca.

Their wine arrived. They raised their glasses, and each took a sip. Luca kept his eyes fixed on Donato. He had graceful movements and gestures. Donato breathed in the wine's aroma before he took a sip. He swirled the ruby red liquid in the glass. He had good posture - his head cocked back slightly, and his long, sensuous nose extended out from his broad forehead. He seemed deep in thought.

From behind the glass, Donato peered at Luca, tracing Luca's pronounced brows with his eyes, observing the contours of a light beard along his jaw, and glancing periodically at the thick dark hair that he had once held in his hand as he kissed him several weeks ago.

"Been to any archaeological sites lately?" Luca asked, chuckling in his head at his line of questioning. Most 21-year-olds would be asking each other about music, movies, and dates.

Donato didn't seem to think the question odd. "No, but I heard there's an exhibit opening at the Capitoline Museum of the Dying Gaul and some copies of it later this month."

"Yes. I read about it. It should be great. Do you want to go together?" Luca asked enthusiastically.

Donato beamed. "That would be nice. Most of my friends have no interest."

"Mine, neither," Luca replied, chuckling.

Donato took a deep breath. He liked Luca. He felt a strong physical attraction for him. That made him nervous, so discovering a common interest that might serve as a pretext of legitimacy was a source of relief.

Their assortment of different bruschetta arrived. Each took a piece and sampled the flavors. "Hmm," Donato began as he chewed his. "You have to try this one," he said, extending a piece to Luca.

Luca took the piece from Donato, feeling the warmth of his hand as they passed the toast. The gesture of exchanging food felt intensely erotic, as barriers of formality melted, and their hands crossed over the table.

"How did your dad end up in Rome?" Donato asked, wanting to learn more about Luca.

"It's a long story, but the short version is that he came here looking for his biological father."

"Did he find him?"

Luca nodded. "He was a priest. He died while my father was visiting. He had advanced stage cancer."

"How horrible! Then what happened?"

"Giancarlo, my papa, was Henry's financial planner. My dads met during Henry's final days. The rest is history or, I should say, love."

"That's right. Your dad is a banker. Does he have any problems – you know, with him being gay?"

Luca realized this was more of a personal question troubling Donato. Could he come out even in the more conservative financial world?

"He's had some issues here and there. But he's good at his work, so people respect him even if they don't entirely embrace him and our family."

Donato looked off into the distance, deep in thought. Suddenly, his face went ashen. "*Cazzo*," he exclaimed.

"What's the matter?"

"Don't turn around. My father just came in."

Luca couldn't help pivoting, and saw Gerardo Bianchi walk into the space with a distinguished man at his side. They were both dressed in tailored suits and talking with great intensity, their hands gesturing excitedly. They were clearly taking a break from a business or political meeting.

Gerardo Bianchi spotted his son and waved his colleague to follow. Donato stood as they approached. Gerardo embraced his son but couldn't take his eyes off Luca, clearly unnerved at seeing him with his son. "Son, this is Federico Luciano, a manager with Lazio Mutual Funds. Federico, this is my son Donato."

"*Piacere*," they both said as they shook hands.

Federico was roughly fifty. He wore a tailored jacket, sporty slacks, and stylish shoes. He wasn't particularly handsome, but he held himself well and had an affable intensity to him.

"And this is a colleague from the university. Luca," Donato added.

Luca extended his hand to Federico and said, "Luca Russo-Monte-Fitzpatrick. *Piacere*."

Federico tilted his head, rubbed his chin, and said, "You must be Giancarlo's son, right?"

Luca nodded.

"Giancarlo and I have begun to work on some projects together. Great guy," he said warmly.

"Thank you," Luca said, beaming. He glanced at Donato's father, who didn't seem particularly pleased.

"See you later?" Gerardo said to his son.

Donato nodded as Gerardo and Federico grabbed a table farther back in the room.

Donato and Luca sat down. Donato hung his head over the table and looked troubled.

"What's wrong?"

"This is going to be a big mess, a big *casino*. My father is all about appearances. You. Me. As innocent as this might look, it will not sit well with him."

"What's the problem?"

"My father is very conservative. He's forged an alliance of people and organizations that oppose gay people and rights for them. He's going to be upset that we are getting friendly."

Luca already knew about Gerardo's political leanings, but hearing Donato give voice to his fear made his heart race.

"But he's friends with Signor Luciano, who knows and likes my father. Shouldn't that make things okay?"

"No. It will be worse. My dad will feel like he is being tugged into a more accepting posture, and he hates that. He has support and funding precisely because he is perceived to be unabashedly conservative."

Donato tensed up, and his eyes darted back and forth, evading Luca's regard.

"I should go," Donato said emphatically. The image he had of a romantic afternoon with Luca had been deflated in seeing his father.

Luca gave him an incredulous look.

"*Mi dispiace*. I'm sorry."

Donato threw 30 euros on the table and stood up. Luca joined him. Donato waved at his father, and they walked out onto the street.

Donato was clearly restless and nervous, his head pivoting back and forth, up and down the sidewalk. He gave Luca a quick embrace. "I'm sorry. I have to go."

"But why?"

"You wouldn't understand. I really like you, but I'm sorry." Donato looked sadly into Luca's eyes, held them for a few seconds, and then slowly turned away.

Luca, dumfounded at the abrupt ending of their date, walked the opposite direction to the historical center of Rome.

Two hours later, Gerardo came home and found his son busy working on the computer, or at least that's what he thought. Donato was trying to give the impression that he was busy, hoping his father wouldn't make anything of having seen him with Luca.

"What are you working on?"

"Oh, just some review of school materials."

"So, that was the Russo boy you were with," Gerardo observed.

Donato nodded nonchalantly, hoping not to get into a protracted conversation with his father.

"I would suggest you avoid him," Gerardo said, more emphatically.

Donato looked up from the computer screen. He knew the motive of his father's admonition but asked nonetheless, "What's the matter? He seems like a nice guy. We have a common interest in archaeology."

Gerardo raised his brows, not previously aware that his son had any interest in ancient history or art, and said, "He and his family are not good for your career."

"You mean it's not good for yours," Donato replied pointedly, wishing as the words came out of his mouth that he hadn't been so prickly and confrontational. Provoking his father was never a good strategy. But his father was up for reappointment, and his political party was posturing itself as one free of scandals.

"Let's not start. I just want to make sure there are no unnecessary questions or problems as you apply for internships and, later, jobs. Banking and finance are a small world – a conservative one – and, well, you know, Luca's family is ostracized."

"Really? Why?"

"A gay couple raising two boys. It's radical and unconventional. Banking and finance are about discretion, integrity, reliability, and connections. People just don't trust them."

"Signor Luciano seems to like Luca's father."

"That's all a façade," Gerardo said, lying to his son. Indeed, Giancarlo had a successful career, and there were many, including Federico, who enjoyed working with him.

"Luca's family is well respected, from what I see."

"Well, maybe in socialist and avant-garde groups. But in my party and in banking, no," Gerardo emphasized.

"*Va bene*," Donato replied without emotion. He wanted to end the discussion, and a simple 'okay' was enough for his father to move on.

"That's my boy. I just want what's best for you. You have a lot of opportunities. A brilliant future ahead of you."

Gerardo went back downstairs to the kitchen where his wife, Laura, was preparing dinner.

Donato remained at his desk and began searching the web for Luca's family. He discovered links to Giancarlo's career in banking and references to Oliver's work as an archaeologist. He couldn't imagine either of those being a problem for his father. He made a few more clicks on other sites and then discovered that Oliver organized conferences and symposiums on gay issues and Catholic theology and that he was active in several organizations advocating for new laws that would permit gay marriage, gay adoption, and laws protecting gays in the workplace.

"Hmm," he murmured to himself. "This would be a problem for my dad's work and public profile." He realized it might be one thing to come out to himself and go out with guys from time to time. But to begin a relationship with a high-profile gay family like Luca's, that was out of the question. He wasn't sure what to do next. He felt good about having given tentative voice to his identity. Luca had been supportive and understanding. But he realized he needed to be discreet.

He scrolled to a few photos he and Luca had taken in San Felice Circeo. The late afternoon sun had cast a beautiful glow on Luca's face and torso. He was incredibly cute and sexy. It just wasn't feasible to pursue him. He resolved to cut off ties and figure something else out.

Luca wandered back home. Fortunately, his fathers and brother were out. He went to his room and laid back on the bed. Donato's hasty exit and retreat stirred painful memories of his earlier relationship with Gino and sent him into a panic. After letting himself feel affection for someone again, he feared the same ending. He closed his eyes and visualized Donato. He could feel Donato's pain and sadness, but he also detected Donato's resolve to sever ties. He was too afraid of his father and too concerned about appearances and his career. Luca's eyes watered, and he felt his chest tighten. He sensed it would be hard to open his heart again.

5

Chapter Five – Longing

Later that week, Donato met up with classmates after work for pizza and beer. Mauro, Nico, and Tino were from Milan and were studying in Rome, too. After dinner, they went to a popular club to see if they might meet some women. It was a hangout for tourists. Mauro was partial to Americans, and Nico and Tino preferred the French. Donato had tried to excuse himself, but to no avail.

"Come on, Donato. It won't be the same without you. You're a chick magnet. We need you."

Donato never considered himself popular with women, but it was uncanny how comfortable they felt around him. He nodded reluctantly, and they headed down the street to the club.

Nico had his arms around Donato's shoulder, already buzzed by the beers they had at dinner. Donato was used to Nico's affection, but given his recent encounter with Luca, it felt different, more laden with ambiguity. Amongst them, there was a playful camaraderie and presumed heterosexual context that made touch innocent. Donato now resented that presumption.

Once inside the packed club, Mauro went to the bar to order drinks. Nico got distracted just inside the door by a cute female student from Spain. He gestured he would catch up later. Tino glanced up and down the bar to see if there might be someone of interest.

"*Dio mio*," he exclaimed in Donato's ear. "*La vedi*? Do you see her?" He nodded toward the end of the bar where a pair of American women stood, chatting with several local guys. One of them stood out – tall, blonde, tan, with long shapely legs. She wore a low-cut top, showcasing her breasts - firm and round.

"*È gia impegnata*," Donato said as he nodded toward the end of the bar. "She seems quite content with her friend."

Mauro glanced over to see what Donato and Tino were talking about. He grinned.

Mauro then said, "*È un culaiolo*."

Donato didn't know the term Mauro used in reference to the guy, but its derogatory and crude meaning was clear. He felt his own butt twitch and wondered if his friends saw through his façade and knew he was gay, too.

The woman glanced toward Tino and winked. Her friend noticed and looked at them. His eyes locked in on Donato's, and Donato felt his legs go weak. Mauro brought them drinks, and they stood to the side of the bar, surveying the room. Tino kept glancing toward the woman and her presumably gay boyfriend. Mauro eyed a group of American women, obviously on summer vacation in Rome, and Donato felt increasingly nervous and ill at ease.

The woman and her companion began to walk across the room toward a sofa. Their path brought them close to Tino, Mauro, and Donato. Tino murmured, as they passed, "*Che bellezza!*"

The local Roman guy paused and glanced at them. He replied, "*Grazie*."

Donato chuckled nervously at the gutsy response and waited for Tino's response.

He didn't miss a beat. He said, "*Sono Tino. E voi?*"

"This is Linda. And I'm Marcello. *Piacere.*"

Tino gazed into Linda's eyes and said, "*Piacere mio!*"

As Linda and Tino began to chat, Marcello glanced in Donato's direction. Donato felt himself perspire. He nodded to Marcello who extended his hand, "I don't think I caught your name."

"Donato."

"Did you say *dotato?*"

Donato laughed nervously.

Marcello glanced up and down Donato's body and said, "Delicious!"

Donato looked apprehensively at Tino and Mauro, hoping they hadn't noticed the exchange. He tried to dissuade Marcello, but he seemed undeterred. He stood close to Donato, uncomfortably close. He leaned toward him and breathed in the scent of Donato's cologne.

Donato turned toward Mauro and tried to chat with him, but he seemed fixated on the women across the room. Nico was near the door with his Spanish friend, and Tino was now leaning up against Linda. Donato said to Marcello, "Excuse me. I've got to go to the restrooms."

"I'll come, too."

"No!" Donato exclaimed excitedly.

Marcello glanced at him with alarm.

"I'm sorry. I overreacted," Donato apologized.

"I'm coming on too strong. You're so handsome. Why haven't I seen you around before?"

Donato didn't know how to respond. There was a protracted silence. Marcello looked at Donato's friends and then said, "Oh. I see."

Marcello's shift in demeanor put Donato more at ease. He asked, "Did I have a sign around my neck or something?"

"Well, *tesoro*. You just have that look."

Donato looked nervously at his chums. Marcello then added, "Do you want to talk? Your friends look occupied. I won't bite. Another?" he asked, looking at the drink Donato had just gulped down.

Donato nodded.

Marcello and Donato made their way to the bar and ordered drinks. They stood at the bar. It was noisy and crowded, an easier place to have a discreet conversation.

"So, new to this, huh?"

Donato nodded timidly.

"You're quite handsome, you know. If you were at a gay bar, they would have eaten you up. You have that exotic northern Italian look."

Donato blushed. "And you?"

"Am I northern Italian?" he asked, chuckling. "No. I'm pure Roman. Dark and fiery."

"Why are you here?"

"Met some women at a local café and recommended this place to them. I wanted to make sure they were okay. Your friends – are they cool?"

"Sure. Harmless."

"And you?"

"Same."

"I don't believe it. There's a lot going on," he said, waving his hand over Donato's torso as if to imply something was active below the surface. "*Fidanzata?*"

"No," Donato replied. He didn't have a girlfriend.

"Well, then?" Marcello asked, grinning.

"But I've met someone," Donato interjected.

"*Mi dispiace.* Too bad."

"My father is a terror, and I've had to sever ties."

"That's horrible."

Donato nodded.

Marcello added, "You can't let your parents run your life. It will end tragically. No matter how painful it is confronting them, it's worse living a lie."

"That's what I keep saying to myself, but you don't know my father."

"No. I don't. But you have to find a way. Are you out to your friends?"

"Are you kidding?"

"Maybe that's a start. Try them first. Learn some lessons and gain some confidence."

Donato looked at Mauro and Tino. He feared coming out, but could at least imagine they might embrace him with some level of understanding.

"And if you come home with me, I can teach you some other lessons," Marcello said, winking at Donato.

Donato felt his heart skip a beat. The idea of having sex with Marcello was both intriguing and frightening. He was not exceptionally handsome, but he had a warm smile, alluring eyes, and an intensity to him that was intoxicating. He realized Luca had made him feel safe, loved, comfortable. Hooking up with a stranger, however tantalizing it appeared, seemed fraught with peril.

Donato furrowed his brow and placed his hand on Marcello's thigh. "Great offer. Bad timing."

"My luck, as usual," Marcello said, lifting his glass to Donato's.

"Come out to your friends first. That will lead the way for more significant steps."

"*Grazie.*"

"*Un bacino?*"

Donato nodded no.

"*Ma dai.* Just a little kiss," Marcello pleaded.

Before Donato could move, Marcello leaned forward and gave him a kiss on the mouth.

"*Cazzo*," Donato said.

Marcello glanced over at Mauro, who witnessed the kiss and said, "Oops! Looks like you'll be coming out to your friends sooner than later."

Mauro walked over. He extended his hand, introducing himself. "Mauro."

"Marcello."

Mauro stared at Marcello and stood close to his face. "If you hurt him, I'll come after you."

Then he turned toward Donato and said, "As for you. It's about time."

Donato looked at Mauro quizzically. Mauro continued, "That's why you're the chick magnet." He smiled and gave Donato a warm embrace.

"Does that mean it's okay for me to take you home?" Marcello inquired, speaking over Mauro's shoulder.

Donato furrowed his brow and nodded no. He was upset and abruptly left the bar. Marcello followed him outside and said, "*Aspetta*. Let's talk. No agenda."

Donato nodded, tears in his eyes.

"Sorry for coming on so strong in there and messing things up. You're cute, and I didn't realize what you are dealing with."

"Sorry I'm so sensitive."

"It's a lot to deal with," Marcello said thoughtfully, as they both walked down the small street, away from the club.

"Without getting too personal, who is this guy you met? Tell me about him."

"He's cute, handsome, smart."

"Shit!"

Donato nodded, then said, "Like you."

"You're just letting me down easy."

"I don't know what I'm doing," Donato added as he walked alongside Marcello over the cobblestone pavement.

"What does your father have against your boyfriend?"

"He's not my boyfriend. We just met, but my father doesn't know I'm gay and Luca's family is a high-profile gay family."

"And the problem?"

Donato hesitated. He didn't like contemporaries to know who his father was. "My father's in the government. He's very conservative."

"Oh!"

"Where did you meet what's his name?"

"Luca. We met at the Vatican Museums."

"Well, that's a curious gay cruising place!"

Donato chuckled nervously.

"Tell me more," Marcello added.

"It was odd, even a bit spooky. I had gone into a section of the museum filled with ancient Christian sarcophagi. Suddenly, I spotted Luca in front of a piece I had just been looking at. It's as if he appeared out of nowhere. Our eyes connected, and I sensed we knew each other. Isn't that uncanny?"

"Not really. I think there are all sorts of people we run into like that – people we may have known in another time."

Donato looked like a deer in headlights.

"You know, past lives. Reincarnation."

Donato continued to shake his head, as if he didn't know what Marcello was talking about.

Marcello continued, "Our souls live, die, and reincarnate. We often have unfinished business with people, and we reconnect with them during another life."

"What about heaven and hell?" Donato asked, still perplexed.

"In most religions, there is a belief that we must live many lives before we achieve some final state of peace, happiness, or beatitude. It is only in Judaism, Christianity, and Islam that there is such a strong emphasis on one life, judgment, and then the consequences. It adds more weight to the idea of right religion."

"I never knew."

"And you thought I was a shallow flirt trying to pick you up," Marcello said, winking.

Donato stared at him, convinced Marcello was indeed trying to pick him up. But he was intrigued by the conversation, not one that would ordinarily presage a tryst. "So, how would we know about our past lives?" Donato asked.

"A regression therapist can hypnotize you and help you connect with significant historical moments. Or you can simply pay attention to peculiar things that happen in your life that suggest familiarity with people and places. In addition, we often discover we have special talents, abilities, and affinities for certain professions or interests."

Donato looked pensive, glancing off in the distance as if in thought.

Marcello noticed Donato's consternation and continued, "Did you feel anything like that with Luca?"

Donato nodded. He wasn't sure he wanted to elaborate more. There was something in Luca's eyes that seemed familiar. He felt at ease and safe with him, as if they had been friends or companions.

"Anything about the sarcophagus that was remarkable?"

"I am not sure. I didn't pay that much attention to it."

"Maybe you should go back. See if there's something there that speaks to you."

"You are one fascinating person," Donato said to Marcello.

"We Romans have a long history of familiarity with the esoteric – with past-lives, magic, premonitions, even spells. It's part of our Etruscan heritage."

Donato nodded.

"Not everyone is into it, but my mother was. She had visitors from the other side and used to do readings."

"You're kidding?"

"No."

They had walked farther down the street. The night air was sensual, and Donato was feeling increasingly at ease with Marcello. He asked, "So, how do you know?"

"Know about your past life?"

"No. How do you know if you are gay?" Donato asked.

Marcello paused and pivoted in place, taking in the charming convergence of small streets. People passed back and forth, arm in arm, heading from dinner to cafes for drinks and conversation. Donato had a sophisticated air to him, and he seemed well-educated and worldly. But he was obviously naïve about sexuality and was struggling with his identity. He peered into Donato's eyes. He found him incredibly sexy and wanted to bring him home. But he sensed Donato was tender and vulnerable. He said, "If you are asking the question, you probably are. Do you catch men's eyes? Do you find yourself drawn to them? Do you notice their attire, their eyes, their physique? Do you hope they will glace your way – a glance of recognition?"

Donato nodded.

"You're young. Take your time. But don't fight things. Follow your heart."

Donato gazed into Marcello's eyes. He was so warm and thoughtful. He wondered if he should go home with him. He hoped Marcello would make another overture, but he didn't. They stood awkwardly near each other in the intersection.

"Well, I better head home," Marcello said, resigned to the fact that Donato was too vulnerable and impressionable to take home.

"It was a pleasure meeting you. Here's my card. Call if you want to talk or have a drink."

Donato looked at the card and smiled. He reached toward Marcello and gave him a warm embrace. "Thanks for the conversation, your understanding, and wisdom."

"Anytime. Good luck to you."

Marcello gave Donato a kiss on each cheek and squeezed his upper arm warmly. He headed farther down one of the small roads. Donato turned the other direction and headed home.

The next day, the bank was closing in the afternoon for an internal audit. Donato decided to head back to the Vatican Museums to revisit the Pio-Christian section of the museums. Marcello's words made him curious. He wasn't sure he bought into the notion of past lives nor was he superstitious, but the experience of Luca appearing so mysteriously in front of a particular sarcophagus intrigued him. Could his and Luca's meeting have been connected to the piece? Did it have a special force? Why had they crossed paths there – of all places? After the bank closed, he quickly made his way across town. Fortunately, the line to the museum was relatively short. He bought a ticket and made his way into the Pio-Christian exhibit hall.

As usual, that section of the museum was practically devoid of people, most tourists making their way to the more popular Raphael Rooms and Sistine Chapel. The empty space felt eerie, as if voices and hands of the past might leap out of the tombs at him. He glanced up and down the aisles, almost expecting to see Luca. He wondered if fate might not bring them together again, unexpectedly. But, alas, Luca wasn't to be seen.

He cautiously approached the marble sarcophagus where he first saw Luca. Compared to some of the others, it was both impressive and primitive. There were extensive carvings of Abraham, Moses, and Jesus. There were countless scenes of Jesus performing miracles.

In the center of the intricate frieze, the faces of the married couple who commissioned the piece had been carved. The images were rustic, and this gave the piece a homier feel, easy for an observer to place himself or his parents in their stead.

As Donato stroked the marble etchings, he was surprised by the presence of a wand in many scenes where Jesus was performing miracles, as if he were a magician. Donato thought it odd. He crouched in front of the piece for a while and then stood, wandering farther into the exhibit hall. He passed the "Two Brothers" sarcophagus and chuckled at the handsome men carved in the center circle. He was about to leave the space when he felt drawn back to the original piece.

He circled back and crouched in front of it. He continued to marvel at how oddly familiar it felt, and recalled Marcello's remarks the night before. He gazed at the images of the married couple and could imagine his own father and mother. He glanced down at the carvings of Jesus performing miracles with his wand. There was a scene where Jesus had multiplied loaves with a wand. In the next scene, he was blessing the bread and distributing it. Unlike the other images of Jesus on the frieze, in this scene, Jesus faced outward. Donato felt as if he were peering at him. Jesus's eyes were haunting. They were caring and warm, as well as mysterious and provocative. Jesus seemed to pose a question, reaching into Donato's soul. Could he be courageous? Could he be imaginative? Did he dare use magic to defy limits? The sensations startled Donato. The sarcophagus seemed alive, and he lost all sense of time.

He finally shook his head to dispel the trance he was in. He stood and hastily exited the gallery. He walked outside and took a deep breath. "Wow," he said to himself. "That was intense."

He walked home, contemplating what had just happened. He recalled Marcello's words the night before. He still wasn't inclined to buy into the notion of past lives and reincarnation, but he had to admit that there was something mysterious about the sarcophagus and about his and Luca's meeting. He couldn't shake the sensation that he was being tested, that he was being given an opportunity. Jesus's eyes continued to haunt him. He knew he was being challenged to stretch, to grow, to be bold. He wasn't sure he had the nerve to do so.

6

Chapter Six – A Close Call

That same afternoon, Luca was sitting on a stool in the kitchen, sipping an espresso. Francesco entered; his long curly hair tousled from a nap. He reached past his brother, affectionately rubbing his shoulder as he pushed a button on the espresso machine to make himself a cup of coffee. The device began to hum. Shortly, caramel colored foamy espresso dripped into a small cup.

"What's wrong?" Francesco asked his brother.

"*Niente.*"

"It doesn't look like *niente* to me. You look sullen."

"It's Donato."

"What about him?"

"He left abruptly from our date the other day. I haven't heard from him."

"And?"

"I don't know. It just feels strange, like he's conflicted, struggling, at war with himself."

"I thought things were good."

"Me, too. But suddenly he left, and I haven't heard from him."

"Anything precipitate it?"

"The only thing I can think of is we ran into his father. Maybe his father told him to break ties."

"Why would he do that?"

"He's very conservative. Wants to groom his son for politics. We're a liability!"

"Hmm," Francesco looked out of the kitchen window. "Do you know where he hangs out? Maybe you can casually bump into him. You're good at picking up vibes. If you see him in person, you can get a sense of what's up."

Luca perked up. He had first run into him at the museum, but it seemed farfetched to run into him again there. But he knew where he lived, and he could imagine casually bumping into him on his street. "You know, for a slacker, sometimes you have good ideas."

"I hide my talents."

They both chuckled. Luca quickly stood, went to his room, and dressed. He grabbed a guidebook of Rome to lend some credibility to whatever pretext he could think of on the spot and headed to Donato's neighborhood.

It was a sunny afternoon. He had on a new pair of shorts that hugged his thighs tightly. The light turquoise pullover contrasted with his early season tan. He hid behind a funky pair of sunglasses with blue rims. Of course, he never left home without a Red Sox cap.

When he arrived at Donato's neighborhood, he walked slowly. He stopped strategically a couple of times on Donato's block and opened the guidebook, giving the impression that he was busy and had a purpose. Donato didn't appear, and he wondered if it was pure fantasy to think he would actually bump into him.

He circled the block a few times. On the third loop, he had decided to head home, resigned to an aborted mission. He rounded the corner and physically ran into Donato.

Each not realizing who the other was, they both exclaimed, "*Scusi!*"

When they recognized each other, they chuckled.

"Luca!"

"Donato!"

"What are you doing in this neck of the woods?" Donato asked, now certifiably unnerved at bumping into Luca after leaving the Vatican Museums. He wondered if fate was forcing them to meet again.

"I had run an errand for my dad and had stopped in the Ara Pacis and the nearby tomb of Augustus to check out the new exhibits," Luca said.

"You look good," Donato said as he stared into Luca's blue eyes and periodically glanced down at his muscular legs. "I'm sorry I haven't been in touch. I've been meaning to, but we were traveling," Donato said, deceptively.

"Yeah. I've been busy, too. Do you have time for a coffee?" Luca asked as he glanced down the street at a café.

Donato paused, not sure if he should encourage Luca or be seen so close to home with him. But his father was out of town and his mother was at a conference, so he said, "Sure. *Andiamo.*"

They walked down the sidewalk to the bar, walked inside, and ordered two espressos. The barista knew Donato and winked at him. He pressed fresh grounds into two pods and pretended to be focused on pulling their coffee, but he furtively studied Luca, a new face in the neighborhood.

Donato walked to the cashier and paid. Luca stared at the back of Donato's head. He had let his hair grow out a bit. The blond hair had turned lighter in the early summer sun, and Luca felt his heart race with affection.

When Donato turned, he was struck by Luca's allure – his casual attire, his pumped physique, and his luscious mouth. All his resolve to sever ties and move on was melting. He wanted to walk up to him and give him a warm, moist kiss. His heart pounded rapidly as he approached the counter. They stood close to each other and sipped their coffee.

Luca could feel heat emanating from Donato and sensed his desire. He felt reassured by the vibes he picked up and said, "So, are you doing an internship? How's it going?"

Donato loved the fact that Luca asked questions. He smiled and said, "Yes. With a fund manager at a bank. It's good. I like the work."

"Cool," Luca said.

"And you?"

"I'm doing some research this summer and some coaching with a psychologist. It's good," he said, avoiding details about Rahel's identity as a psychic.

"*Cos'altro?*" Donato offered as they finished their espressos, wondering if he might extend their time with a drink.

Luca wanted their encounter to seem unplanned. He said, "I really have to go. Maybe we can get a drink in the next couple of days?"

Donato didn't know how to respond. He felt there was something taking hold of his thoughts and words. An idea popped into his head, and he said, "I have a new book I purchased on the sarcophagi at the Vatican Museums. Do you want to see it? It won't take long. My house is right here."

Luca felt his heart skip a beat. There was nothing more he wanted to do than to go upstairs with Donato. He looked off as if in thought and said, "Well, let me text my dad and let him know I'll be a little late. I'm sure a few minutes won't make a difference."

Donato nodded to the barista and led Luca outside and down a few doors to his building. They entered, walked up a set of stairs, and walked inside the large apartment. As Donato closed the door behind them, he turned to Luca, took hold of his shoulders, pulled him close, and gave him a passionate kiss.

Luca glanced around nervously, and Donato said, "My parents are out. My dad is out of town and my mother is at a conference. We're all alone."

"You don't have a book you want to show me, do you?" Luca said, staring into Donato's eyes.

Donato shook his head no, blushing as he grinned. He took Luca's hand and led him up a set of stairs to his room. Luca felt warmth and eagerness in Donato's palms.

Donato couldn't believe what he was doing, and he convinced himself he'd have at least one hot encounter with Luca and then get back on the track his father had laid out for him. They climbed the marble stairs and wandered down the brightly lit hallway filled with modern art.

Donato's room was exceptionally neat, nothing out of place. Mounted on his desk was a large monitor connected to a paper-thin computer. There were artistic lamps strategically placed on his desk, on the bedside tables, and on a dresser. The walls were covered in posters of contemporary musicians – not soccer players, Luca observed.

Donato led Luca to his bed and pushed him down on the fluffy duvet. Luca glanced up at Donato's elegant face - his eyes wide and his skin flush. Donato kneeled on the bed, pushing Luca's legs apart, and reclined on Luca's chest. He leaned forward and encircled Luca's mouth with his own.

"Oh my God," Luca exclaimed, his skin tingling at the feel of Donato on top of him. He cocked his head back, and Donato kissed his neck.

Luca felt himself become aroused, and reached behind Donato, pulling him closer on top of him. He could feel Donato's firm cock pressing against the fabric of his jeans.

Neither wanted to delay the mounting force of their exchange, despite the cautionary messages circling in both their heads. Luca wasn't sure Donato was free from parental controls and shame, and Donato knew he would have to give Luca up. Now, in each other's arms, both simply wanted to devour the other as quickly as possible before their consciences caught up to them.

Donato ran his hands ardently up under Luca's pullover and felt the firm contours of his pecs. Luca, in turn, ran his hands down Donato's back and under the waist of his jeans, feeling the warm skin and firm muscles of Donato's buttocks. With each squeeze of Donato's glutes, Luca could feel Donato's pelvis burrow deeper into his own and their hard shafts looking for a way to connect.

Donato turned slightly and leaned on his elbow, using his other hand to unzip Luca's shorts. He felt his full, warm erection in his hands. Luca, in turn, unzipped Donato, whose cock sprung free of the confines of his undershorts and dangled in front of Luca. In a frenzy of abandon, they took hold of each other, locked their mouths in a wet exchange, and brought each other to a quick and exploding climax.

"*Stupendo*," Donato exclaimed as he collapsed on his back next to Luca, panting heavily.

Luca felt a wave of satisfaction ride through his body. He looked at Donato, stared into his hazel eyes, and smiled contently. "*Si. Veramente.*"

Donato's phone pinged with a text. He casually reached over Luca and picked up the phone off the bedside table. "*Cazzo*," he shouted. "It's my mother. She's on her way home. Her conference ended early."

Donato leaped out of bed, adjusted his jeans, zipped himself back up, and ran his hand through his hair. He gestured to Luca, "*Andiamo. Presto!* We've got to get you out of her."

"Why?"

Donato glared at Luca. The message was clear. Luca and he were not supposed to be together.

Luca felt his heart race as he adjusted his pullover, zipped up his shorts, and looked in the mirror, placing a few errant strands of hair in place. Donato placed his hand behind Luca's back and pushed him out of the room and down the stairs. "We have to get you out of here before she gets to the building. Let's go."

Luca was now getting irritated, although he did his best to hurry. At the door, Donato gave him a quick peck on the cheek, and Luca headed down the stairs onto the street. He walked toward the historical center and his home, noticing Laura cross the street toward her house.

Donato rearranged and fluffed the duvet on his bed and opened the window to let out any perceptible scent that Luca might have left behind. His mother opened the door to the apartment and announced her arrival. "Donato. I'm home. Are you here?"

"Yes, mom. I'm up here working."

As Laura walked inside the apartment, she noticed a book on the foyer table. It was a guidebook of Rome. She opened it and noticed Oliver's name and a flyer for an event featuring a gay activist speaking on marriage laws. "Hmm," she murmured to herself. She looked upstairs, raised her brows, and then walked into the kitchen with the book.

Laura Bianchi had always wondered if her son was gay. His fastidiousness with clothing, furniture, art, and music were not typical of most kids his age. She had always been impressed with his sensitivity and thoughtfulness as a young boy and, as he advanced through adolescence, he showed more interest in spending time with his swim team mates than with girls. She had noticed the spark between her son and Luca at the restaurant and was alarmed when her husband ranted about having seen Donato and Luca together at the wine bar. She slid the book and flyer under some dish towels in a drawer in the kitchen and walked upstairs.

"Hey dear," she said as she walked into Donato's room. "How are you?"

Laura noticed Donato was restless, clicking feverishly through websites. "Good," he said evasively.

"Want to go out to eat tonight?" she asked, giving him a scrutinizing look. "Your father's out of town, and I don't feel like cooking."

"Sure," he said, hoping his mother would leave soon.

She did.

Later that evening, they sat across from each other at a local trattoria. Laura wasn't sure what she wanted to accomplish. She looked at her son. He was handsome. He had noble features – a long face, a tall forehead, and angular jaws. There was a certain intensity to him – alluring hazel eyes, a long sensuous nose, and playful blond hair. He had been well-groomed and had good posture and graceful mannerisms, holding his glass of wine stylishly. He was conversational and had a polished vocabulary and accent. She was proud of him. She loved him.

"How's your internship going?" she began.

"Good. I like it."

She smiled and nodded. "Do you like the work?"

"Sure," he said. "Why wouldn't I?"

"Well. I know your father would love for you to pick up the baton from him – go into finance or banking and eventually a government position. But that's his dream for you. What do you want?"

The line of inquiry surprised Donato. He tilted his head sideways and raised a brow.

She reiterated her question. "What do you want?"

"I guess I've never really thought about it. I like finance, and father's work has afforded us a nice life."

"Hmm," she said. "Yes. But there are other professions. And there are other lifestyles."

Donato felt his throat constrict. He swallowed and took another sip of wine. His mother had always been deferent to his father, and his father had always been quite emphatic about his future, his profession, and the kind of life he would lead.

"Don't mind me," Laura added as she noticed the anxiousness in her son's face. "I just want you to be happy."

Donato wondered if perhaps his mother suspected that he was different, that he was gay. He wasn't certain enough to ask her or to say anything. They ordered their meals and enjoyed their time together, discussing less serious matters such as vacation plans and his mother's work in several charitable organizations.

They returned home, and Donato went to his room. He texted Luca, "Sorry about this afternoon. Close call. Had a good time."

Luca was reading in a chair in his room. He glanced at his phone as the text appeared. He said to himself, "That's it? That's all you got?" He liked Donato. He was sexy, exotic, mysterious, smart, and classy. He was hoping Donato might say, "Wow! Wonderful time with you." Or "Hey handsome. Can't wait to see you again."

He was bewildered. There seemed to be a pattern. Donato came on strong, panicked, retreated, then repeated. He couldn't believe the sex they had, even if it had been quick and over in minutes. Donato's body was hot! He loved the feel of his lean and taut chest, his powerful legs wrapped around him, and the solidity of Donato's cock in his hand. Luca's sexual experiences were limited, but with Donato it was as if his body knew exactly what to do. It all felt so natural and incredible.

He wondered if perhaps Donato felt differently. Sure, he seemed to have liked things, but his hasty exit before his mother arrived and his half-hearted text made him question his initial impression. Was Donato not that into him, or just awkward and reticent, given that he was just coming out to himself?

7

Chapter Seven – A Reckoning

A few days later, Gerardo angrily tossed the guidebook down on the table in front of Donato and yelled, "What is this?"

Surprised, Donato said, "I don't know. I've never seen it." His heart pounded in fear.

"Your mother found it in the foyer the other day," Gerardo said as he opened the front of the book and pointed to Oliver's name. "Oliver Monte-Fitzpatrick!"

Donato tried to think quickly and said, "It must have been mixed in with some materials Luca gave me during his father's tour. I may have inadvertently dropped it when I was unpacking my backpack."

"Hmm," Gerardo murmured. "I trust you haven't seen him again. Look at this!"

Gerardo pulled the flyer announcing a conference on gay marriage out of the book and laid it on the table in front of Donato. "I don't have to remind you that for the sake of your career, you don't want to associate yourself with this," Gerardo said emphatically.

Donato nodded pensively. He knew his father was more concerned about his own career and the upcoming political season than for him.

With a stern, scrutinizing face, Gerardo looked at his son and said slowly and deliberately, "You don't sympathize with this, do you? You don't have any of these inclinations, right?"

Donato shook his head no, trembling inside.

"You know that would be a problem."

"Yes. I realize that. Not to worry," Donato tried to assure his dad. Then he said slowly and thoughtfully, "But I don't understand what the fuss is all about."

Gerardo tilted his head and looked quizzically at his son.

Donato continued, "Luca's family is no different from ours except there are two men instead of a man and a woman. Luca's dads have been married as long as you and mom. Both hold respectable jobs. Luca and his brother are smart and well-adjusted. His brother is straight."

"It's perverted."

"In what sense?"

"Two men. It's not natural. It's against the Bible."

"So is eating pork and shrimp. The Bible permits slaves and multiple wives, yet we no longer consider that acceptable."

"Homosexuality is different. Men need women and women need men to form authentic love. Otherwise, it is just self-indulgent — two people using each other for pleasure."

"How could Luca's dads be together for twenty-something years, and it just be about pleasure?" Donato asked.

"I'm sure they are unfaithful. All homosexuals are. Open relationships and orgies. That's what they do."

"Dad! You must be kidding."

"Check the statistics!"

"I'm sure the statistics are no different from straight relationships – where infidelity occurs all the time."

"They are brainwashing you. It's all part of the liberal secular society. Even more reason to make sure you don't associate with Luca. We Bianchis have a reputation to uphold. We stand for traditional values and families. It is part of why people trust our financial advice and how I got into public office and service."

"But things are changing."

"Not in the banking world, they aren't."

"What about Luca's father, Giancarlo? He's a banker."

"Yes. And there are all sorts of people who won't work with him. He's a liability for the bank. They keep him on because they are afraid of a lawsuit."

Donato's eyes widened. He was certain that wasn't the case, but he realized he wasn't making any headway with his father. He asked, "Are we finished?"

"As long as you agree to cut off all ties with this Luca guy. I don't want you to return the book or anything. No more communication. Do you hear me?"

Donato nodded.

Gerardo Bianchi, red in the face, left the room with the guidebook and flyer. He went into the living room and sat in a chair, opened his laptop, and began doing some work.

Donato went up to his room, passing his parents' room on the way. His mother was sitting in a chair and looked up sadly. She held a finger to her mouth and then placed her two hands on her chest and then extended them to her son. The message was clear. She loved him – just as he was – and she knew.

Although his father's advice was undoubtedly prudent and Donato was unlikely to disobey him, he couldn't shake the sense that something mysterious was going on. The peculiar way he and

Luca met, the sensations he had in front of the sarcophagus, and now their serendipitous meeting on the street all seemed to suggest that something or someone was trying to bring the two of them together. He didn't want to defy his father, but he was beginning to wonder if the fates were more powerful and were already planning their next move.

8

Chapter Eight – Rupture

A week later, Giancarlo and Oliver sat face to face in the living room. The tension in the air was thick, and Oliver's heart raced.

"But we have meetings the next day," Giancarlo insisted as Oliver looked at him sternly.

"You can go to Milan, have your meeting, and then return the same day. I need you here. We have guests in two days, and Francesco needs more supervision. I'm fully booked with tours."

"Well, these are big accounts. We can't afford to lose them. I've got to do some massaging of client relationships the next day. We have some meetings set up."

"I think you're massaging more than client relationships."

Giancarlo turned beet red. He felt like Oliver was hinting at something. He had never been accused of being unfaithful. "What are you implying?"

"You and Riccardo are having an affair," Oliver said emphatically, looking intensely at Giancarlo. He had been holding it in for days, and finally blurted it out.

"No, we're not. We're co-workers. You know that," Giancarlo replied, squinting in disbelief at the accusation Oliver was making.

"That's what I thought. But co-workers have affairs, too. In fact, it's quite convenient. He's gay, single, handsome. You travel overnight for business. It all makes perfect sense."

"What gives you the idea we are having an affair? We've been friends and colleagues for years."

"Apparently rumors are flying."

"What?"

"Hmm hum."

"Who said what?"

"I don't think I need to divulge that. Let's just say there are multiple sources."

"But it's not true. I swear."

"What about these texts?" Oliver pressed, scrolling through a series of screen shots he took of Giancarlo's phone. *I look forward to some quality time together with you – and shall I make reservations at our favorite place?* "These are not things co-workers say to each other. Do I need to continue? There are others, even more suggestive."

"I can see how you might interpret those messages. That's just Riccardo. He's very expressive."

"What about the receipts from your last stay in Milan? A double suite with both of your names listed," Oliver said, pulling out the receipt and waving it in Giancarlo's face.

"I can explain. The city was booked solid for a convention. We had to do an overnight, and that's all that was available. We're ordinarily in two separate rooms."

"Hmm," Oliver murmured angrily.

"I can't believe you went snooping into my stuff. If you had suspicions or concerns, why not just ask me? There are simple explanations."

"And these selfies?" Oliver asked, showing more screen shots of Giancarlo and Riccardo posing affectionately.

"Oliver, you're overreacting."

"Am I? What would you think if you found similar evidence on my phone?"

Giancarlo paused. He felt adrenaline race through his body and his blood pressure rise. "I have never cheated on you."

"Then what are these for?" he asked, pulling a large package of condoms out of his pocket. "I found them in your desk."

"Those are for Luca and Francesco. I was going to give them to them before we went to Ptown. I want to make sure they are safe."

"I don't believe you."

"Ask Riccardo. He'll explain everything."

"Of course, he would. I have no doubt the stories would be similar. That doesn't prove a thing."

"I swear, we are not having an affair."

"Then go to Milan and come back the same day."

"Oliver, I can't. Those meetings are crucial."

"So is our marriage."

"Our marriage is not at risk. I'm not having an affair."

"I can't believe you're taking our relationship so casually. Of course, our marriage is at risk. I should have noticed it before. You and Riccardo are way too chummy. He's always been into you. I just never thought it was reciprocal."

Oliver began to cry. He was exhausted from days of worry and consternation, not sleeping well, and fretting over what to do about the evidence he had found.

Giancarlo was becoming angry. He had been the responsible son who stayed with his parents when his sister moved away for her job in Milan. He had hidden his sexual orientation to shield them from disappointment. He had never been accused of unfaithfulness or dishonesty, and he resented Oliver's accusation as an affront to his integrity. He glared at Oliver, who continued to weep. He began to feel disgust for his partner and said, "You're spoiled and self-absorbed, having an enormous estate handed to you and two wealthy mothers who continue to dote over you. Meanwhile, I'm constantly working to retain our accounts at the bank and fight the bias that the banking world holds against you and me. You don't know how hard it is to keep clients. You prance around Rome hosting conferences on gay topics and gay parenting, making my work even more difficult. And now you want me to cancel key meetings because you're suspicious. It doesn't work that way," Giancarlo said, storming out of the room.

"We're not finished," Oliver yelled at him.

"I think we are," Giancarlo yelled back as he climbed the stairs. Oliver could hear his heavy steps proceed to their bedroom. He felt himself tremble, not sure what to do next.

Shortly thereafter, Giancarlo returned to the living room with a suitcase. Not looking at Oliver in the eyes, he said, "I think it's best for me to give you some space to think about this. I'm not going to stand for false accusations."

Still shaking, Oliver said, "Yes. Maybe it's better. I don't want to live with someone who is cheating and unwilling to be forthcoming when confronted with evidence."

Without response, Giancarlo went out the front door and onto the street. He decided to go to Maria's nearby. He had a key. She and Carlo were away for a few days. He would text her and see if he could crash there.

Oliver collapsed on the sofa, sobbing. He trembled as he realized his marriage might have just ended. He didn't think Giancarlo would be so defiant and just walk out. But, if he was having an affair and wouldn't even apologize or be contrite, then things were worse than he thought.

He was grateful Francesco and Luca were out. It would take

some time for him to recompose himself. His mind was racing with thoughts – would they divorce? Would they sell the house, or would someone buy the other out? Might he return to Boston and give up on Rome? Or had Rome become his home, particularly since their sons were Roman? Still young, he could meet someone else and start all over again.

He glanced back down at his phone, at the images of Giancarlo's texts, his photos, his receipts – and felt rage replace his sadness. No, he would not let Giancarlo's duplicity ruin his life. He had come too far to give up. He would start over again and rebuild his life.

9

Chapter Nine – On The
Fast Ferry to Ptown

A week later, Oliver, Luca, and Francesco were en route to Provincetown on the fast ferry. Giancarlo remained in Rome.

"That guy is totally checking you out," Francesco said to Luca as he glanced up nonchalantly from his phone. Luca glanced at a young man in short shorts, a tank top, and flip-flops walking down the aisle toward the bar.

"Maybe he was checking you out," Luca replied, turning casually toward Oliver to see if he was paying attention to their brotherly exchange.

Francesco shook his head no. "No eye contact with me, but his head swivels your direction each time he passes, and he's wearing out the carpet. He's been back and forth to the bar at least a half dozen times since we left Boston."

The individual stood contrapposto, his weight shifted to one hip and his elbow resting on the bar. He glanced toward Luca and smiled. He ordered a bottle of water and sauntered back to his buddies, casting an unmistakable look at Luca.

"See!" Francesco murmured to him as the guy continued to the back of the fast ferry.

Oliver wanted to see what the fuss was about. He looked over at his sons huddled in conference next to him and then glanced back at the group of young men sitting near the rear of the galley. He smiled, then glanced out the window at the water passing rapidly outside. They were half-way between Boston and Provincetown.

His stomach had been in knots since they left Italy. He and Giancarlo had never reached such an impasse, and it seemed ominous, as if they had irreversibly traversed a line, one neither thought they would ever cross.

Giancarlo remained defiant in his denial of an affair and had camped out at Maria's house until Oliver and the boys left for the States. They hadn't discussed next steps yet, but Francesco discovered Giancarlo was already searching for an apartment. Oliver was unwilling to back off his accusations, noting that Giancarlo couldn't produce credible evidence to the contrary. As he looked back at the last few years, he realized he had perhaps been naïve and overlooked things he should have noticed.

The annual trip to Provincetown was usually happy and exciting, a reunion with Oliver's mothers and an extended vacation on Cape Cod. When the kids were younger, they enjoyed taking part in Family Week activities so that they would see there were lots of other gay families just like theirs. They always returned to Rome with renewed pride in who they were. Although he looked forward to celebrating his mothers' anniversary during this trip, he felt like he had failed at his own marriage and that he was dragging a dark cloud with him.

"He's not my type," Luca said emphatically to Francesco.

"What is your type, *fratello*?"

"I don't have one."

Francesco winked devilishly at him. "Let me guess. Tall, fair, blond, lean."

Luca glared at his brother. The adjectives only exacerbated his sadness at not having heard from Donato.

"Oh, yes. *Un altro – un cazzo grosso.*"

"Francesco. *Basta!*

"At least say hello. It's not like you're asking him for a date or agreeing to a *scopata.*"

Oliver looked at Francesco and gave him a stern look for his crude language. Francesco acknowledged the rebuke, slouched in his seat, and scrolled through his phone. "Don't mind me. I'm invisible here."

"That's hardly the case," Luca replied. "You may not see anything of interest to you, but that doesn't mean they haven't noticed you."

Francesco grinned. He knew he was a head turner and loved being the secret straight boy traveling in a pack of gay men.

"Seriously. You have to lighten up. Say hello to people. Smile. Relax. Donato is past tense."

"But I was certain we had a connection," Luca said. "Something is there. I know it."

Francesco respected his brother's psychic gifts and knew he was extraordinarily perceptive. Over the years, he had learned the lingo and had developed his own sensitivities as well. He said, "Maybe your meeting Donato has nothing to do with forming a relationship and everything to do with nudging you out of your sexual inhibitions. He reignited your sexual desires. That's a big deal. It was about time."

"I still feel like there's something more."

"Maybe. But if that's the case, then nothing you do while you're in Ptown will change that. Have some fun. You're frickin twenty-one-years-old! You're hot. You could have anyone you want this summer!"

Luca glanced evasively toward the window to conceal a smile. He never considered himself attractive, even though everyone said he was handsome. To hear his brother call him hot was both startling and encouraging.

Luca stood up and headed to the back of the ferry, toward the restrooms. He cruised past the young man and his buddies. The young man looked up and smiled, extending his hand. "I'm Ben."

"Luca," he said in reply. "Heading to Ptown for vacation?"

Ben nodded. "These are my friends David, Tom, and Drew."

"Nice to meet you," they all said in unison.

"Come join us," Ben offered.

"Thanks, but I'm hanging out with my brother and father up there," he said, looking toward Francesco and Oliver.

"That's your father?" Ben asked, his brows arched upward.

Luca nodded.

Drew murmured, "Definitely daddy material. Young daddy material!"

"Don't mind them," Ben said, apologizing for his friends. "You must be heading to Ptown for vacation, too?"

"Yeah. We'll be there the month of August."

"Wow! Where are you from? I detect a slight accent."

"Italy."

"First time to Ptown?" Ben asked, having a difficult time controlling the mounting excitement he felt for Luca and the prospects that Luca might need someone to show him the town.

"No. We come here every summer. My father is from here."

"Cool," Ben said, slightly disappointed. "We'll definitely see you around, then. *Ciao*," Ben added.

After going to the restroom, Luca returned to his father's and brother's table by the window. Francesco whispered, "Well done. I'm proud of you."

"All I did was introduce myself."

"That's all you have to do. Things will unfold after that."

"You make it look so easy," Luca said to his brother, Oliver now looking at them with interest. He feared he might have to take tips from his son, too. It unnerved him considerably. He realized he had never been a single gay man, having met and settled down with Giancarlo just as he came out. He wondered what it would be like to walk up to strangers, introduce himself, go on dates, and navigate the inevitable complexities and messiness of new relationships. He furtively glanced around the cabin to see how many age-appropriate men were on board, how many might be single, and whether any were his type. Sighing, he realized most were either much younger or much older. He wondered if he was in an odd twilight zone for gay men – too old to be a young twink and too young to count as part of the distinguished senior crowd.

"Just be yourself. Be friendly. Say hello. Smile. Again, it will all unfold naturally after that," Francesco said confidently to Luca.

Oliver opened a book and looked down to conceal the fact that he was listening attentively to Francesco's coaching.

Francesco gazed at his brother and father, both looking rather discouraged. He never imagined that he would be giving dating tips to them both, particularly his dad. It was hard to imagine his fathers separating and divorcing. They seemed like the ideal couple, and they had always been a rock of support for him, particularly during his childhood illness. He wondered if they could mend their differences and if their being apart might make their hearts grow fonder. Or, if there really were deeper problems, would Oliver meet someone, fall in love again, and begin a whole new chapter? He sensed this summer was going to be significant.

Francesco gave another look at his father and brother and said with consternation, "*Ma guardate*! The two of you look so sad. Lift your heads, smile, enjoy the scenery!"

Oliver looked annoyed but didn't say anything. He looked out of the window and noticed a thin sliver of bright yellow sand appear on the horizon. It was undoubtedly the edge of Race Point, the bend in the cape where the Atlantic Ocean meets Cape Cod Bay. He felt his blood pressure lower. He took a deep breath.

"Are *nonna* and *nana* meeting us at the ferry?" Francesco asked, noticing the approaching shoreline too.

"I told them not to worry about us. We can walk to their place. We need the exercise after the long flight," Oliver replied.

The ferry passed Herring Cove Beach and then hugged Long Point. Light green dune grass waved in the breezes as sparkling blue water lapped at the sandy beaches lined with dunes. The boat rounded the last light house and pulled slowly into the harbor filled with moored sailboats and a few yachts parked against the pier. Luca, Francesco, and Oliver walked out onto the bow of the boat and watched as familiar monuments came into view – the tall granite Pilgrim tower, the imposing public library, the historic town hall, and countless charming homes and taverns nestled along the shore.

The ferry docked, and people disembarked quickly, eager to begin their holiday. Francesco, Luca, and Oliver pulled their large suitcases up the gangplank and onto MacMillan Wharf, passing artist and souvenir shacks on one side of the pier and a dozen large fishing boats on the other.

Ben and his friends were behind them, but they quickly caught up. They waved to Luca as they passed, and said, "*Ciao*, Luca. Hope to see you later this week!"

Luca nodded and waved. Francesco nudged him in the side, so he added, "I hope so. Have a nice vacation!"

It was late afternoon, and people were slowly making their way to Tea Dance at the Boatslip Hotel. Each afternoon, hundreds of people gathered on the hotel deck overlooking the harbor to drink, chat, dance, and cruise one another.

"Hey, let's stop in here to get something for *nonna* and *nana*," Francesco remarked as they approached one of their favorite gift shops.

They all walked inside. Francesco and Luca browsed the merchandise together, looking for a little arrival gift for their grandmothers. They had been trained never to arrive at someone's house empty-handed. Oliver strolled to the back of the store where there were shirts, shorts, and summer accessories. He glanced in a mirror and ran his hand through his blond hair, hoping to minimize the tousled mess caused by the overnight flight and the windy boat ride. His eyes looked tired, and his shoulders were slouched. He arched his back, sucked in his gut, and smiled at himself. "Hmm," he murmured. "Not a pretty sight!"

From the moment Oliver met Giancarlo, he was smitten. Early in their relationship, they both went to the gym and stayed in good shape, but Oliver was never that concerned about looking good, focused more on the responsibilities of parenting and work. For the first time in 23 years, he wondered if people would notice him, if someone might find him attractive, sexy, intriguing. He leaned toward the mirror and examined his brows. He ran his fingers over the deepening creases around the corner of his eyes and lifted his chin to tighten his skin.

"Can I help you?" one of the shopkeepers asked, winking at him.

"Just looking," Oliver replied. He breathed in the intoxicating cologne of the young man and could almost feel heat emanating from him as he stood nearby, folding clothes. Oliver walked around the table and began picking up some brightly colored summer shorts.

"What size are you looking for?" the guy asked. He gave a scrutinizing look at Oliver and said, "Let me guess. A 30."

Oliver blushed. He wore a 32, sometimes a 34, but didn't want to admit it. "Yes, but I'm okay. Thanks."

Francesco and Luca held a couple of decorative bowls and approached their father. "What do you think of these?" Luca asked, glancing at the shopkeeper, who continued to stare at Oliver.

"Perfect. Let's get them and head home. Your grandmothers are probably eager to see us."

The shopkeeper was delighted at the prospect of a sale. He walked around the table toward Oliver, placed his hand on Oliver's shoulder, and continued to the register. "Here on vacation?" he asked as he removed the price tags.

"We have a house here," Francesco noted, hoping to pique the interest of the shopkeeper, who continued to smile at Oliver.

"I haven't seen you before."

"Well, this is our summer place. We just arrived today from Italy," Francesco continued.

The man raised his brows. "Well, welcome back home! Don't be strangers. I'm George."

"This is Oliver, our father, and I'm Francesco, and this is my brother Luca," Francesco interjected.

Oliver blushed. He handed George a credit card, and he processed the sale. He wrapped the bowls in tissue and placed them in a decorative bag. "Here you go! Hope to see you around," he added, looking first at Francesco and Luca, and then peered into Oliver's eyes.

They walked out onto the street. Francesco and Luca both stared at their father, who eventually asked, "What?"

"You know what. That guy was cruising you."

"He was just being friendly."

"If he was," Luca said, "he has redefined customer service."

Oliver blushed. Then he said, "Boys, I want to make something perfectly clear. I still love Giancarlo. I'm angry and disappointed, but I'm not ready to date or pursue someone else. So, let's just drop it. It's nice to be noticed and *basta*. That's it."

Luca and Francesco glanced at each other and chuckled.

The three of them continued walking down Commercial Street. Francesco wore a pair of faded blue shorts that showed off his muscular legs and dark tan nicely. He had stuffed his jacket in a side pocket of his suitcase. His dark, curly hair bounced as he walked down the street. He looked like he could have been a model for the Renaissance artist Donatello – a classic Florentine gem with caramel skin, dark eyes, and a sensuous mouth. He kept his eye out for straight girls, although he knew most were day visitors with their families vacationing in Wellfleet or Truro. As they walked farther toward the West End, the crowd became increasingly gay.

Oliver seemed preoccupied, his head facing down and his body intent on efficiently navigating bicyclists and pedestrians as he made his way to his mothers' home with his suitcase. Luca's head pivoted back and forth, clearly engrossed in the live theater before them. A group of guys in Speedos and high heels were hanging on each other as they made their way to Tea Dance, one of them glancing over his shoulder at Luca. However, Francesco noticed Luca's eyes follow a man who walked gracefully past them. He was tall, thin, and lanky. His legs were cute, and he wore colorful tennis shoes. He had a solitary and complaisant aura, almost as if he was indifferent to the surrounding antics. Suddenly, he turned and smiled at Luca. Luca was caught off guard, smiled back, and the man pivoted and continued his serene walk down the street.

"See!" Francesco said to his brother.

"See what?"

"You're a hottie. Even mister dispassionate and composed couldn't help looking!"

Luca blushed.

As they passed the entrance to Tea Dance, Francesco grabbed his father's arm. "Isn't that *nonna's* friend, Gary? Who's that with him?"

Oliver glanced in the direction Francesco was looking and noticed one of his mother's acquaintances. He was a lawyer. His mother seemed fond of him and always oddly pushy, as if she would have preferred Gary as her son-in-law, and not Giancarlo.

Gary had never paired off with anyone, and he seemed particularly affectionate with the man he was with. Gary spotted Oliver and pulled his companion toward them. "Oliver! Anna mentioned you were coming. Did you all just arrive?"

Oliver gave him a friendly embrace and said, "Yes. We're heading to Anna's and Rita's now. How are you?"

"Good. By the way, this is Jack. Jack, this is Oliver and his two sons, Luca and Francesco. Where's Giancarlo?"

"He had some work. He'll join us later," Oliver said, not sure how he would handle similar questions over the next couple of weeks.

"I hope we can get together sometime while you're visiting."

"Certainly. I look forward to it. Nice to meet you, Jack."

"Likewise," he said, smiling warmly.

Luca, Francesco, and Oliver continued their walk west. Francesco kept a close eye on his father, hoping to detect any hidden emotions or thoughts. Even he sensed Gary's continued fascination with his father.

They climbed a small hill and then turned a corner onto a quaint side street with large antique homes. Francesco pushed his way forward and passed through the picket fence ahead of his father and brother. Despite his reputation for being the wild teenager, he was rather sentimental and couldn't wait to see his grandmothers.

Anna had been sitting in a chair, looking out of the window. She rose quickly and went to the door, greeting her family enthusiastically. "Francesco. Luca. Oliver. I can't believe you're finally here!"

Francesco leaped up the stone steps to his *nonna*. He gave her a hug and kissed her on both cheeks. He pushed through the door looking for Rita, who came around the corner from the kitchen and beamed when she saw her grandson. He set down his suitcase and gave Rita a warm hug and kiss. "*Nana*, how are you doing?"

"I'm fine, Francesco. All is good now that you all are here!"

Oliver waited for Luca to pass in front of him. He looked up and down the garden in full summer bloom – pink and blue hydrangeas, mounds of green hosta, and bright yellow and white cone flowers surrounded by a variety of other perennials. A sliver of the harbor was in view down the street, and majestic maple trees shaded the yard.

Luca gave Anna and Rita warm hugs and kissed them on their cheeks. As he embraced Rita, he cocked his head back and peered into her eyes. He sensed something and wondered what was up.

Oliver, in turn, followed Luca and gave his mothers long hugs and kisses. His eyes filled with tears of joy at seeing them and sadness that Giancarlo wasn't with him. "How are you both doing?"

"We're good. But how are you?" Anna asked, giving him a scrutinizing look and wrapping her arm around Rita's back.

"We'll talk. It's been a tough journey."

"I'm sure. Why don't you all come in, unpack, and we can have some refreshments."

Everyone climbed the steep staircase to the hallway above. Anna's and Rita's home had three bedrooms upstairs and a large master suite on the first floor. Luca and Francesco each had their favorite room – Francesco's facing the road, Luca's facing down toward the water, and Oliver's the larger room in the back, with an ensuite bath. Oliver teared up as he put his underwear, shirts, socks, and other things in the dresser filled with clothes he and Giancarlo had left last summer. He pulled out one of Giancarlo's bright pullovers. He vacillated between wanting to hold it to his nose and breathe in Giancarlo's scent and wanting to throw it out of the window in disgust. He simply pushed it and Giancarlo's other things to the side and found space for the things he had brought this year.

Downstairs, the kitchen opened to a large family room with comfortable sofas, easy chairs, bookcases, and a large coffee table where Rita had set out cheese, hummus, crackers, and nuts. "What would you like to drink?" she asked Luca as he entered first.

"*Vino bianco, se c'e.*"

"Of course, there's white wine," she said as she reached into the fridge and pulled out a crisp, cold bottle of Orvieto Classico, one of the family's favorites. She poured him a generous glass.

Francesco came in behind Luca. "I'll have the same," he said, noticing Luca holding the glass of white.

Rita looked at him curiously. Luca interjected, "He's of age in Italy, you know."

She handed him a slightly less generous pour.

When Oliver descended, Anna came from hers and Rita's bedroom. She placed her hand affectionately on Oliver's shoulder. "It's so good to see you!"

"To drink?" Rita asked.

"Anything stiff."

Rita raised her brows. She reached under the kitchen island and pulled out a bottle of gin for a gin and tonic. She knew it was his favorite summer drink.

They gathered at the coffee table and began to nibble on the appetizers. There was an awkward silence, as neither Anna nor Rita wanted to dive into the unavoidable topic of Giancarlo's absence. Luca rallied and asked, "How are plans for your anniversary? You must be so excited!"

Anna and Rita looked at each other warmly. Anna said, "Everything is set. Our friend, Patrick, is reserving his restaurant for us – a ceremony behind the restaurant on the beach and then a reception and dinner afterwards."

"How many are coming?" Oliver asked.

"I think about a hundred," Rita replied.

Francesco's eyes widened. He was impressed with his grand-mothers and looked forward to seeing all of their friends. They were very popular in town, and it was bound to be a who's who of Provincetown.

"Wow," Oliver said. "Anything we can do to help."

"We'll let you know. At the moment, we just want you to relax and have a good time."

Francesco lifted his glass. He wanted to say, to love and family but, since Giancarlo was missing, he thought it would be in poor taste and only stir raw wounds. He said, "Cheers. To the magic of Provincetown. Thanks for having us!"

Everyone caught up on light news, avoiding more serious issues just below the surface. Francesco and Luca were eager to explore and eventually excused themselves for a walk to the shore and into town. Oliver remained with his mothers.

There was an uncomfortable silence at first as everyone hesitated to bring up the obvious. Finally, Rita began. "So, tell us what happened."

"I don't know where to begin," Oliver replied. "It has been horrible."

"We're so sorry. Do you really think he was having an affair?"

Oliver nodded, choked with emotion. Then he said, "I should have seen it coming. Giancarlo always had a roving eye. I caught him several times at parties."

Anna said, "Everyone looks. We wouldn't be human if we didn't. But what's important is conveying to your partner that you love them. I always sensed Giancarlo adored you."

"Me, too. But things have gotten stale. Maybe he's having a mid-life crisis or something. He is 53."

"Was he, in any way, apologetic?"

"He denies it. He is unrepentant since he doesn't think he's done anything wrong. In fact, he's angry at me for even suggesting that he might have been unfaithful."

"So where are things?"

"Unclear."

Anna leaned forward, eager for him to explain.

"I'm afraid we are both entrenched in our positions. I'm hoping he will eventually admit what he did and apologize. I don't know how I will respond, but it would be a first step."

Anna added, "Sometimes we discover we can do things we hadn't imagined before, not so much bad things, but things that we thought were beyond our strength."

"Could that mean walking away from it all?" Oliver asked, bitingly.

"It could," Rita said thoughtfully. "Or it could mean other things. Making amends. Looking at ways to heal."

"I don't know. I can't imagine walking away from the life and family we built, but I also can't overlook something that threatens that family, particularly if it's likely to be repeated."

Anna and Rita looked at each other again and Rita added, "We don't have to figure it all out now. We're just glad you're here."

"I feel like I'm ruining your celebration."

"How?"

"This is supposed to be a time to celebrate commitment and love. I feel like I failed. I feel like I failed you and Luca and Francesco."

"Honey. You haven't failed. You are a wonderful, loving man and father and son," Rita noted.

"But how can I be an example of love and commitment when my marriage has ended?"

"First of all, unless you're not telling us something, it hasn't ended yet. Second, you didn't fail. Giancarlo did. Your sons will see the difference and follow your example," Anna interjected.

As Anna gave voice to her thoughts, Oliver felt a pit in his stomach. She had blamed Giancarlo, and what he did was wrong. But he wondered if he, Oliver, hadn't done enough to preserve their marriage. Maybe Giancarlo's unfaithfulness was a symptom, not a cause of the breakdown of their relationship.

"We have a couple of weeks until the ceremony. Time and distance will tell. Let's take it a day at a time," Rita said warmly, placing her hand on Oliver's arm.

"You know I hate that expression," he said, raising a brow.

"Maybe it's time to live in the moment."

"But the moment is sad. I miss him."

"We know, dear. Sorry. That's okay to feel sad. But let's also celebrate what you've created — these wonderful boys and the life you have!"

Oliver smiled tentatively. Then he said, "By the way, I saw Gary on the way over. He was walking into Tea Dance with someone – a Jack?"

"Ah, yes. He and Jack are an item now. They both seem very happy," Rita said. She sensed Oliver's curiosity and began going through a mental list of single gay men she and Anna might introduce him to. If things didn't work out, their son was still young and eligible.

"So, fifty years! That's amazing. What's the secret?" Oliver asked with a bit more animation.

Anna wanted to say forgiveness, patience, and gratitude, but she held back. She pondered how to formulate her thoughts and then said, "Everyone says it's about remembering the spark that brought you together, rekindling passion, learning how to forgive. But I think the hardest thing is self-esteem."

Rita and Oliver both tilted their heads and leaned forward, waiting for Anna to continue.

"Yes. As odd as it seems, you have to believe that you can push through the challenges. Love isn't something that happens to us. It is something we create, imagine, and cultivate. Sure, the other person is a gift, often unexpected. We feel like we are drawn into a vortex that is magical and providential, and it is. But as in all magic, our imagination is the force or power that moves it."

Oliver gazed off into the distance, deep in thought. When he imagined the future, all he saw was ending, divorce, rupture. He couldn't imagine a rebirth of their love. Moreover, he didn't feel like imagining a rebirth. He was too angry.

10

Chapter Ten – Boys Beach

"Make sure you lock the bikes, and be careful walking across the moors," Oliver admonished his sons as they pedaled down the street toward the beach. They both wore nothing but Speedos, flip-flops, and towels around their necks. They had slung small chairs and umbrellas over their backs.

Francesco had reluctantly agreed to accompany Luca to Boys Beach, unofficially named for a remote section of Herring Cove Beach frequented by mostly young gay men. During the summer, throngs of guys parked their bikes along the road and walked or waded, depending on the tides, across marshes to a section of pristine dunes and water.

Francesco didn't like Boys Beach. There were no girls, and he had to spend considerable effort resisting proposals from guys who thought his Italian looks were exotic. But he wanted to encourage Luca to get over Donato and find love and romance during their vacation, so he decided to hide behind a dark pair of glasses, survey the terrain for opportunities, and coach his brother accordingly.

When they arrived at the entry to the path, there were already a lot of bikes tied up to the fence. They found a space, locked their bikes, and began the trek across the marsh. The tide was going out, so the water was shallow, and in some places, the path was sandy. They followed dozens of other scantily clad men marching toward the beach.

After a long walk, they climbed bright yellow dunes separating tidal pools from the ocean and peered out over the sparkling blue water before them. A gentle, cool breeze blew from the shoreline, and Luca breathed in the fresh, salty air. The beautiful sandy beach stretched in both directions as far as the eye could see. It wasn't as crowded as the beaches by the parking lot, but there was a festive atmosphere and plenty of handsome men ready for a day in the sun.

"Let's head in that direction," Francesco suggested, pointing out an empty spot a hundred meters south.

Luca had learned not to question his brother's strategies. He followed Francesco past several smaller parties of men, laying in various stages of dress and undress, some in the shade of umbrellas, most exposed to the warm sun. Francesco ignored gazes and occasional comments such as – "delicious" and "hon, are you looking for a place to park?" He kept walking, avoiding eye contact.

Luca, on the other hand, was entirely distracted. Francesco walked them through rather than around groupings, and it was impossible for him to ignore handsome men who leaned forward as they passed, adjusted their crotches, or lowered their sunglasses to gain a better view of his assets.

Francesco led them to a sandy area next to several larger groups of guys. He knew that in such groups, there were more unattached guys looking to meet people. He expected it wouldn't be long before several found an excuse to walk up to them.

They unrolled their towels, erected the umbrellas, and opened their chairs. Rita had packed them sandwiches and water. While

Francesco concealed himself behind dark glasses, Luca continued to be unabashedly curious, turning his head right and left to take in the crowd.

"See anyone of interest?" Francesco murmured.

"Not yet," Luca replied. "Again, I'm not sure what we hope to accomplish."

"Meet people."

"Then what?"

"Luca. You need to relax. Don't overthink this. Don't plan the rest of your life here on the beach. Just be friendly, social."

"Easy for you to say."

Francesco grinned.

A couple of guys from the adjacent group had already glanced their direction. Francesco decided it was time to make sure they didn't think he and his brother were a couple. He stood up and walked toward the group and asked, "Do you guys know if the tide is coming in or going out?"

A cute guy looked up excitedly and said, "Going out. By the way, I'm James."

"Francesco," he replied.

"Italian?"

Francesco nodded. Everyone now looked up.

"First time to Ptown?" another in the group asked.

"No. We come each summer."

"I'm surprised we haven't seen you before," another remarked, lowering his sunglasses and glancing over the rims.

Francesco waved Luca over.

"This is my brother, Luca. Luca – the gang!"

"*Ciao*," several said in unison.

"You guys want to join us?"

Luca was about to say yes when Francesco stepped on his toe and said, "Thanks, but we're waiting for some friends. Maybe later."

Francesco gestured for Luca to follow him, and they returned to their umbrellas.

"Why didn't we stay? Several of those guys were really cute!"

"You don't want to appear too eager or desperate. In increases the intrigue."

"Wow! You're really strategic about this!" Luca said to his brother.

"The gay thing throws me off a bit, but I do okay."

They sat under their umbrellas and watched as guys walked back and forth in front of them. Speedo suits were the uniform, and everyone seemed in perfect shape, undoubtedly having spent all spring going to the gym to get fit for their vacation in Ptown. Luca pulled out a book but found it difficult to concentrate, glancing over the top of the pages to watch the passing parade. His dad's question a few weeks ago echoed in his head – do you have a type? He thought he preferred darker, hairier guys, and they certainly caught his attention. Several passed by, glancing his direction.

One, with a bright red Speedo, dark tan, and trimmed chest hair, stopped at their spot and introduced himself. Etienne was from Montreal. He happened to speak Italian as well as French and a little English. When he first approached, Luca remained reclined on his towel, glancing up between Etienne's legs and obsessing over his abundant package. Francesco nudged him to stand, and he did. Etienne was relieved to find people with whom he could have a good conversation and remained a while before finally returning to his buddies.

Luca thought there was a spark, but when Etienne left, a couple of other guys walked by. Luca picked up Spanish as they jostled with each other at the edge of the water, just in front of them. Two of them were Luca's type — dark, hairy, chiseled. One of them, however, was tall, lean, fair, and had tousled light hair. Luca gasped for air as the guy turned toward him and his brother. He caught Luca's eyes and nodded. He left his buddies and walked toward Luca and Francesco. Luca's heart began to pound.

"I'm Pedro," he said, extending his hand. He had a heavy South American accent.

"Luca. And this is my brother, Francesco."

Pedro squinted, intrigued by their names. "Where are you from?"

"Italy," Francesco replied. But Pedro had his eyes fixed on Luca. "First time to Ptown?"

Luca nodded no. "Our grandmothers live here."

"How lucky!"

"And you? *De donde eres?*" Luca asked. Mysteriously, he had spoken Spanish as a young child. Over the years, he studied it and had become rather proficient.

"*Hablas espanol?*"

"*Si.*"

"*Soy de Miami, pero mis padres son de Cuba.*"

"How is it that you have fair skin with Cuban ancestry?"

"It's unusual, but it happens with some frequency. We probably get it from northern Spanish or northern Italian roots."

"Fascinating," Luca said, still mesmerized by the glowing body standing in front of him. Pedro's skin had a light tan, and his body hair had lightened in the sun and salt water. He wasn't particularly muscular, but his height and broad shoulders were imposing. He had a large head with a pronounced jaw and chin and a strong nose. Luca wanted to devour him on the spot and hoped Pedro couldn't read his mind.

They chatted for a while, then Pedro's buddies waved him along. "*Tengo que irme.* Will I see you around town?"

"Yes. The usual places," Francesco noted with a warm smile.

Pedro and his friends continued their walk along the beach. Luca and Francesco sat back down on their towels and Francesco said, "*Bravo, fratello!* Two hotties in a row!"

Luca blushed. "They're just being friendly."

"And?"

"And nothing."

"I vote for Pedro."

"Why?" Luca inquired.

"He has a good vibe. Good energy. He seems comfortable with himself. He's gentle, but has that Latin spark in him, too!"

"How did you pick all that up?"

"You may be the wizard in the family, but I still share your genes and some of your marrow! I must have inherited something."

"I didn't pick any of that up."

"You were too busy drooling over him. Your mouth was wide open."

"Ugh. I hope it wasn't obvious."

"*Scherzo*! I'm just kidding. You handled yourself admirably."

"Do you think he looks too much like Donato?" Luca pressed his brother.

"Well, I wasn't going to bring it up. But they could be twins."

"That much of a resemblance?" he asked.

"Afraid so. Maybe you're honing in on your type. I still think Donato was a nudge from the universe – and now there's proof. A twin thrown in your path. Maybe he's more compatible."

"How do we know Pedro's parents aren't like Donato's?"

"We don't. But like I said earlier, he seems very comfortable with himself."

Luca nodded.

"*Andiamo in acqua*?" Francesco suggested.

Luca nodded, stood, and ran toward the water, diving in as it got deeper.

"It's chilly but refreshing!" Francesco exclaimed as he bounced up and down.

As they grew accustomed to the temperature, they laid back and floated in the gentle waves. Luca then said, "Thanks for coming with me. You make it all look so easy."

"Anything for you."

"What can I do for you?"

"You already did!"

"That was a long time ago," Luca said, referring to his donating marrow to save his brother when they were both younger.

"I'm grateful each day. I also have a really cool brother."

They eventually finished their swim. They walked back to their umbrellas, picked up towels, and dried themselves.

"What do you think about our dads? Are they going to divorce?" Francesco asked with concern.

"Hmm," Luca began. "It's difficult to get a read. I'm not too good at picking up vibes on our family, and I'm easily thrown off by what I want versus what might be real."

"And?"

"I just wish they would find a way to get past this."

"Me, too," Francesco noted. "I would hate to have to adjust to stepfathers. That would suck!"

Luca chuckled, then turned more serious. "I've never seen dad so sad. He's not taking this well."

"What do you think papa's doing? Why did he just storm out?" Francesco added.

"Maybe he was embarrassed. Or maybe he was angry at being accused," Luca observed.

"Has he said anything to you?" Francesco asked.

"Who, papa?"

Francesco nodded.

"Only that he wished us a safe journey and that we'd talk when we got back."

"Nothing else?"

Luca nodded no.

"Should we send him a text?" Francesco asked. "Maybe we can get him to wish he were here and come after all."

Luca nodded. He pulled out his phone and held it up for a selfie. He leaned into Francesco, their tan torsos pressed against each other and their salty matted hair rustling in the wind. They forced a smile for the camera. Luca took several images. They chose the best and then attached it to a text saying, "We miss you, papa. So does dad. Come if you can."

They both leaned back in their chairs and closed their eyes, each wishing their fathers would reconcile.

Shortly thereafter, they heard a lot of laughter and a group of guys appeared at the top of the dune, surveying the beach and looking for a place to pitch their umbrellas.

Francesco immediately recognized them as the guys on the ferry, particularly the one who had been eyeing his brother. They walked down the dune and onto the beach, walking toward Luca and Francesco. As they got close, one of them said, "Hey. You're the guys from the ferry the other day — Francesco and Luca, right?"

"Ben. Right?" Luca asked.

"Good memory. And Drew, Tom, and David."

They all nodded to each other.

"Do you want to join us?" Francesco asked.

The four looked at each other and nodded. "You don't mind?" Drew asked.

"Not at all," Luca replied, clearly intrigued to learn more about the guy who had been cruising him on the boat. Having just met Pedro and having developed a crush for him, Luca was now starting to wonder if he had gone from a shy introvert to a flirt in just a matter of days.

Francesco glanced at his brother, incredulous as to the monster he had created.

Luca hadn't been initially drawn to Ben but, now with him standing in front of him with nothing on but a tight-fitting swim-suit, he had a new appreciation for what Ben might have to offer – at least from a physical perspective. He had a cute body – a compact frame with strong upper legs and a well-proportioned torso and broad shoulders. He had short dark hair and a light covering of dark hair on his chest. He hadn't noticed his nose before, but it was long and sensual, adding a kind of gravitas to his physique. Ben winked at him playfully, almost seductively. Luca felt his heart race.

Tom and David seemed like they might be a couple. They shared an umbrella and chair and had matching towels. They spread them out along the sand and laid face down, their backs and upper legs gleaming in the sun.

Drew seemed distracted by the guys nearby, and Francesco was relieved, hoping he might play matchmaker but avoid the compli-cated webs people were weaving around him. Francesco stood up and walked toward the water while Ben and Luca visited.

"So, did you guys get settled in the other day?"

Ben nodded. "The place we rented is great. We're happy. Now we can sit back and enjoy. And you all, are you settled in with your grandmothers?"

Luca was impressed that Ben had remembered their connection. "Yes. It's nice to be back. They are excited about us being here, too."

Ben pulled out a bottle of water and took a long sip. He extended it toward Luca and asked, "Do you want some?"

"No, thanks."

"Do you mind?" Ben asked as he pulled out a small sandwich and unwrapped it.

"Not at all. We just ate."

Luca leaned back in his chair and looked across the horizon. The sky was hazy and milky white. A few clouds formed in the distance, and a sailboat passed ethereally in front of them. The sun felt good on his chest, and he could feel himself become slightly aroused as he glanced toward Ben, whose legs were crossed facing him.

Ben and he exchanged a few pleasantries as Ben ate. David and Tom were off to themselves, and Drew laid down face up on his towel, hoping the neighbors might notice him sooner than later. Francesco continued to swim.

Eventually, Ben finished his sandwich, and Francesco returned from the water, dried himself, and laid back on his chair, closing his eyes for a nap. Ben pulled out a paperback from his backpack and opened it. Luca glanced over and noticed it was *A Discovery of Witches*, Deborah Harkness's first book in a series about a woman who unlocks a secret grimoire, a book of magic, and gets entangled in a network of witches, demons, and vampires. Aside from Harry Potter, it was Luca's favorite series.

"Great book," Luca remarked to Ben as he began reading.

"You know it?" Ben asked, his eyes widening in surprise.

"One of my favorites."

"Someone recommended it to me. I'm just getting started, but I'm intrigued. I always love stories like this."

Luca's eyes widened, and he could feel his heart begin to race. He thought - cute body, friendly, and a fellow wizard, perhaps. Hmm.

"You'll have to let me know what you think," Luca added.

Ben nodded and returned to his book. He kept glancing over the top of it at Luca, having a difficult time focusing on the text. Luca began to perspire in the sun, his chest and abdomen gleaming in the light. His turquoise Speedo showcased his dark Italian skin, and Ben fixated on Luca's firm sex pressing against the stretchy fabric.

A couple of the guys nearby shed their suits and ran toward the water, Drew clearly intrigued. He wandered nonchalantly to the water himself, leaving his suit on, but diving into the water and swimming toward the others. They jostled in the water and then remained there visiting.

Francesco glanced up and noticed Charles was now putting the moves on Drew. He was relieved. Ben and Luca seemed fascinated with each other, and Tom and David were snoozing.

Francesco closed his eyes and fell asleep. When he woke, about 30 minutes later, Luca and Ben were laying side by side discussing Harkness's book. At one point, Ben rolled on his side to reach for water. Francesco noticed he had a hard on. His brother's legs were raised behind him, waving contently in the air. Ptown had worked its magic.

Later, it was time to return home, shower, and dress for Tea Dance. Tom and David chose to remain longer. Drew had joined the adjoining gang, and Ben accompanied Luca and Francesco back to town. After parting ways near Anna's and Rita's home, Luca and Francesco entered the house. Oliver was napping on the sofa, Anna was reading a book on a chaise in the garden, and Rita was sleeping in her room.

"Well, *fratello*. Thanks for your help."

"So, you like this Ben guy?"

"I didn't think so at first. But he's into magic, and he's thoughtful and charming."

"Like I said on the boat, he's got the hots for you!"

Luca blushed. "He does seem interested."

"He's more than interested. But don't go matrimonial on me. What about Pedro and Etienne? There were several others who seemed interested, too."

"I'm not like you."

"You could have fooled me today! You thought Donato was the one. Then it was Etienne, followed by Pedro, and now Ben. Take your time and be open."

Luca glared at his brother. He felt that he and Donato had met through fate or destiny, and now he believed he and Ben had come together magically. It was undeniable that providence was at work in both situations, but what were the messages? Was Donato just a nudge? Was he significant, but *basta* - a prelude to Ben?

He liked Ben. They had an incredible conversation, and he could imagine coming out to him as a wizard. That was more important than the sexual connection he felt for Donato. Ben was cute in his own way, too. He was not the lean, muscular type he typically pursued, but he had an adorable face, expressive eyes, and playful mannerisms.

"By the way, we have to leave for Tea Dance in 30 minutes," Francesco said, jolting him out of his thoughts.

"Why don't you go without me," Luca suggested, preferring to stay in his room with his reflections.

"Are you kidding me? It's torture at Tea Dance. I'm there for one reason only – to help you meet other guys."

"I don't need to."

"Oh yes, you do! And we're bringing dad."

"Are you sure that's a good idea? It seems weird to encourage him to meet other guys. I still wish he and papa would make up."

Francesco looked off into the distance. He looked uncharacteristically sad and said, "Me, too. But maybe he needs to take a break. Get his mind off their differences."

Francesco walked down the hall and knocked on his dad's door. "Dad, you're going to Tea Dance with us, right? We're heading down in about 30 minutes."

Oliver hesitated. He was sitting in a chair reading a novel he had picked up in the local bookstore. "You all go without me."

"No. We want you to come with us," Francesco said as he pushed the door open. "Luca needs some encouragement."

"If you insist."

Francesco grinned, returned to his room, and began to clean up and dress. All three descended a quarter hour later, gave hugs to Anna and Rita, and walked toward the Boatslip Hotel.

Chapter Eleven – Tea Dance

Oliver, Luca, and Francesco walked several blocks to the Boatslip. As they approached, Oliver could hear the thud, thud, thud of dance music beckoning countless people lined up to show ID's and pay their cover.

Luca was proud that he was now twenty-one and able to enter without hassle. Francesco had created a fake Italian ID he was certain would pass the scrutiny of the lax attendants. One of them glanced at Francesco's card, glanced up at him, raised his brows, and waved him in. Oliver glared at them both, but was glad to have them along.

They descended the front ramp and walked out on the deck, their eyes widening with amazement at the crowd already gathered. Oliver recalled the first time he had gone to Tea when he came to Ptown with Giancarlo over twenty years ago. They were so enamored with each other, and Anna and Rita were doing everything they could to slow them down. He had just come out and had announced he was moving to Rome to become an archaeologist.

Francesco dragged his brother to one of the bars and ordered three gins and tonics. Oliver approached from behind, took his drink, and wandered toward the edge of the deck overlooking the harbor.

"Let's see if Etienne or Pedro or Ben are here," Francesco said excitedly, shielding his eyes from the strong sun and surveying the deck.

Oliver glanced at Luca and said, "What?"

Luca blushed. Francesco interjected, "Dad, Luca has them eating out of his hand! You should see the hot guys lined up!"

Francesco's remark only made Oliver feel more intimidated by the whole Tea Dance scene. He had never really been a single gay man, having paired with Giancarlo just as he came out. They had gone to Tea Dance as a couple, meeting friends and enjoying the music. Oliver felt awkward and ill-at-ease standing on the deck alone. He hoped his sons wouldn't leave him.

They did.

Oliver decided a good strategy was to look out over the water rather than face the crowd. The late afternoon sunlight cast a beautiful yellow glow on the moored sailboats just offshore. He remained angry at Giancarlo for disrupting their lives.

He felt an unusual warmth near his left shoulder and then heard, "It's beautiful this time of the day."

Oliver pivoted slightly. A distinguished young man stood next to him. The sunlight cast an orange glow on his face and illuminated his dark brown eyes. He extended his hand, saying, "I'm Jonathan."

"Oliver."

Oliver was unnerved and unsure what to do.

"You here on vacation?"

Oliver nodded.

"From where?"

Oliver knew if he said Rome, it would unleash the predictable set of follow-up questions he detested.

"Boston."

"Where in Boston. I live there, too."

"Beacon Hill," Oliver responded, referring to his mothers' neighborhood. "And you?"

"The South End."

Oliver nodded. "Do you have a house here?"

Jonathan nodded no. "I just come and hang out with friends. I'm surprised I haven't seen you before."

"I don't get out that often."

"That's too bad," Jonathan replied as he approached the edge of the deck and leaned on the railing. "I just love the light," he observed, then rotated so that he faced Oliver directly.

Oliver scrutinized Jonathan. He had dazzling deep-set brown eyes and radiant, flawless skin. He had a warm and seductive smile, and his dark, coarse hair blew playfully in the wind. Although Jonathan was handsome, Oliver hoped his sons would return and rescue him. He glanced furtively left and right and saw them chatting amiably with some younger men near the dance area. He was trapped.

A beam of light bounced off Oliver's ring and caught Jonathan's eye. "Married?"

Oliver nodded.

"Where's your husband?"

"He'll be here later," Oliver said, deceptively.

"Too bad," Jonathan said, no longer soft-pedaling his interest.

Francesco glanced across the deck and noticed his father talking with Jonathan, who was now standing uncomfortably close to Oliver's face. Francesco wanted his dad to be happy, but he wasn't prepared to see him flirting with someone so quickly. He hurried toward his father, placed one hand on his father's shoulder, and extended the other. "Hello. I'm Francesco."

"Jonathan. Nice to meet you."

"You've met my father, I presume."

Jonathan gave Oliver a curious look.

"Yep. I have children."

"Good for you," Jonathan said. His eyes no longer focused on Oliver. He began to survey the crowd, looking for his next social opportunity and an exit strategy.

"Dad, I want you to meet someone. Can you excuse us?" he then said to Jonathan.

"Certainly. Nice to meet you."

"The same," Oliver said. Francesco gave him a stern look and took his father's arm and began leading him across the deck.

"Thanks for coming to my rescue," Oliver said.

"He was about to eat you up," Francesco observed, relieved that his father hadn't been interested.

"I don't think I'm up for this. It's too painful on a lot of levels."

"Why don't you come over here with us?"

"I don't know. I feel so awkward. I don't know what to say, and I hate just standing around like I'm a lonely loser."

"First of all, if you are with us, you won't be standing alone. Second, have you noticed?" Francesco asked as he nodded toward several men who were staring their way.

Oliver felt self-conscious.

"Dad, I've never seen so many grown men drooling over someone."

Oliver blushed. "They're drooling over you."

"A few are, but most are looking at you. I hate to say it, but you have that exotic surfer look. It's uncommon on the East Coast."

"I'm just not ready for this."

"I'm glad to hear, but you're going to stay and get comfortable.

Luca needs your support," Francesco said, although it was increasingly evident he didn't.

Francesco dragged his father toward Luca, who was chatting with Etienne in Italian.

"*Papa, ti presento Etienne.*"

"*Piacere*," Oliver said, extending his hand. "*Êtes-vous français?*"

"*Quebecois, ma i miei genitori sono Italiani.*"

"Ahh," Oliver murmured, scrutinizing Luca. He wasn't surprised that his son would gravitate to someone who was multilingual. "*Salute*," he said, raising his gin and tonic. He wondered if Luca might hit it off with someone who could bridge continents and cultures, much as he had done. Someone from Quebec with close relatives in Italy might be a nice fit for Luca.

Luca and Etienne returned to their conversation and Francesco spotted someone who appeared to be a straight girl and approached her. Once again, Oliver was alone.

A husky man approached. Oliver had spotted him earlier, and their eyes had connected briefly. Oliver wasn't typically attracted to bears, even relatively slim ones, but there was something about the guy's smile and eyes that had held his attention.

"*Soy Jorge*," the man said, extending his hand.

Oliver looked at him quizzically. He replied, "*Soy Oliver.*"

"*Mucho gusto*," Jorge replied. "I heard your sons speaking Italian and Spanish with some other guys."

"Sons?"

"Yes," he said, nodding to Francesco and Luca. "I've noticed you and your family over the years. Where's your husband?"

Oliver was now alarmed. "Do I know you?"

"No. We've never met, but I come at the same time each year, and I see you. You and your husband are so handsome. I've always admired your family from a distance. It's something I've always longed for."

"Where you are from?"

"Mexico."

"What part?"

"Mexico City."

"Here with friends? Family?" Oliver inquired.

"Unfortunately, no. I'm recently divorced."

"Woman or man?"

"A man. My husband. He had a midlife crisis."

"*Lo siento.*"

"So, your husband?" Jorge pressed.

Oliver pondered an appropriate answer. He wasn't his type, but he was affable and warm and the idea of having someone to talk to, perhaps go out to dinner with, was intriguing.

"Back in Rome."

Jorge raised his brow. "Permanently?"

Oliver found Jorge's pointed question strangely amusing. "To be determined," he replied.

"Well, if you want some company in the interim, here's my card."

Oliver glanced down at Jorge's card. He was an archaeologist at the anthropological museum in Mexico City. Oliver murmured under his breath, "*Cazzo!* How could the universe be so cruel?"

Jorge gave Oliver an embrace and excused himself. Francesco had been watching the entire exchange and gave his father a curious look. He walked toward him.

"Who was that?"

"Jorge."

"Jorge who? What does he do? What did he want?"

"Jorge, Jorge. He's an archaeologist. He wants companionship."

"Uh oh."

"It's nothing."

"He was smooth. He didn't come onto you like Jonathan. He's not your type, but he's not bad looking, either. Those are the dangerous ones!"

"How did you become an expert on gay relationships so quickly?"

Francesco raised his hands in an Italian gesture of 'I don't know.'

"Let's go. We need to get out of here."

"Try telling that to Casanova over there," he said, nodding toward Luca.

"Who's that?"

"Pedro. He's trouble, too."

"Looks just like Donato."

"I know. It's uncanny."

"Let's rescue him. We need to go home and fix dinner."

Oliver led Francesco over to Luca, who was giving Pedro a warm embrace. Pedro was heading off with friends and Luca already sensed his brother and dad were eager to leave. They threw their empty glasses into the trash and headed out onto the street.

"Well, that was interesting," Oliver began.

"Not cool, dad," Francesco observed, furrowing his brow as they walked toward the West End.

"How so?"

"We know you and papa have your differences, and things might not work out, but we're not ready to see you cruise other guys," Francesco began.

"Precisely. I'm in full agreement. So, why did you drag me to Tea Dance?"

Luca and Francesco looked at each other and shrugged their shoulders.

"I don't think we thought it through," Luca proposed. "We always liked it when you and papa came with us. It gave us a sense of security having you around. Now it's just weird."

"I agree," Oliver added.

"So, you're not going to go out with Jorge, are you?" Francesco inquired.

"You don't like him?"

"Since when have you been into bears?" Francesco asked.

"I haven't. But he seemed nice."

"You don't even know him. He could be a psycho," Francesco interjected.

"I didn't pick that up," Oliver observed.

"I think your filters are rusty. When was the last time you had to sort these things out?" Luca asked.

Oliver looked off into the distance and then glanced back at his sons. He said, "Never. This is all new to me."

"Precisely. You're at great risk!" Francesco said emphatically.

"I'm not entirely naïve," Oliver pleaded.

Francesco and Luca both glared at their father. "Maybe papa will call soon and work things out," Luca said. Francesco nodded. They both hoped there would be a reconciliation.

"I hope so, too. But I'm not going to be a hermit."

"You don't have to be a hermit, but don't go running after every cute guy that smiles at you," Francesco said.

"That's interesting advice coming from you," Oliver said.

"I'm hurt that you would say that," Francesco said, chuckling.

They turned the corner near Anna's and Rita's house and walked into the garden. "Boys, thanks for a fun afternoon. I think you might have to fend for yourselves in the future. I'm not ready for this yet."

Both Luca and Francesco sighed in relief, both hoping their fathers would still reconcile.

Chapter Twelve – Anna and Rita

The next day, Luca and Francesco returned to Boys Beach. Oliver took a long bike ride.

The afternoon light streamed through the blinds in Anna's and Rita's room, the kind of light that made Provincetown such a draw for artists. It cast a vermillion glow on the white quilt of their bed. Rita laid next to Anna and stroked her silky silver hair.

Anna whispered, "So, what do you think?"

"I've never seen him so sad. All these years, he's been the rock for Giancarlo and the kids."

"It's as if he's been beaten down and crushed. Thank God for Francesco's humor and playfulness, otherwise he would be in a deep hole."

Rita chuckled, thinking about Francesco dragging him to Tea Dance. "So, what should we do?"

"Nothing," Anna replied. "They have to work it out themselves."

"I know, but we have to do something."

Anna glanced across the room. She had her own worries. She turned her head toward Rita and said, "How are you feeling?"

"I'm energized by their being here. I'm just afraid the damage to the heart muscle is going to catch up with me. We got through the cancer, but this seems scarier."

"Oh, love. Let's think positive. You'll get better. You're doing all the right things – herbs, Reiki, homeopathy, massage, and diet."

"I hope so. I'm sorry to put you through this."

"Don't worry about me. Let's take care of you. What do you need?"

"Your love."

"You know you always have that," Anna said as she took Rita's hand and massaged it.

Rita wasn't sure. They had had their own rough patches. Rita battled breast cancer twice, eventually having a double mastectomy. Afterwards, she questioned her own sexual appeal and pushed Anna away.

"How did we do it?" Rita asked.

"What?" Anna asked in return.

"How did we get through our difficulties?"

"We almost didn't," Anna said, staring at Rita.

"And?"

"One day I realized that we had overcome opposition from our parents because we believed in each other, we believed we could pull it off - even in the seventies when there wasn't a lot of acceptance. During our duel with cancer, I had grown to doubt myself and doubt us, and realized you probably did, too. It was an epiphany. I realized our intentions are powerful. We can imagine the outcome we want – that's what magic is: imagination, belief, confidence," Anna elaborated.

"I remember that shift. You drew me out of myself. You made me feel beautiful again."

"You still are!" Anna said, leaning toward Rita and giving her a warm moist kiss.

Rita grinned and gazed into Anna's green eyes. Anna reached toward Rita's shoulder and pulled down her sleeve. She adored the contours of Rita's shoulder, how her curly dark hair found places to rest. She ran her finger through the curls and pulled one toward her playfully.

Anna reached up under Rita's dress and pulled down her panties, running her hand over her buttocks, still firm and shapely. Rita arched her back as she felt Anna's smooth hands caress her skin. "What are you doing?" she said in false protest.

"I'm going to tell you how much I love you. It's an early anniversary present."

"Are you sure?" Rita asked.

"Why?"

"The boys."

"They're at the beach. We're alone, and I want to make sure you know you're the most beautiful woman in Ptown."

"Have you been smoking something?"

Anna put her hand up to Rita's dark red luscious lips. "Quiet." Then she traced her hand over Rita's dark brows. "Your eyes have always entranced me. Dark and alluring."

Rita reached over and stroked Anna's hair again, placing her hand behind Anna's head and pulling her toward her. She kissed her passionately, breathing her in and feeling the warmth of her body pressed against hers. She could feel Anna's breast firming up. She reached her hand behind Anna's back and unzipped her dress, letting the shoulders of the dress fall down her arms and her breasts break free of the fabric. They were full and golden. She began to skim the side of Anna's breast with her warm, wet lips. Anna moaned.

Anna laid on her back and let Rita slide her dress off. Rita leaned over Anna and began to kiss the side of her abdomen, taut with arousal and illuminated by the sunlight streaming through the blinds. She made her way down Anna's body and playfully kissed around the edges of Anna's dark blue panties.

Anna pulled Rita down on top of her and unzipped her dress. She felt Rita tense up. She was still self-conscious. She let the dress drop haphazardly, revealing and concealing different parts of Rita's caramel skin. Anna kissed Rita's shoulder, then her upper torso, and then down the center of her chest. She loved the distinctive flavor of Rita's skin. It was like eating chocolate - smooth, silky, and sweet. She reached down with one of her hands and gently began to press her fingers around Rita's vagina, slowly circling it and then, as she became moist, inserting a finger inside, feeling the walls fill with warmth and arousal. Rita began to breathe more heavily, and her heart raced with desire.

Rita rolled over on her side and raised one of her legs over Anna's hip. Anna pressed her finger deeper into Rita, feeling the moistness increase. She felt herself become wet and her pelvic muscles flex in anticipation.

Rita sensed Anna's arousal and caressed her breasts, leaning over and kissing her neck, clavicle, and shoulder. Anna arched her back and moaned. She took Rita's hand and led it to her own sex, pressing against herself as she pressed against and inside Rita.

Rita felt tremors in her hips as Anna continued to stroke her. Her lower body became warm, and she could feel a wave of pleasure mount within. She gazed into Anna's eyes, green and mysterious. Their tenderness made her feel desired, and she let go of all self-doubts. She removed her wet fingers from inside Anna and stroked the contours of her pelvis, watching Anna writhe in pleasure. Her skin had become warm, almost hot. She pulled Anna close to her and felt the warmth invade her.

Anna opened her mouth and surrounded Rita's dark ruby lips with her own, inhaling the warm wetness within. Their tongues slid against each other, and both savored the feel of their bodies pressed close together. Anna continued to massage Rita, finding the spots she knew would bring her to a climax. Rita pressed her fingers inside Anna, sliding them around her clit, pressing, rubbing, and massaging until she felt Anna shudder, waves of intense pleasure coursing through her body. Anna pressed her hand against Rita's pelvis, her fingers still immersed in Rita's wetness, and she watched Rita's hips begin to move as she came, swells of pleasure flowing up and down her lower body.

They both collapsed into each other's arms. Anna nuzzled her nose into Rita's shoulder, breathing in the distinctive scent that rose from her moist body. Rita savored Anna's powerful arms wrapped around her. She felt loved and safe.

Anna whispered in Rita's ear, "I love you. It's as if we were twenty again."

"Not too bad for two seventy-year-olds, right?" Rita replied, chuckling at their exchange.

"It's funny. I thought with Oliver and the boys around, I'd feel old. But they inspire me to dream and wonder and imagine," Anna noted.

Rita had a worried look on her face. She was still apprehensive about her health, but she nodded. "Hmm. Yes," she murmured, as convincingly as she could.

Rita pulled herself up, slid off the bed, and walked toward the bathroom. Anna admired the shapely contours of her hips and the beautiful curves of her legs. She smiled to herself, pulled herself to the edge of the bed and rose, reaching for a housecoat hung on a hook behind one of the doors.

They both paused at the dresser just outside the bathroom door and gazed at a large photo of their family, one that had been taken when Giancarlo and Oliver had celebrated their twentieth anniversary a couple of years earlier. Anna's and Rita's friend Jason, a professional photographer and artist, had taken the picture from their balcony in Boston. The afternoon light cast a luminous glow on them, and Jason had captured their joy and affection as they all glanced at each other playfully.

"That was such a momentous day," Anna noted. She placed her hand on Rita's shoulder and smiled.

"I know. I never imagined that we would celebrate our fiftieth, much less that we would have a son celebrating his twentieth with two sons to boot!" Rita added.

"What do you think will happen?" Anna asked fretfully.

Rita shook her head. "I don't know. Look at all that love and joy. How can it turn sour so quickly?"

"I know. One moment things are solid and certain and then suddenly, they are not. How does that happen?"

"Vulnerability," Anna said without elaboration.

Rita looked at her curiously.

"Vulnerability," she repeated. "You can't love unless you become vulnerable. But if someone betrays that vulnerability either through unfaithfulness or through a thoughtless or insensitive deed, it all unravels. One becomes protective of oneself, building walls."

Rita thought back at their own history. She realized how easy it was to cause the other to retract. "I'm sorry for the times I didn't respect your vulnerability. I always saw you as strong and invincible." She pulled Anna up close to her and gave her another kiss. She rubbed her hands over Anna's shoulder and stroked her silky hair.

"I'm not invincible," Anna whispered.

"I know that now."

"And I know now that your façade of being an easy-going and unaffected Italian is just that — a façade. I never want to take you for granted."

Rita looked curiously at Anna. For the past couple of years, Anna had been intentional about telling Rita how much she loved her and in highlighting all of her best qualities. It had been effective in helping Rita to get over her cancer and trust love and life again. "I appreciate how you nurture us!"

"So, what do we do?" Anna asked.

"About Oliver and Giancarlo?"

Anna nodded.

"I am so angry at Giancarlo. How could he do this to Oliver and the boys?" Rita said. She kept glancing at the photo, shaking her head.

Anna traced her fingers over the image of her family. "I wish I had a magic wand and could fix everything."

Rita's brows rose. Anna didn't ordinarily put much credence into magic.

"Why are you looking at me like that?" Anna continued.

"Magic?"

"I'd try anything at the moment," Anna said, her gaze drifting across the room.

"When I look at the four of them, I see magic. I see love. I don't think we need to cast a spell or conjure up some remedy for them. I think we just model love and trust the process," Rita said.

"Why do you keep using that phrase?" Anna said, grimacing.

"I believe they really love each other. Whatever happened will ultimately challenge them to love more deeply. They will emerge more committed to each other. We did," Rita said.

"It's too painful to watch," Anna continued, not sure she could trust that things would work out.

"Oliver is our son. We've modeled love, forgiveness, vulnerability, fortitude, and commitment. Those virtues are not forged in a vacuum. They are like crystals that take shape under pressure and heat."

"A while ago, you said you were angry at Giancarlo."

"I still am. But I know things will work out. It's an Italian thing. We let things out and then hug and kiss."

"Amazing," Anna said, staring into Rita's dark eyes. It was true. Rita had a mercurial personality. She could be angry and excitable and then become the most loving, affectionate, and tender person in just a matter of moments.

Anna pushed Rita's back and nudged her into the bathroom. "We better get moving. The boys will be back from the beach before long, and they will be famished," Anna added.

"I'm famished," Rita said, chuckling. "You wore me out earlier."

"I have a feeling you could do a second round," Anna said with a twinkle in her eye.

It was now Rita who pushed Anna toward the sink. "Make yourself presentable, dear! We have company."

They both leaned over the pair of sinks and faced the large mirror. They grinned at each other, both aware of how fortunate they were. Rita playfully ratted her hair and slipped a shoulder of her housecoat down on her arm. "How's this?" she asked.

"Perfect. And this?" Anna said as she ran lip stick clumsily over her lips.

"Are you going for the Dina Martina look? It's quite effective. It might take Oliver's mind off things!"

Anna wiped the lipstick off and pulled herself together. She could be playful for a moment or two, but she knew a lot was riding on her shoulders. She was relieved to see Rita comb out her hair and wash her face.

A short while later, they dressed and went into the kitchen, where they readied snacks and beverages for Oliver, Luca, and Francesco.

13

Chapter Thirteen – Praiano

Giancarlo stretched out on the chaise and peered at the sparkling blue water just beyond the terrace. He felt the warm sun penetrate his skin and deepen his tan. He sipped copious amounts of mineral water, nursing a painful hangover. Closing his eyes, he tried to ignore the thoughts swirling in his head. Had he been too quick to dismiss Oliver's concerns? Had he given Oliver reason to suspect things – things he hadn't done, but that he had certainly entertained in his head? What would happen now? Would they divorce? Would Oliver move back to the States? What would they do with the boys?

The Belvedere in Praiano was a classic Amalfi Coast family-run pensione with incredible views of the Mediterranean and an attentive staff who pampered guests with good food and drink. A friend had recommended the place, and Giancarlo was happy to escape Rome and the mess he had made with Oliver and the boys.

Nunzia, the owner of the establishment, fussed over her guests, making sure they had towels, pillows, umbrellas, and drinks. "*Tutto bene*?" she asked as she strolled past Giancarlo.

He nodded silently, avoiding words that jarred his headache.

Patrizio, the manager, escorted some newly arrived guests around the terrace and the deck near the water, showing them the property and its amenities. Patrizio had been particularly friendly the evening before, making sure Giancarlo's room was to his liking, and pouring him generous glasses of a delicious local wine during dinner, obviously contributing to his pounding head.

As he accompanied the new guests back into the main building of the hotel, Patrizio winked at Giancarlo. Giancarlo glanced at his phone to see if there were any new messages. There were none. Clearly, Oliver was upset and not eager to overlook their disagreement.

Most of the clientele were straight and English or Italian. Few had children; most eager to escape family responsibilities and reconnect with each other. Giancarlo realized he and Oliver had become too familiar and complacent with each other over the years, not nurturing their relationship. They were both busy with work and immersed in the responsibilities of raising two lovely but challenging boys. As he looked out over the terrace at the handsome couples lying in the sun, he asked himself when the last time he and Oliver had taken time to be with one another alone in an exotic place? It had been ages.

The sun increased in intensity, and Giancarlo slid his chaise under the shade of the large umbrella. He decided to get some aspirin and find a book to read in his room. He slipped on a pair of shorts over his Speedo and stepped into his flip-flops. He climbed the stairs to the main part of the building and entered the lobby.

Patrizio was standing at the main entrance with his hand on the shoulders of a hunky man who held a box full of wine. A farm truck in the driveway was filled with cases of wine.

Patrizio and the man chuckled and smiled affectionately at each other, and Giancarlo found it intriguing, even a bit arousing. Both were mature, like him, and there was a raw masculine energy between them. The farmer wore a white tee-shirt, and his formidable chest was noticeable as it pressed against the fabric, slightly moist with sweat.

Giancarlo had noticed Patrizio before, but in his exchange with the farmer, he gazed at him with fresh eyes. He had broad shoulders and a trim torso. As he turned toward the door, Giancarlo noticed he had a nice butt and strong, dark legs. "Hmm," he murmured to himself. "Maybe this place isn't as straight as it seems."

The farmer brought more cases of wine into the lobby and stacked them in a corner. Patrizio helped him and took out a clipboard to check inventory.

Giancarlo walked down the hall, entered his room, downed a couple of aspirin, and retrieved a novel he wanted to read. He returned to the lobby, and as he began to head out onto the terrace, he caught the farmer's eyes. Their glance lingered just long enough for Giancarlo to wonder if there might be some interest on the farmer's part. As he pivoted toward the terrace, he realized Patrizio had noticed his and the farmer's exchange. To give his roving eyes some legitimate pretext, Giancarlo asked, "Is this more of the incredible wine you served at dinner last night?"

Patrizio nodded. He wasn't fooled by Giancarlo's attempt to shift focus but said, nonetheless, "Yes, it comes from our family vineyard up in the hills."

"You have your own vineyard?"

"Yes. It's the Benevento vineyard. It's been in our family for generations and produces great wine."

"And you're part of the family?" Giancarlo asked as he gazed at the farmer.

"*Si. Sono Pepe. Piacere.*"

"*Giancarlo. Piacere.*"

Pepe extended his muscular arm toward Giancarlo, and they shook hands. Giancarlo felt the calloused skin of Pepe's hands in his and peered into his deep, alluring eyes. Pepe smiled warmly.

Pepe returned to his truck to retrieve one last case of wine. He placed it in the corner of the lobby and shook Patrizio's hand. Pepe waved at Giancarlo and jumped in the front of his truck, cranked on the motor, and sped off. Patrizio looked up and noticed Giancarlo still staring out the front door. He then said to Giancarlo, "*Non fa parte della nostra squadra.*"

"What do you mean?" Giancarlo replied in protest, although now he knew Patrizio was on to him.

"He doesn't play on our team!" Patrizio said in perfect English.

"*Ma!*"

"But what? Don't pretend innocence, Mr. Russo!"

Giancarlo took a deep breath and asked, "How did you know?"

"Gaydar – as well as the fact that you are here alone, handsome, in good shape for your age, and your wardrobe is more stylish than most of our guests!"

"So, you?"

Patrizio nodded.

Giancarlo smiled, perhaps a little too eagerly for Patrizio, who held up his ring finger. "*Sposato.*"

"With the farmer?"

"No. I told you he's not one of us."

"You could have fooled me."

"Yes. He does have that aura and charm to him. He knows he has an impact on gay men, and he lets them think they have a chance."

"So, does your husband work here?"

"In Positano. In a restaurant. And you, where's your husband?" Patrizio asked as he glanced at Giancarlo's ring.

"In the States. We had a fight. A big one."

"*Mi dispiace.* Do you want to talk? Some coffee?"

Giancarlo nodded.

Patrizio went into the kitchen and made them both double espressos. They sat in two comfortable chairs in the lobby and sipped their coffee.

"So, where in the States did your husband go?"

"To Provincetown."

"You're kidding?"

"No. My husband is American, and his mothers live there."

"Wow! I'm American, too, from nearby."

"You could have fooled me. You look like someone from this part of Italy, and you don't have an accent."

"My grandparents were from here, and I've spent the summers here for quite some time now. I guess I've become a local. So, where's your husband from?"

"Boston."

"Small world! So, tell me. What happened?"

"It's a long story."

"I have time."

"My husband thinks I was having an affair. Someone said something to him."

"And?"

"I wasn't. But I guess I can see how he might think it was true."

Patrizio's eyes widened, inviting Giancarlo to continue.

"I have a gay co-worker who is quite handsome. We get along nicely, and we have to travel for work. We're good friends, but *basta*."

"So, what happened?"

"Someone made some inference that Riccardo was my new boyfriend. Riccardo and I had to do an overnight in Milan, and Oliver insisted we not go. I was upset he accused me and, in principle, traveled with Riccardo overnight."

"Couldn't you dispel the rumor?"

"There was other incriminating evidence – texts, photos, and condoms."

Patrizio's eyes widened, and his mouth stood agape. "That sounds pretty bad. And you say you are innocent?"

"I never cheated on him, and my co-worker and I are good friends but could never be lovers."

"So?"

"The texts and photos look bad, but they are just Riccardo's way of expressing himself. After all these years, I'm surprised Oliver doesn't trust me. I do everything for our family. I work hard and struggle daily with the biases against gay people in the Italian banking world. It really hurt me when he accused me of being unfaithful."

"I'm probably not the best person to talk to. My ex cheated on me."

"But he admitted it, right?"

Patrizio nodded. "So, why are you so upset?" he asked.

"I didn't cheat on him, and he gave me an ultimatum."

"What kind?"

"He doesn't want me to travel overnight with my co-worker. I need to travel to nurture important accounts. And I feel like that's just the start, that I'm going to be on a short leash, always being scrutinized and monitored. At this point in my life, I shouldn't have to deal with that."

Patrizio could see Giancarlo was getting worked up. His face was red, and his hands were shaking. He also had witnessed Giancarlo's roving eye earlier, and wondered if his husband might have seen things, too. Giancarlo was sexy – even for someone in his fifties. Patrizio imagined that if he were his husband, he'd keep a close eye on him, too!

"Why don't you talk with him about your feelings?"

"I think we're probably past that. I stormed out of the house, ended up traveling with my co-worker, and never returned home."

"Hmm. That sounds problematic. Has he reached out to you?"

"Only nominally. He let me know when he left for the States with our boys."

"You have children?"

Giancarlo nodded. "Two boys. Sixteen and twenty-one."

"Wow! How did they take your fight?"

"I don't know. I haven't talked to them."

Patrizio looked off into the distance and rubbed his chin in thought. "Why haven't you reached out to them or to your husband?"

"I don't know. I guess I'm still angry."

"Did he touch a raw nerve or something?"

"What do you mean?"

"Well, have you ever wondered what it would be like if you were with someone else? Or do you fret over getting older? Do you hope others will notice you, make the move on you, even if you have no intention of acting on it?"

Giancarlo blushed.

"Hum hmm. I saw it with my ex, although he ended up acting on it. It's easy to pick up on our partners' doubts and active imagination. Your husband must be very intuitive. Maybe he senses your restlessness."

Giancarlo looked away evasively.

Patrizio asked, "Any photos of him?"

Giancarlo opened his phone and scrolled to a photo of Oliver and showed it to Patrizio.

"Wow! He's really cute!"

"I know."

"Does he know?"

"What? That he's cute?"

Patrizio nodded.

"I thought he did, but maybe he doesn't."

Patrizio rubbed his chin in thought and added, "Do you think you're attractive and sexy?"

"Why do you ask?"

"Let me put this delicately – and it comes from experience. It looks like Oliver might be younger than you. Are you in any way insecure about aging, perhaps feeling less desirable?

Giancarlo smiled. Patrizio had actually hit upon something he was afraid to acknowledge. "Yes. He's younger. 10 years younger. He's also extremely talented. There are times I don't feel I deserve him. I feel like I am not enough for him. He's incredible with our boys – one of whom is talented in his own way."

"Sometimes we sabotage our own relationship not because we are unfaithful or uncommitted, but because we doubt what we bring to the relationship; we doubt ourselves. And the other person can sense that hesitation. If they are perceptive, they might recognize our insecurity. But if someone else makes allegations, the insecurity can look like it has more to do with hesitation about the relationship, and that can become toxic."

"Wow. That's insightful."

"The owner of the pensione, Nunzia, is a wise woman. She knows people well, and she gave me a lot of advice, as Zeno, my husband, and I worked through our issues."

"Is Zeno younger?"

Patrizio nodded. "And handsomer."

"I doubt that," Giancarlo said, glancing at Patrizio playfully.

"We also have a son, and parenting can interfere with romance."

"Hmm," Giancarlo murmured, convinced he needed to work through a lot of things if he was going to salvage his relationship with Oliver.

"Years ago, I was in a similar situation. Nunzia, the owner, sat me down and gave me incredible advice. This place has a special charm to it – as if it forces people to see themselves in ways they had never considered before."

"I used to believe in that, in providence or destiny," Giancarlo said.

"What happened?"

"It's just a way we trick ourselves into thinking a moment or a relationship or a circumstance has more meaning than it really does. It motivates us to value and cherish something as if it is special, as if it is graced. But, in the end, it's all just a matter of accident or luck."

Patrizio gazed at Giancarlo, tilted his head, and said, "Wow. That's cynical."

"It's not cynical. It's just realistic. Oliver and I are two handsome men who met and fell in love. There was nothing providential about it. If it was, why did it fail?"

"Who's saying it has failed? That's a decision you make. You can just as easily say that the challenge you are facing is also providential. It's the universe's way of forcing you to take stock of where you are and see what you need to do to sustain your love."

"So, is providence or destiny just a way of talking about a positive attitude?"

Patrizio looked out of the window at the busy road in front of the hotel. He glanced higher, above the road, at the hills and mountains rising from the sea. He recalled his journey here many years ago and the connections he made; connections that far exceeded his wildest dreams. He turned to Giancarlo and said, "Belief in providence or destiny or magic inspires us to look below the surface and see the unfolding of things in ways that are far deeper than what appears on the surface. I'm sure the circumstances under which you met your husband were improbable. They point to something happening at a deeper level. You can choose to ignore them and simply react to the obvious, or you can embrace them."

"You don't know how surreal this conversation is."

Patrizio gazed at Giancarlo curiously, waiting for him to continue.

Giancarlo hesitated and then proceeded, "One of my sons thinks he's a wizard, a sorcerer. There's some suggestion that he and his brother were connected to each other in a past life. My son speaks multiple languages, can heal people, can travel back in time, and picks up on people's thoughts. So, I've heard all of this before. But, right now, I'm unconvinced. If we were all meant to be together, to continue working through things that started centuries ago, why am I here and they in Ptown? It was a pleasant fantasy, but it's not real."

"As I suggested earlier, why can't the current crisis be a way of challenging you to look deeper, embrace destiny, and heal the wounds you have carried into adulthood – either from your child-hood here or perhaps other lives before?"

"Or it's not."

"Hey, I can't prove providence or destiny. There are things that happen that have too much meaning to be merely accidental. But it's impossible to prove. Ultimately, it's a choice. You can choose to live life magically or not."

"Hmm," Giancarlo murmured, realizing that perhaps Patrizio was right. Even if magic wasn't real, if one embraced it, life would be en-chanted, pregnant with meaning, possibility, wonder, and mystery. He wondered if his life, if his and Oliver's lives, had become flat?

"Let me ask you something," Giancarlo added. "How do couples keep their relationships from becoming boring?"

"You're asking me? Honey, I work at a place where I'm on call 24/7. Zeno works late at the restaurant. We have a son who requires lots of parenting and supervision. Our free days are spent with family in the hills. My life is not a gay cliché!"

"So, is that our destiny — to end up like countless other couples?"

Patrizio nodded no. "Everyone has their strategy. Some couples open things up to outsiders. That's not Zeno's and my thing. Others are constantly moving, buying new houses and doing all sorts of renovations. They avoid boredom or waning affection with lots of projects. I know some couples who travel a lot. And others volunteer or get involved in cultural organizations. I think the ultimate secret is remembering the unique circumstances that brought you together and then doing everything you can to remind the other what you saw in them, and what you have discovered in them over the years. It's amazing how invigorating that is."

Giancarlo nodded. "I think we're probably like you and Zeno. More conventional. But I'm not sure we've ever addressed the question of routine, boredom, tedium. Business trips with my colleague are innocent, but they are also probably a way I've escaped from the routine. When we travel, the bank pays for lavish meals, hotels, and other perks. It's fun. I realize Oliver doesn't have that, and he probably senses there's something I'm fleeing. It's not him, but he doesn't know that."

"I think you've probably hit the nail on the head! Now, as Nunzia once said to me, I think you know what you need to do!"

Giancarlo nodded. He realized he needed to talk with Oliver, let him know how much he adored him, and find a way to rekindle their early romance. But, at the moment, he was still angry that Oliver had questioned his integrity and commitment. He fought competing urges – one to nurse his own wounds and the other to reach out to Oliver and recognize how he might feel betrayed as well. At the moment, he found it difficult to forgive, and he resigned himself to a lonely but much needed respite.

14

Chapter Fourteen – Revelations

Donato was lying on his bed, staring at the ceiling. He scrolled through texts from Luca. Luca had been frantic about the fight his dads had and reached out repeatedly to Donato for solace and company. Donato hadn't responded out of fear of his father. Now Luca was in Provincetown, and Donato realized he had let him down.

He thought back to the discussion he had with his father after finding Luca's guidebook and had resigned himself to letting Luca go. He wondered if he had let himself down, the self that dreamed of love, companionship, and a life that resonated with the deepest parts of himself.

His father's beliefs about gay relationships weren't based in fact or reality. Donato admired Luca and his dads and wondered what all the criticism of gay families and gay parenting was really about. Luca's family was every bit as strong, enduring, and loving as his. But he felt sad and a little disillusioned as Luca's texts conveyed dismay at what had happened. His own sense of stability, love, commitment had been shattered when his fathers parted ways.

Donato scrolled through the texts, entranced by the brightly lit screen and the words flashing in front of his eyes. He felt himself doze off and laid his head on the pillow. When he woke, he picked up the phone to see if there were any new texts. None.

His parents were away at a dinner party, and he wondered what his dad had done with the guidebook and gay flyer he had found. He wandered down the hall to his father's study. He opened the door and breathed in the scent of old books, brandy, and cigars. His father's desk was neat and devoid of papers or files. As a kid, he had watched his father file documents in a cabinet and thought he knew where he might have hidden the key. He reached under one of the bookcases, found the key, and opened the cabinet. He wasn't sure what he would do when he found the book, but it felt like his only link with Luca, who he missed dearly.

He thumbed through the top drawer where there were some small boxes and hanging files. He didn't find the guidebook, but he was intrigued by the brightly colored folders neatly labeled with names of banks, clients, organizations – some of which he knew were active in lobbying against gay rights. Toward the back of the drawer, there was a folder remarkable for its thickness and the name Martina Millefiori written on the label. He pulled it out of the drawer and glanced inside. There were receipts of funds sent monthly to Martina, as recently as last month. The funds were substantial. There was nothing in the file linking her to an organization or to a bank. Donato furrowed his brow as he thumbed through receipts and papers, intrigued by who this might be.

He continued to search the cabinet without finding the guidebook. He closed the cabinet and returned the key.

The next morning, his father was at work, and his mother was doing some chores. He approached her in the kitchen and asked, "*Vuoi un caffe?*"

"Yes. I would love a coffee. When do we ever take the time to sit and chat?"

Donato prepared an espresso for them, and they sat at the center island of the kitchen, taking slow sips. "Mama, do you know a Martina, a Martina Millefiori?"

Donato's mother blanched. She placed her coffee down on the counter and glanced off evasively. She turned back to Donato and said, "Why do you ask? Did you meet her? Read something about her?"

Donato wasn't sure how much to disclose to his mother about having searched his father's files, but he suspected she had tried to conceal Luca's guidebook earlier. "I was looking for something in father's office and ran across her file."

"Hmm," Laura murmured. "I suppose at some point you would have found out about her and that you have a stepbrother."

"A stepbrother?" Donato exclaimed, his eyes wide and his mouth agape.

She nodded. "Martina is someone your father had an affair with. That is why you and I remained in Milan while he took an apartment in Rome, their apartment."

Donato felt blood rush to his face. He was at a loss for words. "An affair?"

Laura nodded.

"How long?"

"Fortunately, only a few years. But it was terrible. Martina was young, only seventeen. She was part of a secretarial team at his bank. She got pregnant, and she was going to report the affair to the managers. Your dad convinced her to keep things quiet. He promised to buy her an apartment and stay with her and the boy."

"Do others know?"

"No. It's been an expensive mistake for him. He has paid Martina a lot of money. He sends her an allowance each month for her up-keep and for the child's education."

"And you stayed with him?"

"What choice did I have? I didn't have a profession, and I didn't come from money. Even if I threatened to expose him, I would have needed a lot of resources to launch a case. He was apologetic about it, and we settled our differences."

"So, everything is good between you and father?"

"It's okay. We have an understanding. We have become companions, although we disagree on a lot of his conservative politics," she said, winking her eye at her son.

"So, he's a hypocrite!"

"Yes. I'm afraid so. I think he genuinely believes what he believes, but his behavior is not in line with his beliefs."

"So, how can he accuse Luca's fathers of being promiscuous and unfaithful when he's done the same?"

"I know. It doesn't make sense. Sometimes people project shame on others to make them feel less shame about themselves. It's perverse, but unfortunately quite common."

"And you?" Donato inquired, wondering where his mother stood.

"Son, I suspect you are so inclined," she began, not quite comfortable using the term gay to refer to him. "Know that I love you as you are, and I always will."

Donato's eyes turned red, and a tear streaked down his cheek. He leaned toward his mother and gave her a warm and long hug. She rubbed her hands over his back. "Let's keep this our secret."

Donato leaned back and looked at her in the face and nodded. He wasn't ready to come out to his father, but knowing his mother was an ally felt deeply comforting.

"Do you know Aunt Teresa?" Laura asked, looking off into the distance.

"You mean the one in Boston?"

Laura nodded and said, "Her daughter is getting married. She sent us an invitation, but we can't go. But you could." She winked at him.

"When?"

"It's next week. She's been insisting that we come, and I keep putting her off. I think I could convince your father that you should go to represent us. I don't think he knows Luca is in the States, near Boston." She winked at him again.

Donato stared at his mother in disbelief, not sure how she knew Luca was in Ptown.

She grinned sheepishly. "Well," she added. "Shouldn't you book a ticket and start packing?"

Donato didn't know what to say. He leaned toward his mother and gave her a warm embrace. "*Grazie!*"

"*Ti voglio tanto bene. Spero che tu possa trovare l'amore* – that you find love!"

15

Chapter Fifteen – Donato Travels to Ptown

Luca stood on MacMillan Wharf as the fast ferry from Boston approached. Bright sunshine sparkled on the water between the pier and the tip of Cape Cod, Long Point, where yellow sand, light green dune grass, and a small lighthouse marked the entrance to the harbor. Luca peered at the bow of the boat to see if he could spot Donato and suddenly, he saw him – his tall lanky body and blond hair.

Donato shielded his eyes from the sun with one hand and waved at the pier as he recognized Luca standing in the crowd. It seemed like an eternity for the crew to tie up the boat and let passengers off. Once on the wharf, Donato ran toward Luca and embraced him enthusiastically.

"*Benvenuto, bello!*" Luca said as he pressed his lips against Donato's. Luca ran his hand over Donato's shoulder and down his arm, squeezing his biceps. Then he slid his hand into Donato's and held it snugly.

"You are so handsome," Donato exclaimed as he gazed into Luca's eyes. "I've missed you."

"I've missed you, and I can't believe you're here, in Ptown," Luca added.

"It is a bit surreal," Donato said, pivoting in place and taking in the sights.

Several handsome young guys walked past, staring at Luca and Donato as they embraced. One winked at Donato, and Luca noticed.

"I forgot to warn you," Luca said. "The fast ferry can be intense. I probably should have chaperoned."

"Not to worry. I'm all yours."

"That's the best news I've heard all day."

"So, where do your grandmothers live? Is it far?"

"No. It's a short walk. *Andiamo.*"

They walked down the pier. It was crowded with people making their way from the ferry into the center of town. Donato continued to gaze at the spectacle – families with kids lining up for Whale Watches, fishermen bringing in catches from the night before, and lots of gay men and women eagerly making their way to the town center.

"I still can't believe you are here!" Luca exclaimed as they approached Commercial Street. "It's just another 10 or 15 minutes to my grandmothers' house."

"I noticed the beaches and dunes as we approached. It looks amazing."

"Yes. We're very lucky. And the town is charming – with galleries, shops, bars, restaurants, and all sorts of venues for stand-up artists and performers."

Donato was still nervous about going around his father's back. The pretext of the wedding in Boston was a stretch, and he would make a quick trip back to Boston for the ceremony, sending pictures to his parents. His mother assured him she would try to soften up his father, but he couldn't imagine him ever changing or welcoming a gay son.

Luca occasionally glanced toward Donato. His golden skin and blond hair glistened in the afternoon sun. Donato concealed his anxiety, appearing confident and self-assured about himself. He was poised and classy, and it was intoxicating. Luca was hooked.

They walked past the town hall, a historic structure with clapboard siding, a steeply pitched roof, and a weathered clock tower overhead. Luca pointed it out and then said, "And that," pointing to a massive granite tower on the hill behind town hall, "is the monument to the Pilgrims landing here in 1620."

"I thought they went to Plymouth," Donato interjected, surprised at his recall of American history.

"They came here first. The tower, inspired by the one in Siena, was built to commemorate their initial landing and the compact they signed, the so-called Mayflower Compact, forming a unique civil society."

The main street of town, Commercial Street, was packed full of vacationers strolling between quaint shops and galleries and stopping at terraces for drinks and food. Donato's eyes widened as he watched scantily clad young men pedaling down the street on vintage bicycles and others arm-in-arm, dressed in tight-fitting shorts and tee-shirts. He observed, "It's like a gay fairy land. I've never seen this many gay people together except at gay pride. And, more interestingly, there are many straight families intermingled, going about their business, shopping, and sightseeing, as if it were all very natural."

"It is a bit of a bubble, but a nice one! That's why we like to come here for vacation. My grandmothers have had a place here for years."

"I can't wait to meet them."

"Hey! Let's stop here. I want to have you to myself before my family descends on you. There's a pleasant bar at the end of this pier. We can get a drink, catch up, and see the sights."

They walked to the end of a covered gallery of shops and restaurants and out onto a deck overlooking the harbor, Long Point, Truro, and Wellfleet in the distance. Luca took Donato's hand and led him up a few stairs to a covered deck and bar. "What would you like?"

"You."

"As an apéritif," Luca emphasized, glaring at Donato playfully.

"What's a good American drink?"

"Martinis, cosmos, gin and tonics, beer, wine."

"I'll have a gin and tonic. It sounds American, or at least English."

Luca ordered drinks, and they grabbed a high-top near the edge of the deck overlooking the water. The afternoon sun was beginning to weave its magic, casting rich golden light on countless sailboats moored in the port. It was low tide, and tourists were walking on the wet sand looking for shells.

"Cheers," they both said as they raised their drinks. Luca gazed into Donato's hazel eyes, filled with longing and excitement. He was eager to play a part in Donato's coming out. He hoped their relationship would develop but, if not, he was certain they would remain close friends. He felt a deep connection with him.

Donato's heart fluttered with excitement. He was overwhelmed with impressions – the picturesque seascape stretched out on the horizon, the sensual bodies he observed around them, and the enigmatic man holding his hand under the table – strong, alluring, and tender all at once.

"I'm sorry for the long silence before," Donato began. "I had a lot to work out, and my father is formidable."

"What changed?"

"I realized he was not the saint I had always considered him to be. Sure, he was never one of those sweet angelic types, but I always thought of him as principled, virtuous, and moral. He had firm beliefs and, even though I didn't always share them, I respected him, even feared him."

"And?"

"Well, as I shared briefly, I found out he had an affair when I was in *liceo*. I have a stepbrother. He criticizes the culture of divorce, extramarital sex, and gay people, but, in the end, he's no different. It's all hypocritical. I realized I needed to forge my own path. Finding out his secrets gave me permission."

"So, does he know you know?"

"Not yet. I'm holding the information in reserve for when I might need it."

"But your mother does."

"Yes. And she was very affirming. She surprised me."

"So, officially you are here for a wedding, right?"

Donato nodded.

"And when you go back? When we go back? What will happen?"

"I don't know yet. Let's not try to get ahead of ourselves."

Francesco's advice echoed in Luca's head as Donato formed similar thoughts. "Did my brother pay you to say that?"

Donato shook his head no.

Luca looked around the deck and noticed a couple of guys looking their way. Their eyes were glued on Donato, undoubtedly drawn to his exotic northern Italian features. His golden hair rustled in the wind, and his long nose and sensual lips were more pronounced as he cocked his head back and took in the sun and cool breeze blowing off the harbor. Luca felt jealous and insecure.

"So, when do we get to meet your grandmothers?"

"Are you ready to go now?"

"One more moment. I want to take all of this in," he said as he waved his hand over Luca.

Luca blushed. He rose from the stool, grabbed Donato's hand, and led him back onto Commercial Street. As they approached Anna and Rita's house, Luca said, "My dad is still very upset about his fight with my father. He may not be as friendly as usual, and it would be good to avoid certain topics."

Donato nodded.

Luca opened the picket gate to his grandmothers' garden. "Wow," Donato exclaimed. "This is beautiful."

"Yes. We're very fortunate."

"Did you come here as a boy?"

"Yes. My fathers and my brother and I came each summer."

Luca pushed open the front door. Donato was immediately struck by the gleaming wood floors and the spacious living area with white sofas and decorative pillows tossed here and there. Anna approached and gave Luca a hug and kiss, her arm over his shoulder. "This must be Donato. *Piacere.*"

"*Piacere mio,*" he replied, shaking her hand. He observed her luminous skin, silky gray hair, and a warm smile.

Rita came up from behind. She immediately reached around Donato and gave him an embrace, kissing him on the cheeks. "*Benvenuto! Che meraviglia,*" she said, looking up and down Donato's body.

"*Nana!*" Luca exclaimed, embarrassed by her unabashed attention to Donato's physical attributes.

She held her hand up to her face as if caught in some misdeed.

Francesco stood in the doorway between the living area and the kitchen, observing everyone. He projected nonchalance and indifference, but secretly delighted at seeing his brother happy with Donato's arrival. Francesco nodded to Donato, and Donato nodded back.

"Let's get you situated, and then we can have something to eat," Rita suggested.

"Where's Oliver?" Luca inquired, realizing he was not part of the mix.

"He ran some errands. He'll be right back."

Anna led Donato and Luca upstairs. "I hope you don't mind. We have limited space. Can you share a room?" she asked, winking at Luca.

Luca turned beet red and glanced at Donato, who smiled bashfully. "Of course, *Nana*," Luca replied, already having discussed this earlier. Luca raised his brows as if to ask Donato if it was okay. Donato nodded affirmatively.

"You can unpack and freshen up. Come down when you're ready."

Anna closed the door behind her and returned downstairs. Luca and Donato looked at each other. Luca approached Donato and ran his hand through his thick hair. His breathing sped up as he leaned toward him. He stared into Donato's eyes and then opened his mouth, kissing him. He tasted the residue of salty air on his lips and breathed in his distinctive cologne.

"Oh my God," he said, as he pulled Donato close to him and felt the firmness of his sex pressed against his abdomen. "You don't know how much I have waited for this."

"Me, too," Donato replied, rubbing his hands over the small of Luca's back and squeezing his buttocks.

Luca was self-conscious about their being in his grandmothers' house and pulled away nervously. "Let's get you unpacked. The shower is just across the hall if you need to freshen up."

Donato seemed frozen in place, not wanting to let go of Luca but realizing he probably should deal with the practicalities of unpacking and meeting Luca's family.

Luca heard the door open and close downstairs and realized his father must have returned. He heard him coming up the stairs and knock on the door.

Luca opened the door and Oliver peered inside. "Donato. Welcome," he said, extending his hand.

"*Grazie, Signor Monte-Fitzpatrick.*"

"Call me Oliver, please. How was your trip?"

"Uneventful. Glad to be here."

"We're glad you are here, too. Make yourself at home! We'll see you two downstairs in a bit?"

Luca nodded. Oliver left the room.

"Your dad is so cool," Donato said as he returned to unpacking his bags.

"He's really upset, though. It's such a strange time – celebrating my grandmothers' anniversary and processing my fathers' relationship problems. Happiness and sadness all at the same time."

Donato nodded. He felt the similar conflicting emotions about learning of his father's affair and yet now being in Luca's arms.

Later, they went downstairs where Anna and Rita had put out cheese and hummus and were pouring drinks for everyone.

"All unpacked?" Anna inquired as she waved Donato into the kitchen.

"Yes. And thank you for your hospitality."

"We're glad you're here. Luca's glad you are here! Something to drink?"

"*Un po' di vino. Rosso se c'e.*"

"*Subito,*" Anna said, having become fluent in Italian over the years.

She handed him a glass of red wine and Luca poured himself a seltzer. They joined Oliver and Francesco and Rita in the family room.

"So, you're from Milan?" Rita began what would inevitably be a lengthy interrogation. She was eager to scrutinize Luca's new boyfriend.

Donato nodded. "And now, Rome."

"And your father is a minister of finance in the government?" Anna continued. "That's impressive."

"Yes, and unfortunately, part of several conservative cultural organizations."

Oliver raised his brow and took a long sip of wine.

Donato glanced toward Luca and added, "It was so interesting meeting Luca at the Vatican Museums a while back. We have a lot of common interests."

"And he was a swimmer," Luca added, looking at Francesco, who seemed indifferent to the conversation, scrolling through social media on his phone.

"And how exactly did your father allow you to come to Ptown?" Oliver asked with concern.

"Well, he thinks I'm at a cousin's wedding in Boston. I will go there later in the week. My mother concocted the plan."

"Did she?" Rita asked, smiling. "I like her already!"

"So, have you come out to your parents?" Oliver asked, not having been briefed yet on all the details of recent events.

"No. My mother and I had a good talk, and she's fine. My father still thinks I'm straight, although he asked me the other day if I had certain leanings. It was his roundabout way of probing. It was during a heated discussion, and it was clear that saying yes was not the correct answer."

Luca felt a knot form in his stomach. He came from a long line of gay activists, and dating a closeted guy wouldn't be tolerated for long. He could foresee Gerardo being quite a force to be reckoned with, and he wasn't sure Donato would stand up to him.

"What was the source of the heated discussion?" Oliver pressed Donato.

"Dad! Donato just arrived. Let him get acclimated. Let's just get to know each other," Luca pleaded.

"No. It's okay," Donato interjected. "If it doesn't bother you, I don't mind talking about it. I don't have anyone to talk to, and it's been an eventful couple of weeks."

Francesco glanced up from his phone. Anna and Rita both took deep breaths. Everyone focused intently on Donato, who was leaning forward, his elbows resting on his knees.

"When Luca visited the other day, he inadvertently left one of Oliver's guidebooks in our foyer. A flyer for an event on gay marriage had been tucked in the pages. My mother discovered the book and tried to hide it, but my father found it. He was alarmed and angry and confronted me. I couldn't believe the venom he spit out about gay people. I knew he was conservative, but he seemed especially hateful toward gay couples." Donato paused. "I'm sorry," he said. "Maybe I shouldn't continue."

"It's nothing we haven't heard before," Rita said. "Sorry you had to feel the brunt of it so directly."

"He said gay couples are promiscuous, unfaithful, and spend their lives going from one orgy to the next. I couldn't believe it, and I pointed out that you and Giancarlo have been together for the same length of time as my parents, that you have two upstanding boys, and that for all intents and purposes, there is no difference between your relationship and my parents' relationship."

Oliver felt a lump form in his throat. He had always been proud of his marriage, and the example he and Giancarlo had been to others. He now felt embarrassed and sad at having failed.

"What happened next?" Luca inquired.

"He said gay people can't love authentically. That it's all a façade and that if I wanted to have a future in banking and government, I would need to sever my relationship with Luca."

"Thus, the silence," Luca hypothesized.

Donato nodded. "*Mi dispiace.*"

"When did you have this conversation?" Oliver asked.

"About two weeks ago. Why?"

"Just curious. It's nothing."

Francesco stared at his dad and immediately knew what he was thinking. Everyone else seemed intent on getting to know more about Donato and were oblivious to Oliver's shift in demeanor. Anna and Rita continued to ask questions of him - more superficial ones – like where he went to school, what he was studying, what he planned to do when he finished school, and what he liked to do in his free time.

Oliver stood up and went to the kitchen to refill his drink. Francesco followed.

"Dad! I know you made the connection, too. Do you think Mr. Bianchi might have tried to sabotage your relationship to prove his point?"

"I can't imagine someone doing that," Oliver said, even though the thought crossed his mind.

"Neither can I, but I can't imagine someone holding the views he does, either. Who told you papa was having an affair?"

"Lorenzo."

"And where did Lorenzo find that out?"

"I don't know. He said he was at a reception or something."

"Can we find out more? Maybe papa wasn't having an affair and was set up by Mr. Bianchi. Wouldn't that be ironic given where his son is now?"

"But there's other evidence."

"I know. You mentioned the texts, photos, and receipts, but maybe they have less value or could be discounted if we knew more about the original allegation."

"I'll see if Lorenzo has more information."

"Do you promise?"

Oliver gave Francesco a warm hug and said, "Yes. I'll follow up. But don't worry about papa and me. We'll work this out. You just need to have a good summer."

"What? In frickin gaysville?"

"I know it's a sacrifice for you to come here. Why don't you go into town? Meet some people your age and of your persuasion. We'll continue the interrogation of Donato. Just come home for dinner."

Francesco nodded, ran upstairs, changed his clothes, and sneaked out the back door into town.

Oliver returned to the family room to hear more about Donato. Eventually, Luca decided to walk him into town, and Oliver and his mothers remained to prepare dinner.

"So, what do you think of him?" Anna pressed her son after they left.

"He's nice. He's obviously well-educated, handsome, smart, and adores Luca. I'm still concerned about his father. He's not a nice guy, from what I gather."

"Sometimes that's what motivates someone like Donato to make a big shift. And, who knows, if Mr. Bianchi loves his son, maybe he can make the shift, too," Anna noted.

"I doubt it, but we'll see. By the way, what's for dinner?"

"Rita wants to do some pasta, and I'm going to grill local sea bass. Can you make some of that wonderful green sauce you make – isn't it with parsley, garlic, capers, lemon, and olive oil?"

Oliver nodded. He was deep in thought and looked at his watch. It was five o'clock, and eleven in Rome. Lorenzo would still be up. He walked out onto the back patio and dialed Lorenzo's number.

"*Pronto*," Lorenzo responded. "Oliver?"

"*Si. Sono Io.* I hope I'm not getting you too late."

"No. But what's up? How are you doing?"

"It's been difficult. We're here in Ptown for the month. I have no idea where Giancarlo is."

156 ~ MICHAEL HARTWIG

"*Mi dispiace.* Is there anything I can do?"

"Yes, as a matter of fact. Where did you hear Giancarlo had a new boyfriend?"

"Hmm. Let me think. Yes, it was at a reception for the ministry of finance. There were a lot of bankers and politicians and various other types there."

"And?"

"Well, I was talking with one of my colleagues, and I overheard someone mention Giancarlo. My ears perked up. I glanced over my shoulder casually and noticed several politicians chatting. Someone said, 'Is that Giancarlo's new boyfriend?' I looked across the room and noticed Giancarlo with Riccardo. I was incredulous since I have always known them as colleagues. Someone interjected the same sentiment, saying, 'Oh, that's his colleague at the bank.' Then this other person, who had made the first comment, responded, 'Oh. That's not what I hear. Things have changed.'"

"So, that's it?"

"Yes. That's what I shared with you before."

"Did you see who made the original comment? Do you know who he is?"

"Yes. He's Gerardo Bianchi, one of the ministers of finance. I thought it odd. He tends to be pretty prickly about gay people. That he was making comments about someone's new boyfriend was out of character. But I thought you should know. So, I told you. Did I do something wrong?"

"No, no, no," Oliver said. "It was good that you told me. I appreciate it."

"So, when are you all back?"

"End of the month."

"Anything I can do for you?"

"No, thanks. You've been a big help. *Ciao.*"

"*Ciao, bello. Buona notte.*"

LOVE UNEARTHED ~ 157

"Well, that changes things," Oliver murmured to himself. He walked back into the kitchen.

Anna looked up and asked, "Who were you talking with?"

"A friend in Rome. When Donato was talking about his father, I made a connection. The date at which I learned of Giancarlo's affair and the tense conversation Donato had with his father were a few days apart. I just confirmed that it was Donato's father who made a comment about Giancarlo having a new boyfriend."

"You're kidding!" Rita said, dropping the head of lettuce on the cutting board and giving her full attention to her son.

"Maybe I overreacted," Oliver said pensively.

"But wasn't there other evidence?" Anna asked.

"Yes, and those are problematic. But it's possible Mr. Bianchi tried to sabotage our relationship."

"Maybe he was the messenger, not the cause," Anna continued.

"Maybe. But what if he was the cause?"

"How are you going to find out?"

"I don't know," Oliver said. "I'd like to see Giancarlo take more initiative and responsibility. He just stormed out of the house as if I had affronted his integrity."

Anna and Rita looked at each other.

Anna put her hand on Rita's forearm and said, "Son, it's almost always a two-way street. Both parties play a role."

"But look at you two. Fifty years!"

"We've had our bumps, too."

"But not like this."

Anna and Rita looked at each other again.

"No. Did you face this, too?" Oliver asked.

Anna and Rita both nodded. "It was a long time ago. Well, maybe not so long ago. It was when your ma first discovered she had cancer," Anna began. "She resented my health, success at work, and social network."

"I went to a really dark place," Rita continued. "I was angry, and I was sick, and I wanted to blame someone. Anna's life was, from my perspective, flawless and carefree. It wasn't fair, I thought."

"So, what happened?"

"I pushed her away," Rita said.

"We both accused each other of being too chummy with a few of our mutual friends. I thought Rita and Jean were too close. Jean was doing all sorts of things for Rita during her illness, and it just seemed too intimate from my perspective."

"And, in response to my anger and prickliness, Anna spent more time with colleagues at work. She had to travel, and she went on a couple of trips with Frankie. Again, I thought it was curious that precisely when your mom had to travel, she and Frankie began to work on projects together."

"So, how'd you get through it?"

"It wasn't easy," Rita said. "When I went into remission, I felt better about myself. I confronted Anna, and she confronted me. We went to a counselor and worked things out. We totally love each other, and we realized how easy it was to become complacent and even calloused, shielding ourselves from disappointment and resentment."

"I love you both, and I can't imagine our family any other way."

"What about you and Giancarlo? What about Francesco and Luca? What do you want?"

"I want us to be the family we always have been."

"You're all older now. It can't be as it was before. But you can reimagine it for the stage in life you find yourselves at now. How do you rekindle love, passion, friendship? How do you find ways to strengthen bonds?"

Oliver nodded. He realized he and Giancarlo were at a cross-roads, but the hurt he felt at Giancarlo's response to his concerns was still tender, and he needed time. He just hoped the time apart wouldn't reinforce Giancarlo's indifference.

16

Chapter Sixteen – Young Love

Everyone settled into vacation mode. Oliver wrestled with conflicting emotions, anger over Giancarlo's abrupt departure and possible infidelity, and yearning that they could heal their differences, that perhaps Giancarlo had been faithful and merely the victim of a vicious attack. He took long walks, read books, and helped Anna and Rita cook for the gang each evening.

He resisted the urge to reach out to Giancarlo, hoping he would make the first move. It seemed important for Giancarlo to take responsibility and to fight for their marriage. His mothers continued to insist that Oliver needed to do his part, too, but for the moment, he had dug in his heels and kept waiting for a text or call.

Anna and Rita fussed over their family, worrying about Oliver, encouraging Francesco and Luca in their romantic exploits, and double-checking arrangements for their anniversary ceremony. Rita refused to let her health issues interfere with their celebration and decided not to share new information with Oliver, particularly considering what he was going through. Although her cancer remained in remission, during a checkup, the doctor had detected heart problems. Rita's heart valves weren't working as they should, resulting in increased fatigue, shortness of breath, and dizziness. They were monitoring things, but the doctors were looking at interventions if things continued to worsen. Luca seemed particularly solicitous of her, and she feared that with his psychic abilities, he already had picked up on things. Neither felt the need to name it and simply expressed their affection for each other.

Surprisingly, or perhaps not, Francesco met a lovely and affable person during his wanderings about town. Taylor's mothers lived in Boston and had a place in Ptown, so they were on the Cape during the weekends. Taylor and Francesco had spotted each other on their bicycles, riding up and down Commercial Street. After passing each other several times over the week, Francesco swerved in Taylor's direction, forcing Taylor to stop. He used the opportunity to apologize and introduce himself, and there was an instant connection.

Taylor and Francesco discovered they shared an interest in art. They sat in front of Town Hall and sketched people walking by. Both were quite talented. People asked to see their work and were amazed. They sold a few drawings on the street.

Taylor was roughly Francesco's age and made it clear early on that Taylor was non-binary. Taylor had firm, round breasts, shapely hips, and an angular face with short blond hair. Radiant golden skin, blue eyes, and whimsically painted nails punctuated an alluring androgyny.

Taylor and Francesco sat close to one another; their hips pressed firmly together. Francesco loved the feel of Taylor's skin next to his, and Taylor melted as Francesco peered into their eyes and conveyed his affection.

Luca and Donato strolled past Taylor and Francesco on their way to the water shuttle for Long Point.

"*Francesco, come stai?*" Luca asked.

"*Benissimo, e voi?*" he replied, standing up and giving Donato a hug and kiss.

Taylor rose, too, and asked, "*Ciao, Luca e Donato. Come va?*"

"*Bene, grazie.* I see Francesco's teaching you Italian!" Luca said.

Taylor blushed and nodded.

"Can I see what you've drawn?" Donato asked, glancing down at their sketch pads.

Taylor picked theirs up and showed it to Donato.

"Oh, my God. Amazing!" he exclaimed. "I can't believe you can do this so quickly. You've captured the energy and form of people walking by. And yours?" he asked Francesco.

Francesco picked his up and gave it to Donato who had his arm around Luca's back. They both stared at the work. "*Bella! Non ci posso credere!*"

"We should get you both in a show! Doesn't *nonna* know one of the gallery owners?"

"I don't think we're ready," Taylor said.

Luca noticed Taylor had used the pronoun 'we' and raised his brow. Francesco didn't pick up on it, but then he said, "Do you think we could at least show *nonna's* friend our work?"

Luca nodded enthusiastically. "Let me talk with *nonna*. Meanwhile, we have to get to the shuttle. We're going to Long Point to swim."

They all hugged. Taylor and Francesco sat back down, and Donato and Luca walked toward the pier. "Did you notice they both used the term 'we' regarding each other and their work?"

"Yes. I thought that was curious. I thought your brother was the inveterate playboy."

"Me, too. He seems to be serious about Taylor."

"And Taylor about him," Donato added.

As they spoke about Francesco and Taylor, both realized their own relationship was getting serious. Neither wanted to say too much out of fear they might jinx things. Donato was still apprehensive about what to do when he returned to Rome, and Luca sensed his apprehension each time he held his hands.

Luca was reluctant to use magic – either to sense the direction of things or to influence Donato's affections. It was always difficult to get clear messages about one's own relationships, and he definitely considered it unethical to cast a love spell on Donato. But each time he touched Donato, he felt a surge of current course through his hands and a scramble of messages he tried to decipher. At night, as they held each other in bed, Luca tried to still his racing mind and listen. But it was impossible. His heart invariably accelerated, pressed next to Donato's warm skin, and his imagination went wild planning their life together.

Donato and Luca walked to the Long Point shuttle. There were half a dozen people embarking on the pontoon boat with coolers, umbrellas, and towels. The boat backed out of its slip and headed into the harbor and across the water toward the tip of Cape Cod.

As they approached the beach, a few seals surfaced, curious about interlopers to their terrain. Donato asked, "Don't sharks follow seals?"

"Yes, but not to worry. The sharks rarely enter the harbor."

"That's reassuring."

"I'll protect you," Luca added, winking.

The boat ran up onto the beach, and people disembarked. Most wandered a few meters from the shoreline and pitched umbrellas. Donato and Luca walked farther down the beach, hoping for solitude. "And why didn't we go to boy's beach?" Donato inquired as they trekked along the sand.

"Are you kidding? Did you see the way they devoured you with their eyes the last time we were there? It wasn't the sharks I was keeping my eyes on!"

Donato blushed. He loved the attention and affection Luca showed him. He knew he was handsome, but no one had ever fussed about him the way Luca did. "Shall we sit here?" Donato asked as they found a quiet, empty space near the water.

Luca nodded. He put up their umbrella and laid out their towels. Donato put their cooler under the shade and then stood in the sun, stretching. "Shall we go in?"

Luca ran for the water and leaped in. It was clear, cool, and refreshing. Donato swam up next to him and wrapped his long legs around Luca's torso. "Hey, handsome," Donato said to Luca, his blue eyes sparkling in the light.

Luca leaned toward Donato and gave him a kiss. Donato looked around nervously.

"Don't worry. We're alone and in Ptown."

"It's a reflex."

"You're worried, aren't you?"

"You mean about Rome, about my father?"

"Hmm, hum," Luca replied, gazing into Donato's hazel eyes.

"I've been thinking."

"Yeah?"

"Maybe my father doesn't have to know."

"You mean hide this from him?"

Donato nodded. Then he added, "At least for a little while. When we are back at school, we can get together relatively easily without notice. I will work with my mother to soften up my dad. I've also thought about talking with Signor Luciano. He seems like he might be an ally, even one of us."

Luca didn't respond at first. He wasn't keen on the idea of lurking about clandestinely with Donato. His family had worked too hard to go back into the closet. Donato detected Luca's hesitation and added, "Sorry. I'm just thinking out loud. We have some time to figure this out. We can come up with a plan you're comfortable with."

Luca smiled. He pulled Donato up close to him and felt his chest press against his own. He could feel Donato's hardness under him and knew it wouldn't take much to get him going. Since they weren't at the Boy's Beach, it was probably prudent to keep things calm.

As he released Donato and swam out to deeper water, he could feel the impressions he had picked up from Donato and was certain Donato didn't have the courage to come out. Luca felt sadness. However, the words of his brother echoed in his head – have fun, relax, don't plan your whole life. He waved Donato forward and gave him a warm embrace. He reached behind him and slipped his hands down inside the seam of Donato's suit, feeling his firm, round buttocks.

Donato peered into Luca's eyes and felt himself stiffen. He laughed to himself as he imagined dragging Luca to shore and entering him on the warm sand. He kissed Luca and said, "I'm so in love with you."

Luca's heart melted and whatever hesitations he had about their future floated away in the gentle waves. They swam back to shore and laid out in the sun, absorbing its warmth, and watching their bodies tan.

Later that afternoon, they returned home. As they entered the house, Oliver glanced up from the novel he was reading and asked, "How was Long Point? The water must have been amazing!"

"It was incredible," Luca replied. "We had a good time. Are you up for going to Tea Dance in a while?"

"Sure. You?"

Oliver nodded, although he continued to have mixed feelings. He enjoyed the festive scene of a deck full of handsome men overlooking the harbor and the play of late afternoon sunlight on the moored boats. But, as he wandered about the deck, he felt a deep sadness and wished Giancarlo were with him.

Donato and Luca headed upstairs. Once inside Luca's room, they stripped. Luca's tan line accentuated his firm, round buttocks. Donato walked over to him and took his firm sex in his hand. Luca, in turn, ran his hands over Donato's smooth chest and around his back, pulling him up close.

Luca was growing to appreciate how illuminating touch was. Yes, the contours of Donato's muscles engorged with arousal were sexy and delicious. Donato's skin took on a unique sheen and color as he abandoned himself to their mounting union. But Luca detected embedded memories enfolded in Donato's cells, countless lives and experiences inherited and aligned in his body. He had learned to recognize those early in his own life – languages, skills, knowledge, personality traits, unresolved conflicts, and familiarity with places and objects. He skimmed the surface of Donato's flesh, torn between wanting to read the underlying narrative and simply devouring him.

He wasn't sure if it was his imagination or intuition, but as he ran his hand down Donato's side, he sensed an ancient Roman man, someone in his thirties - smart, handsome, and privileged. He enjoyed a good life. Luca ran his hands up the backside of Donato's legs and felt power and confidence. Whoever Donato had been, he was a man of action, not leisure.

Luca nuzzled his nose into the side of Donato's neck, breathing in the residue of salt from their swim. He nibbled at his ear and ran his hand along the back of his neck into the coarse folds of his dirty blond hair. His neck was strong but stiff, and Luca perceived he had been principled in a past life, even when it wasn't convenient or lucrative.

Donato's mind was racing, and the surface of his scalp was warm to the touch. Luca leaned his head back and peered into Donato's hazel eyes. They were filled with longing and passion, but as Luca continued to gaze at them, he sensed doubt and apprehension.

"Are you okay?" Luca asked.

Donato nodded quietly, not wanting to disturb the increasing arousal he felt as Luca caressed him. Luca's touch was comforting, the sensation of finally being held, loved, and recognized. As an only child, he had enjoyed inordinate attention as he grew up, but neither his mother nor his father had been physically affectionate. He never realized how much he craved the warmth of someone's hands on his skin, how deeply he longed to be held and kissed.

Luca delighted in Donato's radiant smile - the luscious contours of his lips, the brightness of his teeth, and the dark stubble of beard that contrasted with the blond hair on his head. When Donato grinned, Luca felt like he had reunited with a long-lost friend or companion.

They abandoned themselves to their newly found camaraderie, to an innocent joy at being in each other's arms. Luca felt Donato's firm sex pressed against his abdomen and marveled at how natural it felt. He savored its power, suppleness, and raw determination.

Luca wanted Donato inside of him, to fill him, and to erase all boundaries between them. He took Donato's hand and tugged him toward the bed. He reclined and pulled Donato on top of him. The solidity of his body was intoxicating. Luca felt his skin vibrate.

It amazed him how Donato could read his mind. He gently and tenderly ran his warm hands under Luca's balls. He then spread Luca's legs, caressing the insides of them until Luca moaned. Luca glanced at the bedside table. Donato reached into the drawer and extracted a condom. Luca's eyes widened in anticipation as Donato opened the package and unfurled it over his throbbing sex.

Donato was gentle and warm. His chest was moist, and he glided back and forth on top of Luca. Luca closed his eyes and abandoned himself to their intimacy. He could feel the throbbing of Donato's heart pressed against his own, and as they kissed, they breathed each other in.

Donato's body flexed with strength and grace. Luca's reciprocated, his legs wrapped tightly around the back of Donato's upper legs, pressing him deeper and deeper. Luca felt the tip of his own erection tingle in the warm moistness of their torsos gliding against each other. He squeezed Donato again with his powerful legs and felt him explode, his body writhing in waves of intense pleasure. Luca jostled under Donato's body and felt himself come as well, releasing a torrent of sensations in the tight cavity between them.

Donato collapsed onto Luca's body. He laid his head on Luca's chest.

Luca laid his head back and regained his breath. As he did, he detected a familiar scent – an earthy odor mixed with the moist air of ancient bricks and marble. It was a sensation connected with Rome, with archaeological tours, not something he had ever smelled in Ptown surrounded by the sea. He thought it odd and took several deep breaths. It became even more pronounced.

Donato stirred and rolled over. He smiled contently at Luca, saying, "*Ti voglio bene!*"

"What a gift you are!" Luca replied, running his hand over Donato's shoulder.

Donato stood and reached for a towel hanging on the back of the door. He wrapped it around his waist and said, "I'll take a shower?"

Luca nodded. As Donato opened the bedroom door and walk out into the hallway, Luca felt as if he had hallucinated. From the back, Donato's hair appeared darker and longer. His body seemed shorter, slimmer. He turned to glance at Luca, and Luca could have sworn he said something to him in Latin.

When Donato returned, his body gleamed in the late afternoon sun streaming through the windows. Donato's frame was, as usual, tall and imposing. His blond hair fell playfully on his forehead. His eyes sparkled. He leaned over and gave Luca a kiss. Luca breathed in his cologne and smiled.

"My turn?" he asked.

"For what?" Donato inquired with a worried look.

"A shower, silly."

Donato sighed, unwrapped the towel from around his waist, and tossed it to Luca. Luca sniffed at the cotton fabric. No smell of earth, brick, or marble. He glanced up and marveled at the handsome body in front of him, wrapped the towel around his waist, and walked out of the door.

Later, they headed downstairs and accompanied Oliver to Tea Dance.

It was a Thursday afternoon, and the deck was packed. The DJ was cranking good techno music, and people were milling about. Oliver got them drinks, and they gathered at the far edge of the deck overlooking the water. Oliver pivoted and faced the deck and then leaned toward his son and said, "Isn't that the guy we saw on the ferry the other day?"

Luca followed his father's gaze and noticed Ben approaching.

"Yes. That's Ben."

"He's handsomer than I remember."

"He is," Luca said with some consternation. "And no less pushy."

"Hmm," Oliver said.

Ben approached and said, "Luca, what a surprise to see you here. I haven't seen you at the beach much lately."

"Ben, do you remember my father, Oliver?"

"Sure. Nice to see you again."

"And this is Donato," Luca said, with his hand behind Donato's back.

"Pleasure," Donato replied, giving Ben a territorial look. Donato realized Luca had not identified their relationship. He was neither a friend, a colleague, nor a boyfriend. He took that as a perplexing sign.

Ben waved his companions forward. "You remember my friends, right?"

"Good to see you all again. This is Donato and this is my father, Oliver."

They all nodded and raised their glasses.

"So, what have you been up to?" Ben asked, looking curiously at Donato.

"I've been showing Donato around Ptown. It's his first visit."

"What do you think?" Ben asked.

"I love it. The beaches are beautiful. Tea Dance is fun, and it's such a cool place."

"So, you're from Italy, too?"

Donato nodded. Ben glanced at Luca and then back at Donato. He sensed their connection and realized he wasn't getting the full picture from Luca. Luca wasn't very talkative, so after a few more pleasantries, Ben excused himself and his friends, and they headed to the dance floor.

Oliver looked at his son, who gave him a look back as if to say, 'What?'

Oliver then glanced over at Donato and raised his brow. Luca realized his father wanted to know what was developing. Luca pivoted toward the water and pointed out sights to Donato. His father got the message. Don't intrude.

"So, who was that?" Donato inquired.

"Someone we met at the beach the other day."

"Hmm," Donato murmured.

Luca detected Donato's concern and said, "Not to worry."

"I'm not worried about you, but he seemed pretty keen on you."

Donato wanted to ask a more pointed question. Why hadn't Luca introduced him, Donato, as his boyfriend? He hesitated, knowing that if he pressed the issue, he might feel pressure to introduce Luca as his boyfriend in Rome.

"Again, not to worry. My heart is yours."

Donato gulped.

Luca detected the internal war Donato was fighting. He held his hand. It was tingling.

Luca glanced across the deck and spied Ben talking with friends. Ben sensed he was being stared at and looked over, smiling at Luca.

Luca took Donato's hand and led him to the dance area. They squeezed into the crowd of people dancing on the small wooden floor. It was warm, and people were perspiring. Handsome guys were taking off shirts.

Luca stood close to Donato, who moved adroitly to the music. Periodically, their chests grazed each other. Luca glanced across the crowd and then back to Donato - infatuated with his smile, the broadness of his shoulders, and the solidity of his body moving in front of him. He took one of his hands and felt the intensity of affection coursing through them.

It felt good to let go, to resonate with the beat, and to feel part of the passion and joy of the crowd. Luca remarked to himself that it was an odd sensation – one in which he lost a sense of his own individuality and yet, at the same time, felt so focused on the man in front of him. He smiled contently at Donato, who leaned forward and gave him a passionate kiss.

17

❦

Chapter Seventeen – Marriage Renewal

Oliver rose, slipped on his shorts and flip-flops, and headed downstairs.

Anna was in the kitchen, sitting at the table and drinking coffee as she read the paper. "There's a fresh pot over there," she said as she watched her son stumble into the room.

"I need a big cup!"

"What's wrong, dear?"

"I don't know. I had a rough night. I couldn't sleep."

"I'm the one who should be nervous, not you!"

"I know. Not sure what it was. I had some weird dreams, but I can't recall them."

"Were you and the boys drinking?"

Oliver nodded no. He poured himself a cup and sat next to his mom, putting his hand on her forearm. "It's a big day today! Fifty years! Wow!"

"I know. It seems like yesterday that we met. What an incredible journey."

"And there's more ahead," he added.

Anna tried to conceal the twitch she felt course through her body, the apprehension she felt for Rita and her health. She looked at her son and wondered if everyone would face new choices soon.

"Where's Rita?"

"She sleeps late," she said, without explanation. "She'll be down soon. And the boys?"

"They are all eager for the ceremony, even Donato. I'm glad he could stay. He and Luca seem to be getting along nicely."

"Yes, but I'm still concerned about what will happen when Donato goes home and confronts his parents."

"Yes. I know. What a mess."

"Do you need anything today?"

"No. We will start getting ready this afternoon. Our dresses are here – simple white summer attire. Patrick has things under control at the restaurant. Everything will be set up. We just have to show up."

"Well, if something comes up, don't hesitate to let me know what I can do."

"You're being here is an enormous gift. I still remember the day we picked you up. We were so thrilled. You resembled both of us, and we always marveled at that, as if you were destined to be our son."

"It is interesting how those things work."

Oliver seemed troubled, and his mother knew why. She reached over and held his hand. "We don't regret your having gone to Rome to meet Henry, nor your having fallen in love with Giancarlo. We love our grandsons, and we love Giancarlo. You guys will work it out."

"I'm not so sure. He doesn't seem to be taking any initiative."

"He will."

"How do you know?"

"Luca's not the only one with a keen sense of intuition," she said, grinning.

"I wish I was convinced."

Anna leaned over and gave her son a kiss. "It's time for me to get Rita up."

She left the room. Francesco came down next, his face buried deep in a stream of text messages on his phone. "Taylor?" Oliver inquired.

Francesco nodded without looking up.

"Are they coming today?"

He nodded again.

"And your brother. Is he up?"

"I heard him and Donato moving around. I imagine they will be down shortly."

A short while later, Francesco, Donato, and Luca were pressed against each other at the kitchen table, sipping coffee and eating granola and yogurt. Everyone held phones in hand, texting friends, checking social media, and reading news.

Oliver wrestled with the idea of texting Giancarlo. He had been on his mind all morning, and even with all the distractions of getting ready for the ceremony, he kept feeling something stirring within.

Luca sensed his dad's unsettledness and gave him a warm embrace. "You must be excited about your moms' anniversary. What an amazing accomplishment."

Luca's remarks only made Oliver feel more wretched. He nodded unconvincingly.

Francesco noticed an article about Donato's father in the online Italian newspaper. He raised his brows as the article recounted an interview with Gerardo about the upcoming political season and the importance of doubling down on traditional values. Francesco glanced at Donato and shook his head, realizing how ironic it was that he was off shagging his boyfriend in Ptown. Francesco wondered if Luca or Oliver had seen the article and what they thought might happen when Donato returned to Rome.

Rita sauntered into the kitchen, her hair a tangle and circles of darkness around her eyes. She walked to the coffeepot, poured a large cup, and sat down at the table. "Buon giorno," Donato said, smiling warmly at her. "Buon anniversario!" he added.

"Thank you, Donato."

"Yes, nana! Happy anniversary!" Francesco added.

Luca gave her a hug and sensed her fragile health.

"Anything we can do for you today?" Oliver inquired.

"No. I think everything is in order. We can relax, take our time, and head over to the party later this afternoon."

Anna came into the kitchen and walked up behind Rita, placing her hands on her shoulders. She looked over the table and felt a deep sense of satisfaction at seeing her family gathered. She couldn't believe that she had been with Rita for fifty years, had a son, and now had two grandsons! In her wildest dreams, she would have never imagined this.

Francesco went upstairs and returned with a large package. Anna's and Rita's eyes widened. "What's this?" Anna inquired.

"A little something we got for your celebration," Francesco noted.

Rita took the package, opened the card, and began to tear up at the sentiments written inside.

Anna opened the paper. Inside was a large, framed photograph of them during the visit they made last summer – Anna and Rita, Oliver and Giancarlo, and Luca and Francesco. The picture had been taken during a sunset beach party. Everyone's faces were aglow in the vermillion light.

"Happy anniversary, mom and ma!" Oliver said, giving them both kisses.

"Yeah, nonna and nana. Happy anniversary," Francesco said. Luca smiled at them and gave them warm kisses on their cheeks.

Oliver glanced at the picture and felt a twitch in his heart, seeing Giancarlo in his arms. It was a painful reminder of his absence.

Donato admired them all. Their affection and love were palpable, and it only emphasized the incongruence between his father's views and reality.

Later that afternoon, everyone walked down Commercial Street to Patrick's restaurant. He had created a unique space along the beach with a small awning over a podium where the renewal ceremony would take place. Chairs were set at round dining tables spaced on the sand and decorated with fresh white and blue hydrangeas.

People arrived, ordered drinks, and took their seats. A small ensemble of musicians played background music as people greeted one another and waited for the ceremony to begin. The musicians got a nod from Patrick, paused, and then struck up the traditional wedding march. Anna and Rita processed arm in arm from the main part of the restaurant out onto the beach.

The sun was low, casting an orange and yellow glow on countless boats moored behind them in the harbor. The sky was clear, and a gentle breeze blew across the water.

The minister welcomed Anna and Rita and invited everyone to take seats. She began, "Welcome friends and family from nearby and from far away. It is a new phenomenon for us to be able to celebrate milestones like this in our community. Anna and Rita were part of an early wave of those who formed households and raised families. It wasn't easy. They were pioneers and trailblazers. We now see the fruit of their love." The minister glanced toward Oliver, Luca, and

Francesco. Oliver nodded back, but continued to feel disturbed by Giancarlo's absence.

He looked over at his sons, who seemed untroubled, focused as they were on their grandmothers' celebration. They all had big smiles on their faces, and Luca had his arms around Donato's back. He hoped that his mothers' celebration of fifty years together would dispel any doubts Donato might have about his sexuality and about the options he had before him.

As Oliver took a long look at Luca and Donato, he glanced up and noticed Giancarlo standing at the edge of the restaurant, his hands in his pockets and his hair tousled from what he imagined must have been his recent arrival by ferry or small plane. Oliver's heart skipped a beat. He wasn't sure if it was out of fear, shock, or affection. He stared at Giancarlo, who looked back and smiled. Oliver feigned a timid smile and waved him toward him. There was an empty chair at a nearby table. Oliver grabbed it and moved it to his table, and Giancarlo sat down. Francesco and Luca turned around to see what the commotion was all about and saw their papa. Their eyes turned red, and tears streaked across their faces.

Oliver reached his hand under the table and took Giancarlo's. He mouthed to him, "*Ti voglio bene.*"

Giancarlo was choked with emotion and simply nodded.

The minister continued the service, reading passages from Anna's and Rita's favorite poems, and recounting stories of their meeting, their professional work, and their service to the community. Anna and Rita each recited vows, renewing their commitment to each other. They kissed and turned to the crowd.

"We're so happy you are here to celebrate with us. You have strengthened our relationship over the years, and we are grateful for your love and support!" Anna said.

Rita glanced toward Oliver and saw Giancarlo. She turned to

Anna and whispered the news in her ear, and Anna glanced up. She then whispered to Rita, "The magic of Provincetown never lets us down, does it?"

Rita nodded. They kissed, and then walked to Oliver and Giancarlo.

Oliver gave his mothers each a warm kiss. "Congratulations!"

Anna leaned toward Giancarlo and said, "*Grazie*! It means so much to us you are here."

"Thank you for embracing me so many years ago. I won't let you down," he whispered back.

Rita looked at him curiously, almost sternly. She wasn't so quick to forgive and made it clear he would have to prove himself again. Giancarlo smiled at her reassuringly, then grabbed Francesco and gave him a warm hug.

"We missed you papa."

"I missed you, too. We'll work this out."

Patrick stood in front of the crowd and said, "I'm so happy to welcome you here for Anna's and Rita's anniversary. As you undoubtedly know, Anna and Rita are two of the most welcoming and loving people in our community. I came to Ptown twenty years ago, nursing wounds from an abusive relationship and looking for a fresh start. Anna and Rita welcomed me into their home and helped me find my way in this incredible town. They helped fund my first restaurant and promoted it so successfully that I could purchase this place. They have done that for countless others. The town is what it is because of people like them who are generous, supportive, visionary, and loving. To Anna and Rita," he concluded, raising his glass in a toast. "Help yourselves to food and drink inside, and then return here to the beach to continue the celebration."

Francesco eagerly led Taylor, his brother, and Donato into the restaurant, and they quickly filled plates with pasta, lobster, shrimp, grilled vegetables, and salad.

Oliver took Giancarlo's hand and led him to a quiet place near the edge of the water. He traced his finger along Giancarlo's temple and over his brow. "What are we going to do?"

Giancarlo found it difficult to speak. He nodded as if to say, 'I don't know.' His eyes were filled with sadness, embarrassment, and longing. He finally managed to say, "I'm sorry. I have never been unfaithful to you, but I should never have stormed out of our argument, and I need to do more to assure you of my affection for you."

Oliver began to sob. He pivoted away from the crowd, and away from Giancarlo. He rubbed his eyes and took several deep breaths. "I'm sorry I didn't give you the benefit of the doubt."

"I can see how the evidence would concern you. I'm sorry."

"Let's not talk about this now. I want to celebrate my moms' anniversary. Can we pick this up later?"

Giancarlo nodded. He pulled Oliver toward him, gave him an enthusiastic hug, and then kissed him. "I love you."

"I love you, too," Oliver replied. "I hope we can celebrate fifty years sometime. Given that you snatched me at a young age, we might even make sixty or seventy!"

Giancarlo chuckled. He glanced over at Francesco and Luca and smiled.

"It looks like Luca is hitting it off with Donato," Giancarlo speculated.

"That's a long story, and there's a sordid aspect of it. I'll explain later."

"Now you have me intrigued."

Oliver held his finger up to Giancarlo's mouth and said, "Later."

"And who's that with Francesco?"

"Taylor. A local. He's head-over-heels in love."

Giancarlo tilted his head to the side and furrowed his brow. He wasn't used to thinking of Francesco in terms of love.

Oliver walked inside the restaurant to be with his mothers and their friends. Giancarlo walked to his sons' table and caught up with them, introducing himself to Taylor and reinforcing his previous introduction to Donato.

Soon, all the guests were seated on the beach. As the sun set, the sky transitioned from blue to vermillion to a purplish pink hue. The wind died down, and the water took on a glassy sheen. A few remaining rays of sunlight caught the top of some sailboats and the edge of the structures on the piers.

The beach and tables were bathed in the glow of patio lights strung across the area. The string ensemble packed up, and a DJ began to crank out classics from the 70s and 80s. Some people danced. As people finished eating, they refilled glasses and visited with one another.

Anna and Rita were radiant and seemed to enjoy floating from one group to the next, expressing their affection for one another, and conveying how much their friends and family meant to them.

Once the last guests had left, Anna and Rita thanked Patrick and headed home. Oliver and Giancarlo accompanied them. Francesco and Taylor met up with friends at Taylor's mothers' house, and Donato and Luca went dancing.

Anna, Rita, Oliver, and Giancarlo sat in the parlor. "Amazing celebration," Oliver said. "You must be so happy."

Anna looked at Rita and then at Giancarlo and said, "We are. Thanks for celebrating with us!"

There was an awkward pause as everyone tried to process Giancarlo's arrival. Rita interjected, "So, you flew from Rome today? You must be exhausted."

"I am, but I'm also excited to be here. I'm sorry for the pain I must have caused everyone."

"We'll work it out," Oliver assured him and his moms.

Anna was tired and wanted to go to bed. She also knew Oliver and Giancarlo needed some time alone. "Well, folks. I'm tired. You ready for bed, love?" she asked Rita.

Rita glanced at Oliver and Giancarlo and picked up on Anna's hint. "Sure. I'm ready for bed, too."

Anna and Rita stood, gave Giancarlo and Oliver kisses, and headed back to their room.

Giancarlo slid over close to Oliver, put his arms around his shoulders, and said, "I miss this. I miss us. I'm so sorry."

"Me, too," Oliver replied. "Are you tired? You want to go to bed?" he added, raising his brows.

Giancarlo nodded. He stood, took Oliver's hand, and led him upstairs.

18

Chapter Eighteen –
Reconciliation

Large swells caused by a storm out at sea crashed against the shore. Race Point Beach was Giancarlo's favorite — a broad expanse of pristine yellow sand with unobstructed views of the Atlantic Ocean. Magnificent dunes rose from the beach. Near the entry of the park, the dunes were broad and gentle. Farther east, they were steeper and dramatic.

A gentle breeze blew through the bright green dune grass, and piping plovers raced in and out with the coming and going of the waves, pecking for food in the wet sand.

Giancarlo and Oliver found a quiet place away from other beachgoers to plant their umbrellas and set down chairs. They spread towels and laid in the sun. Oliver glanced at Giancarlo's body, already dark from his time on the Amalfi Coast. Although he had gained weight and lost some muscle mass over the years, he

LOVE UNEARTHED ~ 183

still looked good in his red Speedo. He had muscular legs, a firm abdomen, and a broad chest covered in dark hair.

Giancarlo was relieved that his and Oliver's reunion had gone better than anticipated. He expected Anna and Rita to have been bitter and cold, but they were ecstatic when they spotted him during the ceremony. Oliver had welcomed him enthusiastically, and the boys couldn't stop hanging on him during the reception.

"We need to talk," Oliver said, breaking the tranquility of the moment. Giancarlo had almost dozed off, lulled to sleep by the sound of the waves on the shore.

Giancarlo rolled onto his side and looked at Oliver. He reached his hand toward him and ran his finger on Oliver's nose and over his lips. "So sexy," Giancarlo said.

Oliver blushed. He felt his sex stiffen slightly. Giancarlo noticed and raised a brow.

"I'm sorry," Giancarlo continued. "I can see how you would be alarmed, and I shouldn't have been so defensive. I realized I was carrying a lot of anger deep inside."

Oliver squinted. "Tell me more."

"It all seems so easy for you. I'm sure it isn't, but it looks like you glide through life. I feel like I'm always looking over my shoulder, ready for the shoe to drop and the house of cards to collapse."

"But you're the successful one."

"It's a challenge, and I feel like I'm always under intense scrutiny."

"From me?"

"Not initially. But, when you raised the questions you did, it stirred my resentment at the scrutiny I'm under at work. I just blew up."

"I'm sorry," Oliver said, reaching over and stroking Giancarlo's chest.

"I'm sorry for what you must have gone through after hearing the rumors. I can see how that would be a problem."

"So, are we okay?" Oliver pressed.

"I hope so," Giancarlo replied. "But this has made me realize that I can't take you for granted. I can't take us for granted."

Giancarlo scooted toward Oliver and pressed his torso up against Oliver's and reached around his back, giving him an enthusiastic embrace. He loved the feel of Oliver pressed against him. He ran his hand through Oliver's blond curly hair and gave him a moist kiss. He could feel their shafts hardening and rubbing against each other through the thin material of their swimsuits.

"Should we take a walk?" Oliver suggested, raising his brows.

Giancarlo nodded. He knew what was implied in Oliver's suggestion and smiled.

They stood, hid their phones and wallets, and began walking east, away from the crowd.

They held hands and walked along the wet sand. Occasionally, a large wave crashed nearby and sprayed them with water. Oliver savored the raw elements — sun, sand, ocean, and their bodies turning dark in the sun.

"I still remember the day Henry first introduced us. I tried to remain professional and detached, but I feared you saw right through me, saw the desire mounting in my eyes," Giancarlo recounted.

"I have to admit, I had expected Henry's financial advisor to be an old accountant with yellow teeth, gray hair, and wrinkled skin. When I saw you, I gasped for air, and my legs grew weak. I thought you would notice my eyes undressing you, exploring the contours of your body. You were an Adonis, and I was in awe."

"I was thirty and depressed that my twenties were behind me. You reminded me of my younger self, and I wanted to have you. That's probably not very noble of me in retrospect. It was raw, unadulterated desire. I quickly came to appreciate how thoughtful and multilayered you were – and are. That's when lust turned to love and affection."

"And you were everything I wanted to be – a successful financial advisor and gay, classy, and sexy."

"Look at us now! Two aging gay men with kids. Whew!" Giancarlo said in jest and with some seriousness.

"But you're still the hot sexy man I met twenty-two years ago. Look at you!"

"I don't feel that way," Giancarlo lamented. "I'm fifty-three. That's old."

"Tell that to the guys cruising you on Commercial Street. You're still a head turner."

"They're looking at me to see who they have to fight to get you."

Oliver blushed but didn't refute Giancarlo's statement. Then he said, "We have to deal with this. I don't want you to resent me or to feel you are inadequate. You are my rock. You inspire me to be the best I can be. I keep trying to live up to your achievements."

"And I need you to trust me," Giancarlo replied. "Yes, I'm an insecure middle-aged Roman queen, but there's no trading up. You're more than I could ever imagine."

"So, we're good?" Oliver inquired.

"Yes, and we can do better. I want to take you to this quaint but exotic inn on the Amalfi Coast and spend quality time with you."

"Is it a gay place?"

"Well, not really. But one of the owners is gay, and there's a lot of eye candy."

Oliver furrowed his brow.

"Not to worry. I was on a diet. I noticed, but didn't indulge," Giancarlo said playfully. "Really. I think we need to spend time alone. Rekindle things. Pay attention to each other."

"That sounds good to me."

"And, in the future, I want to take you on my business meetings."

"What?" Oliver said, squinting at Giancarlo.

"Yes. Some of the others bring their wives to these meetings. I think unconsciously I was trying to protect us from the scrutiny of a conservative banking world. In the end, it only set us up for more innuendos. I think we need to stand out, stand proud, and help others feel more comfortable with us. They will meet you and instantly feel comfortable and engaged."

"Are you sure?"

"Absolutely. If, after playing it safe for so many years only set us up for a nasty rumor by Gerardo Bianchi, then that strategy is not working. You're traveling with Riccardo and me next time we go to Milan."

"What does Riccardo think?"

"He's all for it. He's thinking the three of us can go to a bar, and you and I can help him meet someone."

"Amazing," Oliver observed.

They wandered farther down the beach. It was remote and pristine. A few precipitous dunes rose from the beach. Years before, they used to climb them with the boys and look out over the water, spotting whales feeding just offshore. Giancarlo glanced at Oliver and took his hand, pulling him up the steep incline. Nestled between a few undulations in the sand, Giancarlo stripped off his suit and started yanking on Oliver's. "*Ma dai!*" he said, as Oliver protested.

Oliver loosened the string of his Speedo, and Giancarlo reached his hand in the loose front, stroking Oliver's increasingly stiff cock. He pulled him down onto the sand. He laid back, his arms behind his head, and gazed up at the blue sky. Oliver removed his suit and laid next to Giancarlo, both baring their nakedness to each other and to the world.

The gentle roar of the waves and the whisper of the breeze through the dune grass lulled them both to a light sleep. They woke a while later, both semi-erect. Oliver glanced toward Giancarlo and watched his chest rise and fall as he breathed. "Hey sexy," Oliver whispered to Giancarlo.

Giancarlo felt his heart flutter. *"Andiamo in acqua?"*

Oliver nodded. They left their suits on the sand and walked down the dune to the edge of the water. The water was unusually pleasant, and both waded in. The briny water and the gentle thrashing of the waves were soothing.

Giancarlo approached Oliver and pulled him up next to him. The feel of his hard shaft against him was electrifying. He felt his own sex throb, and he pressed it up under Oliver. Oliver wrapped his legs around Giancarlo's waist and gave him a deep kiss, breathing him in. Giancarlo extended his tongue deep into Oliver's mouth, savoring the warm, moist, and salty space between them.

Their bodies rose and fell with the undulating water. Oliver felt his erection slide back and forth on Giancarlo's torso. He felt himself become increasingly excited and flexed his buttocks around Giancarlo's thick cock under him. The edge of Giancarlo's penis quivered as it grazed Oliver's firm, round bottom.

Oliver closed his eyes and felt the warmth and strength of Giancarlo's embrace. He let his doubts and inhibitions float away. Giancarlo entered him. Giancarlo's muscles tightened and blood rushed to the surface of his skin. He kissed Oliver with abandon.

Oliver continued to flex his muscles around Giancarlo's sex. Giancarlo moaned. With one hand placed under Oliver's butt, he used the other to stroke Oliver's erection, gliding his hand up and down the long shaft. Giancarlo felt Oliver's cock grow increasingly hot and engorged. He slowed his hand, feeling his own sex ready to explode inside Oliver. As swells of intense pleasure traveled the length of his shaft, he gave Oliver one more intense tug, and they both came. Oliver felt Giancarlo's thick sex shudder inside him and his own sex writhe with spasms of bliss.

They both let go of each other and let the waves gently edge them toward the shore. Both gazed into each other's eyes. Giancarlo laid back on the wet sand and let the swells wash over his body. Oliver sat with his arms wrapped around his knees. He caressed Giancarlo's chest and said, "I love you so much!"

Giancarlo peered up at him and smiled. "*Ti voglio tanto bene!*"

They eventually stood, retrieved their suits, and made their way back to the main part of the beach. Both were famished, and quickly opened the sandwiches that Rita had prepared for them.

"That was intense," Oliver said as they ate.

Giancarlo nodded, chuckling. "I'm still sorry for overreacting."

"I'm sorry for not trusting you. But, you know, you underestimate how alluring you are."

Giancarlo blushed.

They finished their sandwiches, eased back in their beach chairs, and pulled out books they wanted to read. Both immediately dozed off, content lying next to each other in the warm sun.

A couple of hours later, they returned to Anna's and Rita's.

"Did you have a good time at the beach?" Anna asked as they walked in the door.

Oliver put his arm around Giancarlo's back and nodded. Giancarlo turned to Oliver and smiled.

"Want something to eat or drink?" Rita inquired, rising from the sofa.

"Don't go to any trouble," Giancarlo protested. "We can help ourselves."

"I was going to put out some cheese. Maybe some hummus?"

"That would be nice," Oliver noted. "I'll open some wine?"

"There's a bottle of red in the cabinet there," Anna said to Oliver.

Rita prepared a small platter of nibbles, and Oliver poured everyone a glass of wine.

"And the boys?" Giancarlo asked.

"Well, Luca and Donato are on a bike ride, and Francesco and Taylor are drawing," Rita noted.

"Everyone's in love!" Oliver said, chuckling.

"Yes, it would seem," Anna added.

"See what you missed?" Oliver said, poking Giancarlo on his shoulder.

"I have to say, Francesco is the big surprise," Giancarlo observed. "He seemed like he enjoyed casual flings here and there. Do you think this is serious?"

Rita nodded. Anna glanced at Oliver, who nodded, too. Then Oliver said, "I find it interesting that Taylor is non-binary. Francesco always seemed to gravitate to women who were gender conforming. He seemed to play the classic role of a handsome man pursuing gorgeous women. And he never seemed interested in settling down with one."

"What do you think happened?" Giancarlo asked.

"I've been asking myself that for the last couple of weeks. Do you have any theories?" Oliver asked his moms.

They both shook their head no. Then Rita noted, "Francesco is more thoughtful than I remember. He's been very solicitous of us since you all arrived. He also seems to be very protective of and concerned about Luca."

They all nodded.

"I remember growing up and feeling a lot of conflict. If I turned out straight, I feared people would think I was just protesting my mothers' orientation, trying to be different. If I turned out gay, I feared people would think it was just because I grew up in a gay household, conditioned to be that way. I wonder if Francesco feels the same conflict. He's surrounded by gay men. He is always making sure people know he's not gay. But I wonder if deep down, he's not as traditionally heterosexual as people think. Maybe he's more fluid, but has had a difficult time embracing that," Oliver remarked.

"Tell us more," Anna said.

"Maybe he's never been serious because he's not as traditional as people think. He finally found someone who gets him and allows him to be different," Oliver said.

"He's also just sixteen," Giancarlo noted. "Who gets serious that young anymore?"

"Yes, but even sixteen-year-olds have their favorites and pair off. Until Taylor, Francesco hadn't," Oliver said.

"I don't know what non-binary really means," Giancarlo stated as he took a sip of wine.

Anna and Rita looked at Oliver.

"Why's everyone looking at me?"

"You run workshops on this stuff. You're the expert," Rita said.

"I'm no expert. From what I understand, there's a lot of pressure in society to be male or female and to conform to gender roles – dress, professions, relationships, mannerisms, and other things. A person who is non-binary is someone who doesn't feel that gender is always either/or – that some people feel both male and female inclinations and seek to integrate them into some unique configuration, a non-binary one."

"Is it transgender?" Anna asked.

"No. That's different. A transgender person is someone who identifies as male or female but was assigned a different gender at birth. They seek to affirm the gender they feel on the inside, not the one they were assigned."

"So, is Taylor just a butch female?" Giancarlo asked.

Oliver glared at him.

Giancarlo protested. "I know. I'm not very politically correct, but I'm just trying to understand."

Anna and Rita leaned forward.

"I think in the past, we thought everyone fit a male or female designation. Even in gay couples, people thought there had to be a husband and a wife. There were feminine males and butch females. We assumed gender ordinarily took a binary and complementary gender form. A non-binary person evades traditional gender categories. Some would argue there are more than two genders. At least at this point, a non-binary person is someone who doesn't want to identify as male or female, someone who is forging a unique expression of gender."

"So, what does this have to do with Francesco?" Giancarlo asked.

"Maybe being with Taylor allows him to be queer without self-identifying as gay or straight," Oliver hypothesized.

They all nodded pensively.

Giancarlo stood and asked, "Anybody for a refill?"

Everyone nodded enthusiastically, ready to let the discussion go.

"So, are we all just going to avoid talking about this?" Oliver pressed.

"Dear, my head is hurting. It's too complicated," Anna said, placing her hand on top of Oliver's.

He nodded and smiled. He raised his glass as Giancarlo poured.

They all raised their refilled glasses. Rita said, "Here's to being queer!"

"Cheers," they all said in unison.

Giancarlo's enthusiasm was curbed by an underlying apprehension. What would it mean to celebrate queerness in the conservative banking world of Italy? Oliver glanced his direction and noticed his reticence and realized more terrain would have to be traversed for them to be okay. He realized Donato's father could still be a problem, particularly when he found out his son was queer, too! Oliver took a long sip of his drink, excused himself, and went upstairs to shower.

Giancarlo nervously fussed with some appetizers, checked emails on his phone, and followed Oliver upstairs.

Rita and Anna cleared the table. As they carried platters into the kitchen, Rita said, "I'm glad things seem patched up, but I'm not convinced everything is good."

"Me, either," Anna said. "I can feel something in the pit of my stomach; something on the horizon. I hope everything will be okay."

"Me, too," Rita replied. "We have to trust that they all have the resources to face whatever challenges come their way. We can't shield them."

"I know. I wish I could, though."

Rita placed a platter in the sink and turned around. She ran her hand through Anna's silky gray hair and said, "Thanks for a wonderful life!"

"You sound like you're going someplace," Anna said, furrowing her brow.

"You never know. I just want to make sure you know how much I love you."

"You're going to be fine," Anna said, holding Rita's shoulders in her hands. She wished she could breathe assurance and strength into her, but she realized Rita's condition was tentative at best. She kissed Rita and gave her a warm embrace.

19

Chapter Nineteen –
Choices

The next week was Carnival. The town was full, and excitement was mounting for the parade that would take place two days later, on Thursday. Meanwhile, Luca had convinced Oliver and Giancarlo to join him and Donato at Boys Beach for the day.

"I'm still not sure why we're trekking all this way to the beach," Giancarlo lamented as they hiked through ankle deep water in the marshes. "I prefer my *lettino* at San Felice Circeo and a bit of pasta and vino for lunch."

"Rita has done her best to accommodate you," Oliver said, pointing to his backpack filled with pasta salad and wine.

"And think of all the eye candy," Luca said, winking at his father.

"I have all the eye candy I need right here," Giancarlo said, nodding at Oliver.

"It's Carnival. A time to loosen up!" Oliver noted.

"That's a trick statement. I'm on a short leash," he said, chuckling.

Donato wasn't sure what to make of the banter between Luca's fathers. They had obviously patched their differences, but he sensed raw emotions still under the surface. He also was apprehensive himself about heading out to Boys Beach with Luca. Things were going well, and he didn't want some cute flirt to come between them.

As much as Giancarlo complained about the walk and the lack of services he was used to at an Italian resort, secretly he looked forward to time with Luca and Donato, and he always enjoyed the procession of incredibly handsome men strutting back and forth in front of them on the beach.

The tide was coming in. By the time they arrived at the dunes, the tidal pools were filling. They waded through one of them and made their way up a steep and narrow path of sand. The dune grass waved in the gentle breeze. From the ridge of the dune, they glimpsed the festive spectacle before them. Hundreds of colorful umbrellas concealing scantily clad bodies stretched along the narrow beach.

"The water must be warm," Luca noted. "Look how many people are in the water!"

"*Grazie a Dio*," Giancarlo murmured, unable to tolerate the usually cold water surrounding the Cape.

"There's an open patch down there," Donato observed, pointing down the beach.

"*Andiamo?*" Luca suggested.

The four of them walked toward the water and then along the shore. Donato and Luca held hands and seemed oblivious to the heads turning their direction as they hiked along the sand. Oliver, ordinarily prudish, seemed unusually curious. He scrutinized each clumping of bathers they passed and was surprised how many gave him an intense look back. Giancarlo followed. He was being extra careful, and kept his eyes fixed on Oliver. He observed his broad tan back and the curvature of his buttocks pressing against the fabric of his swimsuit. Oliver's blond hair, now even lighter from days in the sun, blew in the breeze. He turned around to see if Giancarlo was still with them, and Giancarlo gasped for breath. Oliver was stunningly handsome, and he realized how fortunate he was. They found a place, set up their chairs and umbrellas, and carefully laid out towels on the soft yellow sand. Donato and Luca raced to the water, while Oliver and Giancarlo sat in the shade and unpacked lunch.

"What do you think of them?" Giancarlo began.

"They seem perfect together. I haven't seen Luca happier."

Giancarlo nodded and smiled. "*Vino?*" he offered to Luca.

"I'll have some with the pasta salad, thanks."

Giancarlo opened a small container and gave it to Oliver. He poured him a glass of wine. They sat back in their chairs and glanced out over the horizon.

"And us?"

"I'd pick you over all of these?" Oliver said, waving his hand over the beach.

"Even those?" Giancarlo remarked, nodding toward two exceptionally handsome men frolicking in the water, their erections bouncing up and down as they groped one another.

"Even those!" Oliver said matter-of-factly.

Giancarlo smiled.

Luca and Donato came out of the water and walked toward them. Oliver threw them towels, and they dried themselves. They both grinned at one another, clearly in love.

"*Volete mangiare?*"

"*Si, ho fame!*" Luca remarked, having worked up an appetite. Donato nodded yes as well.

Luca and Donato sat in the shade and picked at Rita's pasta salad. Oliver leaned his chair back and began reading a novel. Giancarlo closed his eyes for a nap.

Donato's phone pinged. He pulled the phone out of his backpack and said, "*Cazzo.*"

"What's wrong?" Luca inquired, leaning toward Donato.

"My father."

Giancarlo opened his eyes and leaned forward in his chair. Oliver set his book down. Donato read the text from his mother. His father had uncovered their scheme and was furious. He demanded that Donato return immediately to Rome.

"Does she elaborate?" Luca asked.

"Not really. She just says he's furious and that she's sorry." Donato began to tremble. He felt exposed and vulnerable. He was on a gay beach in a gay village with his gay boyfriend. There would be no way to mollify his father.

"I thought your mom had covered for you; that you were at your cousin's wedding," Giancarlo noted.

"She did. But my father is a master at sniffing things out. I should have known better," Donato said, shaking his head.

Luca felt horrible, guilty at having lured Donato to Ptown. "What are you going to do?" Luca inquired.

"I have to go back. How soon could I get a flight out of Boston?"

"Thursday is the parade. Can't you stay until Friday?" Luca pleaded.

"Screw the parade. I have to get back," Donato said, clearly agitated and upset.

Oliver and Giancarlo looked at each other with alarm. Luca stood up and started pacing.

"You could get a flight tomorrow afternoon," Giancarlo said. "We can get you on an early ferry tomorrow and you could easily catch any number of flights to Europe or even the non-stop to Rome."

Donato began typing on his phone. He had an open-ended ticket and checked to see if he could confirm a seat for the next day. About ten minutes later, he said stoically, "I found a seat for tomorrow." Then he added, "Sorry to put a damper on things."

He stood up and approached Luca. "Sorry, *tesoro*."

At first, Luca pushed his hand back, angry and annoyed that things were unraveling. Then he peered into Donato's eyes and could see the pain and fear mounting. "Let's take a walk," Luca suggested.

Luca took Donato's hand, and they walked to the edge of the water.

"What are you going to do?" he asked Donato.

"I don't know. This is going to be bad."

"Can't your mom do something? Can she soften him up?"

"I think she's probably already tried, to no avail. He's such a terror."

"You're alarming me," Luca observed. "He wouldn't hurt you, would he?"

Donato just looked at Luca, saying nothing.

"No. You can't go back, then."

"I have to. I have to face the music one way or the other."

"And?"

"I don't know. We'll see how bad things are."

"I'll go back with you," Luca offered.

"No. That would be worse."

"I won't come to your house, but I'll be in Rome to support you after you meet with him."

Donato shook his head no. "I couldn't have you cut short your time with your family. It's too important – your grandmothers' anniversary, your fathers' reconciliation, and your time with Francesco and Taylor. I'll take care of this myself."

"We're in this together," Luca added.

Donato glared at him. He appreciated Luca's gesture and sentiments but, at the moment, he didn't feel they were in this together. There could be no 'we.' It was impossible. There was no future in this, as long as his father objected and was the source of his financial support.

Luca felt the shift in Donato's energy and realized he was losing

Donato again. He felt his chest grow heavy. They continued to stroll along the water. Donato grew withdrawn and quiet. Luca didn't know what to do.

They returned to the umbrellas. Oliver and Giancarlo abruptly quit what they were discussing and glanced at them both. "Well?" Oliver inquired.

"I'm sorry for spoiling your vacation," Donato began. "I probably shouldn't have come."

"Donato. It was brave for you to come, and we hope it was a good experience. I know your father is intimidating and has strong views. Hopefully, you have a new sense of who you are and what is possible, having met Luca's grandmothers and spent time here. Don't let go of the strides you made in your self-understanding," Giancarlo said.

"Signor Russo, how is it in the banking world?" Donato interjected, clearly already calculating the impact of things on his career. "My father warns me it is unforgiving."

Giancarlo looked over at Oliver and then turned back to Donato. "I have to be honest, it's a conservative world. Early in my career, I was closeted and hid my identity from my father and from my colleagues. Even when Oliver and I first met, I was discreet and careful. But if you are good at what you do, and if you don't let people create doubt in yourself, you can be successful. You mentioned Federico Luciano the other day. He's one of the most successful mutual funds managers in Rome. People are begging to be his clients, and they don't care if he's gay or not. You're smart, handsome, and have good connections. You will be as successful as you want to be."

Luca scrutinized Donato's face to see how he reacted to his father's thoughts. He remained nervous and afraid. He reached his hand over to Donato and held it. Luca felt his fear.

"Should we head back?" Luca suggested. He no longer felt like relaxing on the beach. Everyone nodded and packed up umbrellas, chairs, towels, and backpacks.

The next day, Luca stood with Donato at the pier, waiting to embark on the ferry. "You'll text me when you get to the airport, and let me know when you arrive in Rome, no matter the time."

Donato nodded. "I'm sorry," he whispered to Luca.

"Don't apologize. We'll get through this," Luca assured him.

Donato wasn't convinced, and Luca sensed his lack of confidence. The crew announced boarding, and Luca gave Donato an affectionate kiss and held his hand as long as he could before Donato finally extracted himself and headed down the ramp to the ferry. Donato waved as he walked inside. He took a seat in the front of the boat and leaned his head back, tired from the war raging inside himself. He was inspired and encouraged by what he had seen in Ptown – Luca's grandmothers, the strength and resilience of Giancarlo's and Oliver's relationship, and the gay-affirming town he had grown to love. But his father had all the power. He depended on him for financial support, and it was his father's connections that would be the ticket to a successful career in banking and finance. He couldn't defy him.

Luca stood dazed on the edge of the wharf, waiting for the ferry to pull away from the dock. Oliver, Giancarlo, and Francesco watched Luca from a distance.

"This will not go well, will it?" Oliver inquired.

"Nope," Giancarlo murmured. "Gerardo Bianchi is a force to be reckoned with. He's vindictive, and I imagine he will bring his son to his knees."

"That's too bad. Donato's a nice guy," Oliver said.

"He's nice, but he's not very self-confident," Francesco observed.

Oliver and Giancarlo looked at their son.

"Don't look at me. I'm just a silent observer."

"Why do you say that he's not self-confident?"

"I've watched him and Luca. Donato is tall, poised, and seemingly calm and self-assured. But I can sense a lot of insecurity below the surface."

"Like what?" Oliver asked.

"Little things. The deference he gives to Luca and the self-deprecating way he talks about himself. He's also clueless about how handsome he is, and he seemed extraordinarily reliant on Luca during their time here."

"But he's new to the place. You know Ptown. It's intimidating."

"Yes. But everyone reacts differently. He's not self-assured, and I wouldn't be surprised if his father has berated him before. It's the classic case of a homophobic father who senses his son is different and puts him down all the time."

"Hmm," Oliver said, rubbing his chin thoughtfully.

"He's going to cave," Francesco added.

"How are we going to help Luca through that?" Giancarlo inquired.

"I don't think it will take much. Take a look," Francesco re-marked, nodding toward the ramp of the ferry where Luca was talking with Ben.

"Who's that?" Giancarlo inquired.

"Ben," Francesco replied.

"Ah, yes. Ben from the ferry," Oliver noted. "We met him on the way in from Rome."

"I gather there's more to the story," Giancarlo added.

"Ben was flirting with Luca on the ferry from Boston. We also ran into Ben on Boys Beach several weeks ago. He went back to Boston but apparently has returned at an opportune time," Francesco ex-plained, raising his brows.

"And is Luca interested in him?" Giancarlo inquired.

"Not as much as he likes Donato, but they have a common inter-est — magic."

"Ahh," Giancarlo noted.

Luca and Ben approached them. "Look who just showed up," Luca said.

"Ben. Great to see you again," Francesco said. "You remember our dad, Oliver? This is our papa, Giancarlo."

"Nice to see you again, and nice to meet you," he said, extending his hands to both Oliver and Giancarlo.

Francesco leaned toward Ben and gave him a kiss on his cheek.

"So, you just came in on the ferry?" Giancarlo inquired.

Ben nodded. "Here for Carnival!"

"It would seem so is half of Boston!" Giancarlo said, chuckling.

"*Andiamo?*" Oliver suggested.

They walked toward town. Crowds continued to grow in anticipation of the Carnival parade in two days. The ferry coming from Boston had been full, and the pier was now crowded with people dragging suitcases and meeting friends. The day was sunny and pleasant, and tan and buff men were in abundance. Giancarlo's head pivoted back and forth at all the eye candy. Oliver squeezed his hand tightly to remind him who he was with.

"Are you meeting up with Taylor?" Oliver asked Francesco.

"Yes. We're meeting the gallery owner *nonna* introduced us to. She's going to show our sketches this weekend."

"That's so exciting. Will there be a reception?"

"Friday night."

They arrived at the center of town. Francesco headed east to meet Taylor and the gallery owner. Oliver and Giancarlo pretended they had an errand at Town Hall to give Ben and Luca a chance to be alone. Ben and Luca stood in front of Town Hall. People were sitting in the shade watching people pass back and forth.

Luca said to Ben, "Where are your friends renting? I'll walk you there."

"It's in the West End."

"That's where my grandmothers have a house. We can walk together."

"Do you want something to eat?" Ben inquired. "I'm starved."

Luca nodded. "A burger? At that place just past Spiritus?"

Ben nodded.

In a few minutes, they arrived at the restaurant, were given a nice table on the deck overlooking the street, and quickly ordered drinks. Luca began, "Such a pleasant surprise to run into you."

"I know. I thought you might already be back in Rome."

"We have a couple of weeks more."

"Wow! And were you seeing people off at the ferry?"

"Yes. A friend from Rome."

"Donato? The one I met?" Ben asked, raising his brows. "Is he a friend friend or a special friend?"

Luca didn't know how to respond. He didn't have much confidence Donato would stand up to his father, and he couldn't believe how uncanny it was to see Ben disembark just as Donato left for Rome. It was as if the universe was hitting him over the head with a sign, a big sign. Sure, Donato made his heart pound and his pulse race. The smell of Donato's cologne lingered on his shirt collar, and he savored the memory of their bodies entwined overnight. But he also sensed Donato was heading for a reckoning, and it wasn't likely to go well. He sensed their story might end, once and for all. Could a new one be in the works?

"It's complicated," Luca said, deciding it was better to be honest, particularly with a possible fellow wizard.

Ben squinted his eyes, and his grin relaxed a bit.

"He was someone I met in Rome. He's closeted and seemingly unable to come out to his conservative and stern father. So, there's not much future in it."

Ben took a deep breath. He felt encouraged by the news but

slightly disappointed he might be second choice, a backup plan. "So, how did you leave off?"

"He's heading to Rome. His father is angry he came here. Not sure how things will unfold."

"I'm sorry," Ben said genuinely, albeit with a bit of relief. He still liked Luca. He gazed into Luca's deep set blue eyes. They were melancholy and distant. While Ben didn't want to be second choice, he felt like he and Luca might be a good match, a fortuitous match. He also realized if Luca had just seen Donato off, it wasn't a good time to be overly forward and aggressive.

The server came and took their orders. Luca then turned toward Ben and asked, "So, did you finish Harkness's book?"

"Oh, my God! I got hooked. I've read all three in the trilogy. I couldn't put them down."

Luca's eyes widened. "And?"

"I love the whole process by which Diana comes to terms with her abilities, her identity as a witch."

Luca could relate to Diana's story, the gradual discovery of her identity as a sorcerer and the struggle to come to terms with her powers. It was his story, and he wondered if it was Ben's too. But he didn't want to frighten off another prospect and said, "It's almost like the process of coming out. One discovers that one experiences the world and sexuality differently as a gay man. In many cases, others don't know who you are, but you know you are different. You occupy another realm with its own language and ways. Sometimes there are those who mentor you. You eventually learn how to move and function in two parallel universes."

Ben couldn't believe how accurately and poignantly Luca had expressed his own story. For Ben, the process of coming to terms with his identity was both that of embracing his sexuality and that of accepting that he was a wizard. He wanted to confide in Luca, but he feared Luca would think him odd.

Both took sips of their drinks to minimize eye contact. Their burgers arrived, and Ben quickly picked up a few of the incredibly delicious fries and plopped them in his mouth. Luca peeled the bun off the meat and squeezed mustard and ketchup on it and replaced the bread. "*Buon appetito.*"

"I love that you speak Italian," Ben remarked, grateful for a segue to change the subject. "What was it like growing up in Rome?"

"I loved it. It was nice having the connection with my grandmothers here — growing up in two worlds and two languages."

"And your fathers and grandmothers are all gay!"

"Yes. It was an accepting environment but didn't lessen the tension I felt with the broader environment. Yes, Rome is relatively accepting and affirming, but not always. My friend Donato's situation is a prime example."

"I thought it was interesting that in Harkness's books, Diana's parents try to protect her, but fate forces her to come to terms with things. I loved the moving back and forth in time. I even think the whole notion of vampires is a metaphor for past lives. Their accumulated knowledge – such language skills and the information they know – could easily be a way to explain how people who have lived many lives come into this incarnation with inherited abilities and wisdom."

Luca's heart skipped a beat. One of his special gifts was the ability to move back and forth in time, in different past lives. That Ben could so easily talk about that was extremely encouraging. He decided to take a risk and ask, "So, do you believe in past lives?"

Ben was almost certain Luca did and decided it was worth the risk, too. "Yes." He paused, and then asked, "And you?"

Luca nodded. "I can't believe it."

"What?"

"That you are into this stuff."

"Why?"

"I don't meet many who are, and it's odd that we would meet so randomly."

"It's never random," Ben said solemnly.

"My dad keeps saying that."

"So, your interest in Harkness?"

"Personal."

"Personal as in, I don't want to share, or personal as in it is relevant."

"Relevant," Luca said simply.

"I love your elaborate answers," Ben said jokingly.

"I guess I'm just a little cautious."

"Understandably. Did Donato share these interests?"

Luca nodded no.

Ben's heart raced with excitement.

Luca glanced across the table and peered into Ben's eyes. They sparkled. They weren't haunting or alluring, like Donato's. And Ben was a less imposing figure — cute rather than handsome and affable instead of mysterious. He recalled from their afternoon on the beach that he was well-endowed, not that he considered himself a size queen. But it helped. Could he grow to love Ben the way he loved Donato? It was a question that kept coming up. He wondered if that was the lesson that he was being taught during his vacation in Ptown.

They finished their burgers. Luca then said, "Well, sorry to have distracted you en route to your friends."

"I'm not."

Luca blushed. "I'll walk you to your friends?"

"I'd love that," Ben said. In fact, he hoped Drew, Tom, and David would be home and see him with Luca. They all thought he should have been more aggressive and pursued Luca earlier. He sensed there wasn't enough chemistry and had already been through enough bad breakups recently.

They walked through town into the West End. Ben led him down a side street and then said, "Here it is. You're not far from here?"

"Just around the corner and a couple of streets down."

"Amazing."

"Do you rent here often?"

"We have a few times before," Ben noted.

"And we've never crossed paths?"

"Curious, isn't it?"

Luca nodded. He leaned over and gave Ben an affectionate kiss. "I enjoyed running into you. How long are you here?"

"At least through the weekend," he said, raising his brows as if to suggest he could remain longer.

Luca blushed. "I think you have my number, right?"

Ben nodded. "I'll text you."

Ben climbed the steps to his friends' condo, and Luca returned to his grandmothers. When he entered the house, Francesco, Oliver, Giancarlo, Anna, and Rita were all gathered in the family room nibbling on snacks and enjoying some cool beverages. There was a protracted silence as everyone glanced up and stared at Luca.

"Looks like the inquisition," Luca said lightheartedly.

Francesco breathed a sigh of relief and said, "*E allora?*"

"What do you mean, *allora?*"

"Fascinating meeting Ben," Francesco noted, the adults all looking on.

Luca realized, as his brother spoke, that the sadness associated with Donato's departure had lifted. In fact, he had forgotten to check his phone. He pulled it out of his pocked and noticed several texts from Donato and one missed call. "*Cazzo,*" he said. "I have to make a quick call," he said, excusing himself.

He dialed Donato's number, and it went to voicemail. He texted him and said, "Hope you arrived in Boston safely. Text or call me before you board."

Luca went back to the kitchen, fixed himself an espresso, and joined the others.

"How are you feeling?" Giancarlo asked, patting his hand on Luca's knee.

"I'm okay. Why?"

"With Donato leaving and all."

"It's funny. I'm not as upset as I thought I would be."

Giancarlo and Oliver both took a deep breath and leaned back on the sofa.

"It wouldn't have anything to do with Ben's arrival?" Francesco asked provocatively.

Luca glared at his brother in protest, but he realized he was right. He didn't answer.

Oliver and Giancarlo looked at each other and nodded. Oliver cleared his throat and timidly said, "We liked Donato. You guys seem like a good match. But we're still not convinced he'll be able to stand his ground against his father."

"I have the same feeling," Luca said.

"I guess we'll see, right?" Oliver asked.

Luca nodded.

"Any vibes you're picking up?" Rita inquired, wondering what psychic messages Luca might have received.

"It's difficult when you're dealing with matters of your own heart."

"Have you thought about doing a reading with Carolyn?" Anna inquired.

Luca looked off across the room. He smiled. "Thanks, nanna. That's a great idea."

She smiled. She wasn't usually the one pushing the psychic stuff, but it occurred to her that Luca needed some outside help.

Luca excused himself and walked into town. He approached the office of a family friend and psychic, Carolyn. He knocked and heard a voice inside say, "Come in."

He pushed the door open. The spacious loft was full of books, crystals, and stacks of various kinds of tarot cards. Carolyn looked up and said, "I was expecting you."

Carolyn had a sheepish grin. She had bright gray hair, a penetrating gaze, and a calm demeanor as she sat on an easy chair in front of a round brass decorative table. Luca was, at first, skeptical of Carolyn's remark. But Carolyn was usually on target, and it wouldn't have surprised him if she had been expecting him.

"So, what can I do for you?" she asked.

"I need a reading."

"Sit," she said as she pointed to a chair in front of him. She kept her eyes focused on him as she shuffled a deck. "Cut the deck," she added, and then continued, "What do you want to know?"

"I have a dilemma. It's a matter of the heart. Romance."

"What's the question?"

"Is it Donato or Ben?"

"Can we reframe the question? Let's ask about each one separately."

Luca nodded and then said, "What can you tell me about Donato and me?"

"Let's see," Carolyn said. "Pick a card."

Luca did. It was the 'Lovers' card. "Oh my God," he said in surprise at the beautiful card decorated with two lovers bathed in flames of light and fire.

Carolyn maintained a neutral and stoic face. She said, "Let's pick another."

He did. It was the 'Tower' card. "Hmm," he lamented. "Not a good sign," he said, aware that the tower symbolized a sudden overturning of things.

"Don't judge it yet. Who's the other?"

"Ben."

"So, what about Ben, right?"

Luca nodded. He pulled a card. It was the 'Two of Cups,' a card with two lovers facing each other. "This isn't helpful," he said, clearly disconcerted at the fact that with both Donato and Ben, a card suggesting love appeared.

Carolyn just smiled. "Pull another."

He did. It was the 'Magician.'

At first, Luca was surprised. The two lovers and a magic card were uncanny in their representation of his and Ben's relationship — love and magic. But, on further consideration, he wasn't surprised. The cards were always very informative, and the fact that they were so on target only confirmed his intuition.

"So, we have the 'Lovers' and the 'Tower' for Donato. And we have the 'Two of Cups' and the 'Magician' for Ben. What does that say to you?" Carolyn knew Luca, and she knew he was gifted at interpreting Tarot. She didn't need to help him much.

"It would seem one is headed for a showdown, and the other confirms our connection — love and magic."

"Pull another."

Luca pulled another card. It was the 'Two of Swords,' a woman blindfolded with two swords crossed.

"Hmm," Carolyn said. "Very interesting. It doesn't appear that the answer is known yet. You're at a critical juncture, a crossing of sorts, but you are still blindfolded, unable to see the outcome."

"So, what do I do?"

"What does the 'Tower' card suggest to you?"

"It's the tough encounter Donato faces with his father," Luca said.

"I imagine that is the outcome we don't know yet," Carolyn suggested.

Luca nodded.

"But with Ben, there is love and magic, the perfect combination."

"Maybe," she said with a grin. "But the 'Lovers' card is a more significant card – one of the major arcana. It indicates not just love but also personal identity, a coming into your own, perhaps Donato coming into his own."

"And?"

"And I'm afraid you have to sit tight and wait for the outcome. I'm sorry."

Luca sighed, realizing he had no more information than when he arrived. He was drawn to both Donato and Ben and had to wait to see how things unfolded. "You've been very insightful, as usual. I sensed that was the case."

Carolyn raised her brows. She wasn't convinced the reading was over. She pulled a card from the deck and flipped it over. It was the 'Star' card. "That's you," she said affectionately. "Don't ever doubt yourself. Keep your chakras open and clear. A lot of information is forthcoming soon."

Luca nodded pensively. He thanked Carolyn, paid her, and walked back onto Commercial Street.

"*Pazienza*," he said to himself. But he didn't feel patient. He was restless and wanted firm and quick resolution.

20

Chapter Twenty – Facing the Music

A car service was waiting for Donato at Rome's Leonardo da Vinci airport. He placed his bag in the trunk, and the car sped off to the city. The countryside was a dramatic contrast to the New England coastline. The August sun had parched the fields to a crisp light brown. The roads into the city center were empty. Most people were at the beaches or in the mountains. The driver adroitly maneuvered around several ancient monuments – the Baths of Caracalla and the Circus Maximus. He made a turn at Santa Maria in Cosmedin and passed the archaeological site Luca had taken him to only a few months earlier.

As he thought of Luca, he felt a small pinch of his heart. He wanted to be resolute in the strides he had made coming out to his friends and to himself, but he feared he would ultimately acquiesce to his father. He felt trapped, unable to imagine an alternative narrative, one where he could pursue his interest in banking yet be proud of his identity as a gay man. He struggled with competing voices in his head, his father's winning out.

The familiarity of Rome passing outside the car window was comforting, a city steeped in history and time. Donato breathed in the scent of Roman air – a mix of roasted coffee and earth – centuries of stone, cement, and brick, releasing their odors into the crowded urban center. He had enjoyed his journey to Provincetown. Charming and historic in its own way, the town jarred the senses with its array of bars, clubs, restaurants, shows, galleries, and the parade of humanity walking up and down the main street. As stimulating as Ptown had been, Donato felt a certain satisfaction in his connection to Rome and to the quotidian habits of life as he was accustomed.

The driver continued along the Lungo Tevere, under shady trees lining the Tiber River, until they passed the Ponte Sant'Angelo and then turned left over a modern bridge into the Prati neighborhood. Soon they were in front of Donato's home. He retrieved his bags and headed upstairs into the apartment. He was trembling and his heart raced.

He opened the door and walked inside. His parents had been expecting him and were sitting quietly and sternly in the parlor. Donato's mom looked up. Her eyes were red. She tried to convey warmth and affection, but her face was apprehensive and sad.

Donato glanced at his father. His eyes were piercing. He inched forward in his chair, his body stiff, as if poised to strike. "Sit," his father directed.

Donato set his suitcase down, draped his jacket over the handle, and walked into the parlor, taking a seat in front of his parents.

"Your mother has filled me in on her little scheme."

Donato glanced at his mother, who stared back at him, emotionless.

"I'm surprised at you both," he continued. "I feel betrayed. You have been deceptive, dishonest, and have done something that could cause irreparable harm to your future career and to our family's livelihood."

Donato began to tremble. When his father was angry, there was little restraint. It was also best to nod and agree.

"I thought I told you to sever all ties with the Russo boy."

Donato nodded and said timidly, "When mom suggested I go to Giorgia's wedding, I realized I wouldn't be far from where Luca and his family would be on vacation. I have always wanted to see Cape Cod and thought it wouldn't be a problem to make a quick visit."

"Don't try to spin this favorably. You both knew what you were doing. So, you thought going to one of the most notorious centers of depraved gay culture in the world wouldn't be a problem?"

"It's not depraved," Donato replied. He glanced over and noticed his mom nod her head almost imperceptibly. "It's a historic town and a major art destination."

"And where did you stay?"

"With Luca's family."

"And you don't think that's a problem?"

"How?"

"Do I have to remind you they do not have a good reputation? Getting involved with Luca and his dads will only bring question to your own orientation and integrity."

Donato swallowed nervously. His father's line was the perfect segue to come out, to declare that he was gay. He looked over at his mother and she nodded no.

"Luca's grandmothers were very hospitable and couldn't have been nicer. They are lawyers in Boston."

Gerardo stood up and paced. He said, "I don't care who they are. Luca's fathers live here, and if word were to get out that you spent the summer with them in Provincetown, it would be all over. I'm really disappointed with your judgment and lack of respect. I explicitly told you not to associate yourself with them," he said, slapping the back of his son's head sharply.

Donato turned his head to the side and held his hand up to his cheek. His father had never hit him, and he was stunned.

"And I expected much more of you," he said, turning to Laura. "This wasn't a casual trip to Giorgia's wedding. It was a deliberate way to circumvent me and give license to Donato's folly." He took hold of Laura's hair and gave a long, hard tug and held his hand up as if he were about to strike her.

Laura screamed, "*Fermo!*"

Donato's eyes widened. He had seen his father stern and angry, but he had never seen him out of control like he was now.

"*Tu fermi!*" Gerardo said in reply. "Both of you have to stop this nonsense."

Donato stood up and walked toward his father. "Do not hit or touch mom!"

"I'll do what I want. You've both disobeyed me. I work hard to make sure you have a good life and a bright future and look what you both do!"

Donato walked up to his father and stood inches from his face. He could smell the odor of cigar and brandy on his breath. "Who is Martina Millefiori?" Donato asked. His voice was strong, but he was shaking inside.

Gerardo turned to his wife and slapped her. "We had a deal."

"I've never broken it," she screamed, weeping.

Gerardo turned back to his son. "So, going through my stuff, then?"

"That's not the point. The question is – who is Martina Millefiori? You talk about honor, integrity, faithfulness, and family values. And yet you are a hypocrite – an abusive and nasty one at that," Donato said forcefully.

Donato couldn't believe the words coming out of his mouth. He had never confronted his father like that, and he had not intended to do so. But witnessing his father's abuse was too much. He had had enough.

"I made a mistake, and I am paying for it. I don't want you to make a similar one."

"I don't intend to. I'm not going to live a double life or pretend I'm something I'm not. If the Bianchis stand for integrity, then I want to make sure people know who I am and what I stand for."

Gerardo looked with horror at his son. He knew what was to follow.

"I'm gay."

Laura burst out in sobs, fearful of what was to follow, yet proud that her son had finally voiced his truth.

"You filthy piece of shit," Gerardo replied, striking his son's face with a powerful blow. "You're on your own then. I want nothing to do with you. Go back to the Russos or to whomever, but don't come back here."

Donato composed himself and gazed at his father in the face. "No. I think you have that all wrong. Now I want you to sit down," he said, pointing his finger at the nearby chair.

Gerardo looked defiantly at his son.

"Sit. There's more."

Gerardo reluctantly sat. Donato began to pace. He gathered his thoughts and said, "You are no longer in a position to tell mom or me what to do. I don't want to ruin your reputation or career, but I am only a few steps away from taking evidence of your affair to the press if you touch mom again or if you do anything to disinherit me or kick me out of the house."

Gerardo trembled, but he said defiantly, "You don't have the balls to do it."

"I used to think I didn't, but I'm fed up and ready to do whatever it takes."

"This is my house, and neither of you contributes to the budget."

"What do Martina and her son contribute?"

Gerardo turned ashen.

"Hmm hum," Donato murmured. "I don't know what kind of relationship you and mom have. You can work that out. If she wants a divorce, you either decide on a favorable settlement or I'll make sure you do. I imagine a judge would not look favorably on a finance minister who is paying a woman to stay quiet about an affair and a child. I also expect the same support you've been providing while I'm in college – housing, an allowance, and recommendations for internships and jobs. Again, if not, there will be publicity."

"That's blackmail and illegal."

"Father, do you really think someone would convict me of black-mail for threatening to make public information about his father's infidelity and abuse?"

Gerardo just starred at his son.

"And one last thing. Actually two. First, if you ever try to sabo-tage Luca's fathers' relationship again, I'll divulge your affair. Second, you can cavort with your conservative colleagues all you want. But I don't want to see your name on any bills against gay people or your support and endorsement of lobbying efforts to block gay rights."

"You're a fool," Gerardo said with a sinister smile.

Donato peered at his father.

"If you come out, I'm finished. There's no incentive for me to back off. I will have lost everything, and so will you and your mom."

"Actually, that's not true. It's your choice how you react to me. I have no intention of publicizing my coming out. It's possible some tabloid may find it curious and interesting, but you have the power to salvage your career by how you spin it. You are a pro at that."

"I'll be finished no matter what. Your threat to go public with my affair doesn't dissuade me. You're coming out is what will do me in."

"That's a bluff. You are a survivor, and you will spin the

information to your advantage. You always do. I know you don't want to lose your fortune, your political power, or future opportunities. An affair is something you did. Keeping it secret by paying off the woman is a huge scandal for someone who has professed conservative values and integrity. Hiding an illegitimate son, even more damning. Having a gay son is trivial today. No one will bat an eye. Your conservative crowd might even sympathize with you, feel compassion for you. But an affair that you've paid to keep secret – now that's something for the tabloids!"

Gerardo knew he had been cornered. His face turned a deeper shade of red. He glared at his wife and sneered at his son. He stood up and walked upstairs to his study.

Donato walked toward his mom, sat next to her, and gave her a tender hug. They were both trembling.

"Mom, I love you. He'll never treat you like that again."

"I love you, too," Laura said, wiping tears from her eyes. "I can't believe what you just did!"

"I can't either. I had no intention of doing it. In fact, just the opposite. I had resigned myself to playing by the rules, keeping my nose clean, hiding my orientation. It's curious how dad's actions, particularly his abusiveness, inspired me to come out and challenge him."

"I'm proud of you," she said, running her hands through Donato's blond hair.

"So, what are we going to do now?" Donato asked, almost chuckling.

Laura wiped her eyes and looked off across the room. "Well," she began softly, almost in a whisper. "I've never been to Cape Cod."

Donato stared at her, raising his brows.

"There's still two weeks till school starts. I don't want to go to Courmayeur with your dad, not now. Why don't we take a little trip?"

"But I just got back."

"Then you know how to navigate the airport in Boston, how to get to Provincetown, and know where we should stay," Laura noted.

All night Donato had been mentally making the break with Luca. The momentum of those thoughts and emotions was difficult to reverse. He rested his head on the back of his hand, looking grim. Laura placed her hands on his shoulder and said, "I thought you'd be excited to go back to the States. What's wrong?"

"I don't know. I guess I was moving in a different direction. I didn't expect all of this."

"Well, we don't have to decide right away. I'll send your father to the mountains. You and I can compose ourselves and decide later. It's been an emotional day."

21

Chapter Twenty-One – Healing

The water passed swiftly outside the window as the ferry glided across Massachusetts Bay. Luca held his grandmother's hand. He could feel her apprehension.

"It's going to be okay, nana," he remarked.

"Are you sure?" she inquired, her eyes sullen and worried.

Luca nodded, but it wasn't clear to him she was out of the woods.

Luca hadn't heard from Donato. He didn't receive a text when he would have arrived at the Rome airport, and two days had passed since his expected head-to-head with Signor Bianchi. Rita had a check-up with her cardiologist, and Luca offered to accompany her on the ferry. He needed something to occupy and distract himself.

The ferry slowed as it pulled into Boston harbor, passed the airport, and pulled into Long Wharf. Luca called a car service, and the driver met them at the ramp of the ferry, whisking them off to Mass

General Hospital. Luca felt Rita's heart pound as she prepared for the appointment.

The cardiologist did some imaging and ran some tests and met them in her office for the consult. She glanced down at the reports and looked up at Rita. "Well, Mrs. Monte-Fitzpatrick, it would appear things have changed."

Rita squeezed Luca's hand, expecting the worse. She stared at the doctor, who continued, "The valves are all opening and closing normally. The flow is good, and there is no evidence of any permanent damage."

"What?"

"Yes. It looks like a full recovery," she said emphatically. "I'm baffled."

Luca looked at Rita and smiled. "Congratulations!"

"But I don't get it. Things looked bad the last time we spoke," Rita said.

"Yes. They did. Whatever was going on, it has resolved itself."

Luca grinned.

"So, what's next?"

"I'll see you in six months for a follow up. Keep doing whatever you're doing – diet, exercise, meditation."

Rita stood, extended her hand to the doctor, and said, "Thanks so much. I appreciate your care over the past couple of years."

Luca took Rita by her hand and led her outside. Rita jumped up and down gleefully. "I can't believe it," she exclaimed.

Luca knew his grandmother was more empathic than she realized and had probably taken on a lot of family hurt and pain around her heart. Since everything had all been resolved, she was better. Even though he wasn't surprised, he still found it amazing when things like that happened, confirming a world of magic and energy.

"I'm happy for you," he said warmly, giving Rita a tender embrace.

They called a car service and headed back to the ferry for the return trip. They had time to kill, so they took a table at a nearby restaurant on a terrace overlooking the harbor. It was on the first floor of an old wharf that had been converted into offices. They sat on a beautiful deck with unobstructed views of the harbor and boats coming into and leaving Long Wharf.

Rita ordered a glass of wine and a salad. Luca ordered a burger and a beer. "So, nana. What fantastic news today!"

"Yes. It's wonderful. A great conclusion to a special week!"

"When I first embraced you a couple of weeks ago, things were not good. I sensed something was up."

She looked at him quizzically, but knew he was usually spot on.

"And earlier today?"

"I felt your apprehension, but I didn't get a read on the underlying medical condition."

"Now?" she asked, still not fully believing the abrupt change.

He reached his hands across the table and took hers. He closed his eyes and felt her energy. "It's all clear. I keep seeing the image of a heart. It's almost as if it is dancing."

Rita chuckled. Then she said, "I know Anna isn't into this stuff, and she's been worried sick. But when Giancarlo showed up at our anniversary, I felt my heart calm down. Maybe I was picking up on things."

"I'm sure you were. You learned a lot from your Aunt Rosa – maybe you inherited her gift."

Luca retracted his hands and took a bite of his burger. He gazed out over the harbor and thought of Donato. He still had knots in his stomach, worried about him, worried about them. Was it over? Had Donato cowered in the face of his father?

Rita noticed the concern on Luca's face and said, "You know, it wasn't just Giancarlo. It was seeing you finally happy and in love that made my heart leap with joy."

"Oh, nana. That's so sweet."

"Really. I was so happy. It's not easy coming out and trusting your heart."

"But look where it got me."

"What do you mean?"

"Donato's gone radio silent, and Ben lost patience."

"I liked Ben. He seemed like a nice guy, and you had that rapport with him around magic. But your heart beat stronger for Donato, and I can see the pain."

Rita took a sip of her wine. She reached over and placed her hand on Luca's. As much as she lamented what he was going through, there was something inside of her that was calm, relaxed, even a bit giddy. She thought it an odd sensation. Why did she feel glee when he seemed so glum? She wondered if things might not work out after all.

They finished lunch and strolled to the entrance of the ferry. It was a glorious afternoon. The air was pleasant, and the sun was shining. Long shadows cast by the nearby skyscrapers cooled the busy wharf as people made their way to boats – some going to Ptown and others heading to the harbor islands, Charlestown, and various cities south of Boston. Luca glanced up at the iconic skyline and realized he hadn't spent much time in Boston. He pondered whether to send Rita back on her own. He could stay at his grandmothers' apartment on Beacon Hill and go out to a few clubs in the city.

Ben had given him an ultimatum. He liked Luca and wanted to be with him, but he didn't want to be a backup plan. Their affinity for the esoteric was compelling, and Luca had grown to like Ben and enjoy his company. But he kept seeing the 'Two of Swords' tarot card in his head, the image of two swords crossed in the hands of a blindfolded woman. He still didn't have clarity. Ben left angry, and Luca wondered if he should call him, pursue him.

As the crew opened the rope for embarkation, Luca took Rita's hand and proceeded forward. From farther back in line, he heard "*andiamo.*" He glanced back to see if there weren't some Italians boarding. Two people were bent over, wrestling with their suitcases. He turned back around and helped his grandmother navigate the ramp. Then he heard, "*piano, piano – ci penso io.*" The sound of his native language made his heart flutter. He felt a little homesick.

Once his grandmother was safely on the boat, he glanced back to see who might be speaking Italian.

His eyes widened and his heart pounded as he spotted the tall lanky body of a man dragging a couple of suitcases and holding the hand of a young woman carefully navigating the rough ramp. It was Donato and his mother. He gasped for air as his chest constricted with excitement.

Luca stood at the edge of the boat, waiting for them to approach. Suddenly, Donato looked up. He spotted Luca and froze in place. Then he said slowly and emotionally, "*Non è possibile.*"

Donato wrestled with the suitcases as Signora Bianchi placed her feet on board. She turned around to see what the commotion was and followed her son's eyes to Luca. "*Dio mio,*" she said as she recognized him.

Luca leaned forward and took Laura's hand. "Signora Bianchi. Let me help you."

"*Molto gentile,*" she replied as a curious look stretched across her face.

Donato came up behind her and approached Luca. He leaned toward him and said, "I can't believe it." He gave him a warm kiss on both cheeks.

Rita had already gone inside but noticed the exchange just outside the window. She leaped up and ran toward Luca and Donato. "*Donato! Come mai?*"

"*Signora Monte-Fitzpatrick, ti presento mia madre, Laura. Mamma, questa è la nonna di Luca, una delle due nonne.*"

"*Piacere,*" the two women said in unison.

"Come inside. Let's put your suitcases here. Have a seat," Luca invited them.

Rita gestured to a table near the windows, and everyone took seats – Donato and his mother on one side, and Luca and his grandmother on the other.

The foghorn of the ferry sounded as the boat pulled away from the wharf. It slowly navigated the busy harbor. As it reached open water, the captain sped up the motors, and the ferry raced toward Ptown.

"What happened?" Luca began, beaming at Donato.

"It's a long story. The short version is that my father is a nasty and abusive man, and I stood up to him."

"He was amazing," Laura said excitedly, beaming at her son. "I don't think we will have any more trouble from Gerardo."

Donato blushed.

"And you're here. *Come mai?*" Luca pressed.

Donato stared at Luca. His eyes were warm and tender. It was clear he was there for Luca. Then he said playfully, "My mother has never been to Cape Cod. I thought it might be fun to show her around."

"Your father?"

"Courmayeur. Alone. Presumably."

Rita grinned, then she said, "You'll stay with us, right?"

"That's very generous of you, Rita, but we reserved rooms at a small inn. We didn't want to disturb you," Laura said.

"It's not a disturbance."

"We're fine at the inn, aren't we?" Laura said to her son.

Donato and Luca looked at each other. Luca was already planning a sleepover.

"Everyone is going to be so surprised!" Rita said gleefully, resisting the temptation to text Anna in advance.

"Can I get you something to drink?" Rita asked Laura. "You must be exhausted from the trip."

"It was an easy flight. I feel light-hearted. Relieved."

Rita nodded. "Some wine or something?"

"Sure. *Vino bianco, grazie.*"

Rita glanced at Donato and Luca. Luca said, *"Lo stesso."*

Rita stood and headed toward the bar. Laura followed.

Donato faced Luca and smiled warmly. *"Ti voglio bene!"*

"Anch'io."

"What a coincidence that you were on this boat," Donato added.

"There are no coincidences!"

Donato smiled, convinced the universe was throwing them together again, a forceful message hitting them over the head. Then he said, "I want to eat you up. You look delicious!"

Luca blushed. He extended his legs toward Donato's. Donato wrapped his legs around Luca's and squeezed them. Donato extended his hand toward Luca's and held it, feeling its warmth. Luca sensed Donato's confidence, a stark contrast to what he felt just a few days before.

Laura and Rita returned with drinks. They sat by the sunny window, watching the shoreline recede. Laura felt an instant affinity for Rita, who channeled her Italian heritage with witty Italian phrases and gestures. Donato and Luca caught up on the events of the past few days.

Soon the shoreline of Cape Cod appeared. "That's the outer edge of the Cape," Rita said, pointing to the sliver of sand appearing on the horizon.

"The Atlantic is on the left side, and Massachusetts Bay on the right," Luca added.

"Donato has been telling me so much about Provincetown. Isn't your brother having an art show?"

Luca nodded and smiled at Donato. "We'll have to go. He and Taylor are so excited."

"Do you enjoy going to the beach?" Rita asked Laura.

"Yes. I grew up in Liguria, along the sea. My husband hates the beach, so we are always in the mountains on vacation. Are the beaches nice on Cape Cod?"

"Oh my God!" Rita began. "They are pristine and beautiful."

"Ma, they're not like Italy, though. No *lettini* or *ombrelloni*. They are simple but magnificent."

"Anna and I will take you," Rita said excitedly, already planning an outing to Herring Cove with food, drink, and friends.

Laura perked up.

Rita gave her a curious look and wondered if Laura might not be open to women. It was going to be an interesting week ahead.

The ferry traversed the blue water along Herring Cove and Boys Beach. Donato glanced out of the window, trying to focus his eyes on the shore. Luca reached over and turned his head back toward him playfully. Rita laughed.

The boat pulled into Ptown harbor. Oliver had driven to the wharf to pick up Rita and Luca. It was a long walk home for a seventy-five-year-old with heart problems. As he saw Luca and Rita exit the ramp, he honked his horn. He shielded his eyes and tried to focus. He thought he saw Donato.

Luca opened the hatch of the mini-SUV. Oliver thought it odd given the two of them had just gone to Boston for the day – presumably without suitcases. Oliver opened his door and stood, almost bumping into Donato. Donato stood facing him, grinned, and reached his arms around Oliver, giving him a hug. "I bet you thought you had gotten rid of me," he said playfully.

"*Ma, come mai?*"

"Unfinished business."

Oliver nodded, glancing over the car at Rita, who opened the back door for Laura. Oliver stooped and looked through the car as Laura slid into the back seat. "*Signora Bianchi. Benvenuta!*"

Oliver stood back up. Luca stared at him from the back of the car and said, "*Sorpresa!*"

"A surprise, indeed," Oliver said.

Rita slid into the passenger seat, and Luca and Donato sat behind Oliver with Laura.

"Dad, can we make a stop at the Bayberry Inn?"

Oliver just nodded. Then he said, "Can someone explain to me what just happened?"

"We picked up a couple of extra passengers in Boston."

"I see that. What's the backstory?"

"Well, Rita had a good checkup. We had lunch and then boarded the ferry, bumping into Laura and Donato on their way to Ptown."

"And Signor Bianchi?"

"In the mountains," Laura said gleefully.

Oliver shook his head as if he might be in a dream. "I take it you must have come out to your father," Oliver inquired of Donato.

"Yes."

"And more," Luca added.

"I want to hear all about it, but first, let's get you settled. Why aren't you staying with us?"

"We didn't want to disturb you," Donato said.

"It's no disturbance," Oliver noted.

"I said the same," Rita chimed in.

"Well, let's get you checked in and then we'll gather for a drink at Anna's and Rita's."

Luca stayed with Laura and Donato, helping them get checked in. Oliver brought Rita back to the house, and they prepared Francesco and Anna for the surprise. An hour later, Luca walked Laura and Donato to the house, and they gathered in the parlor for appetizers and beverages.

"So, let me get this straight," Anna began. "You stood up to your father's abuse, called him out on his hypocrisy, and came out – all within a few minutes."

Donato nodded.

"And he's not likely to seek revenge of some sort?" Giancarlo inquired, looking at Donato and Laura with concern.

"He's got too much to lose," Donato said. "We hold the trump card."

Giancarlo took a deep breath.

"And your exam showed a full reversal of heart problems?" Anna asked Rita, holding her hand.

"The doctor was baffled but delighted," she replied, nodding at Luca.

"Well, I'd love to stay for this celebratory love fest, but Taylor and I have to get to the gallery for the show," Francesco interjected.

"Oh yes," Oliver said, placing his hands on his knees and standing up. "The opening is at 6 tonight, during Gallery Stroll. Why don't we go out to eat afterwards? Perhaps to the Red Inn?"

Everyone nodded. "I'll make reservations," Giancarlo noted. "I know it's Carnival Week, but the owner owes me. I think I can get us a table. There's too much to celebrate!"

Francesco excused himself and headed into town. Laura asked her son if she could take a nap at the inn. Donato was glad to be with Luca alone. They walked her to the inn and then took a long walk along the beach. Anna and Rita retreated to their room, where Rita relayed the good news about her heart. Giancarlo called the restaurant, and Oliver listened in nearby, placing his hand affectionately on Giancarlo's shoulder.

"Well, we have a table for seven. I don't know how they did it, but we're all set," he said, as he ended the call.

Oliver looked into Giancarlo's eyes. They sparkled. "I wasn't expecting this, were you?"

"No," he said, shaking his head. "I hope Gerardo won't be vindictive."

"Sounds like his wings have been clipped," Oliver noted.

"I'm still not sure about Donato. I like him, but he's just come out. There's a lot that could unfold in the forthcoming months."

"Ultimately, we can't protect our boys from hurt and disappointment," Oliver said.

"I know, but I want to be vigilant!"

22

Chapter Twenty-Two – Magical Knots

"She's all set?" Luca asked, as Donato closed the door behind him.

Donato nodded. He had been eagerly waiting to slide into bed with Luca. It had been a long day, an emotional one. He feared he would arrive too late in Ptown, Luca snatched up by some cute local guy. He wasn't sure how his mother would take to Ptown and Luca's grandmothers, but she seemed to feel right at home and formed an instant bond with Rita. He hadn't realized how difficult it would be to tell Luca and his family about his encounter with his father. He trembled as raw emotions surfaced.

He plopped himself down on the bed and stared into Luca's eyes. He took his hands and rubbed them affectionately. "Hey handsome," he said, leaning toward Luca and giving him a moist kiss.

"*Tu sei bello!*" Luca echoed in reply. "I can't believe you're here."

Donato pushed Luca over on his back and laid his head on Luca's chest. He could hear his heartbeat and watched his chest rise and fall as he breathed. He slid his hand through an opening in his shirt and felt the warm skin underneath. It reassured him that Luca wasn't a phantom or figment of his imagination. He was there in flesh and blood.

Donato unbuttoned Luca's shirt. He slid his hand below the waist of Luca's jeans and felt him stir. Luca moaned and arched his back. He closed his eyes. Donato slid on top of him and affectionately kissed his eyes, nose, ears, and neck.

Luca could feel Donato's hardness pressed against his. He reached back and felt Donato's firm, round buttocks flexing.

Donato reached down, unbuttoned his jeans, and slid them down. Luca felt an instant charge of electricity course through him as he felt Donato's warm skin against his abdomen. He reached his hand behind Donato's head and ran his hands through Donato's thick, blond hair. He breathed in Donato's scent and leaned forward, giving him a deep, wet kiss.

Donato rose and slid his shirt and underwear off. He helped Luca remove his. In the soft ambient lighting, their bodies glistened. Donato sat on top of the blanket and spread his legs. He pulled Luca toward him and wrapped Luca's legs around his own waist. He nuzzled his erection under Luca and gazed into his eyes.

Suddenly, Luca felt himself tighten up. His chest constricted, and his heart raced. He felt himself sweat and his face become flush. He felt like he was going to faint.

Donato noticed and asked, "What's wrong?"

Luca put his hand to his head and said, "I don't know. I feel dizzy and faint."

Donato took Luca's legs and laid them on the bed. He pulled back the blankets so that Luca could lie on the sheets. He placed his head on the fluffy pillow, placed a blanket over him, and rubbed his hand over Luca's forehead. "What's the matter?"

Luca shook his head.

"Maybe it's too much excitement for one day," he suggested.

"We don't have to do this," Donato said with concern.

"Can you just lay here next to me?" Luca asked.

Donato turned Luca over and spooned him, squeezing him snugly in his arms. Donato could feel Luca's heart race. "I'm worried about you."

"I'll be okay," he said. "I love you."

"I love you, too," Donato said.

Luca closed his eyes. They both fell asleep.

Around six the next morning, Luca was startled by a noise in the inn's kitchen. Donato's arms were wrapped around his shoulders, and they were both lying next to each other under the covers.

As Luca regained consciousness and glanced around the room, he realized he had just had a dream, a disturbing one. He had been standing in the Bianchi's house in Rome. He had felt exposed, and Laura and Gerardo were laughing at him. Donato stood to the side and snickered, too.

"What the fuck?" Luca murmured to himself.

Donato stirred and caressed Luca's arm and side. "Are you up?" he asked.

"Yeah," he murmured.

"How do you feel?"

"Okay, I think. But I had a horrible dream."

Luca turned toward Donato. He kissed him and savored the feel of Donato's body pressed against his own.

"What was the dream?"

"You're going to laugh. I was at your home in Rome. Your mom and dad were staring at me. I think I must have been naked. You were snickering from the side."

"How horrible!"

"It was all very embarrassing."

"It must have been the stories I recounted last night. I'm sure they were terrifying."

"Hmm," Luca said. He closed his eyes and tried to recall more details of the dream. He clearly saw Gerardo and Laura. Gerardo didn't frighten him, but he was embarrassed about being exposed. The fact that Donato was snickering was more troubling. He couldn't imagine being embarrassed in front of Donato, so what was it?

He took a couple of deep breaths and used his imagination to glance around the room inside the dream. There was nothing out-of-the-ordinary. He decided to look at himself. He assumed he was naked and expected to see himself thusly. He closed his eyes again and used his mind's eye to look at himself. It surprised him to see he was fully clothed. But, in his right hand, he held a wand, a magic wand.

Startled, Luca opened his eyes. Donato was leaning over him, concerned. "How are you feeling?"

"Better," Luca said, lying. He didn't feel better. In fact, he started perspiring more. He realized that he was feeling vulnerable and exposed because of his magical abilities — his identity as a wizard. It was one thing to be an out gay man. It was an entirely different matter to come out as a sorcerer. The last time he did, his lover ran.

Luca sprang out of bed and went to the bathroom. He rinsed his face, brushed his teeth, and came back into the room, searching for his jeans, shirt, and undershorts. He put them on and said to Donato, "Why don't you and your mom have breakfast here? I'll check on my family, and we can meet up later."

Donato looked at Luca incredulously. Something was up, but he wasn't sure what it was. He nodded, put on his own clothes, and walked Luca to the hallway. They kissed, and Luca returned home.

He walked inside Anna's and Rita's house and saw everyone sitting at the dining table sipping coffee and eating breakfast. They all looked up and smiled.

Francesco detected Luca's under-the-surface anxiousness and got up to pour his brother a cup of coffee.

"*Ecco, un po' di café.*" Francesco gave his brother a scrutinizing look. Luca didn't say anything, still in a daze.

"What's wrong?" Francesco pressed his brother.

"*Niente,*" Luca replied.

"I know it's not nothing. What's up?"

"Nothing. It was just an emotional day yesterday. By the way, how was the reception at the gallery?"

"Good," Francesco replied. "We sold six pieces."

"Wow! Congratulations."

"So, back to you. What's up? Second thoughts about Donato?"

"No. I like him a lot."

"*E, allora?*"

Luca rubbed his hand nervously over his face. He began to hyperventilate.

"Tell me."

"I'm afraid."

"Of what?"

Luca widened his eyes, as if Francesco should know what it was. It was then that Francesco nodded. "Ah, yes. He doesn't know, does he?"

Luca shook his head no.

"He'll be okay with it."

"I don't know," Luca observed. "It took him a lot to get to this point. Now there's another whole set of issues he has to deal with."

"Give him a chance."

Luca could feel his heart race. "And what if he laughs, as he did in the dream?"

"What dream?"

"I had a dream. Everyone in his family was snickering. I had a wand in my hand."

"Change the dream."

Luca looked curiously at his brother. "You can't just change the dream."

"Why not? It's not a past event. And as something in the future, it's not cast in stone. It's being created in your imagination, so use your imagination to change it."

Luca stared at his brother incredulously.

"I have to talk with him."

"Of course you do. And he'll be understanding."

"I'm not sure."

"Change the dream. Use your imagination."

Luca took a long sip of his coffee and walked toward the dining room table. "How did things go?" Giancarlo inquired as he looked up at his son.

Before Luca could answer, Francesco interjected, "He's nervous about coming out to Donato."

"Coming out?" Anna asked, confused.

"Coming out as a wizard," Francesco clarified for everyone.

They all looked at Luca, whose head was hanging low.

"Dear, it will go well. He loves you," Rita assured him.

"I hope so."

"How are you going to tell him?" Oliver asked.

"I don't know. We've never had a conversation that even came close to the topic."

"Just be honest with him," Giancarlo remarked.

"Yeah, the last time I did that, Gino took off. I'm not sure I can deal with that again."

"Give it some time. He just arrived yesterday. Enjoy each other's company and let your relationship develop," Rita added.

Luca looked preoccupied, pacing back and forth.

"I think I need to just get it over with. Tell him straight forward. Maybe at lunch."

Francesco shook his head no. "Brother, take your time. Donato loves you, but don't overwhelm him too quickly."

"No. I think I need to tell him right away."

Francesco glanced at Oliver and Giancarlo. Both shrugged their shoulders.

Luca then said, "Nonna and nana, can you take Donato's mother out for lunch and shopping? I'll have lunch with Donato and tell him."

They both nodded. They would take care of Laura.

Luca continued to pace and then went upstairs to shower and change. He texted Donato. "Let's get together for lunch – just you and me. I'll have Rita call your mom and take her shopping in town."

Donato replied, "Good. Where?"

"The place on the water where we ate when you were here last. We'll get a quiet table. At noon?"

"*Perfetto. A dopo.*"

A couple of hours later, Rita and Anna picked Laura up for a stroll through town, and Luca walked into the restaurant and noticed Donato already seated. He approached, gave him a warm embrace and kiss, and sat down.

The server came and took their orders.

Luca was nervous, his head darting back and forth evasively. Donato kept trying to catch his eyes, hold his regard, keep his attention.

"*Che c'e?*"

"I'm still troubled by the dream?" Luca began.

"You don't have to worry about my family anymore," Donato assured him. "That's past tense."

Luca looked at Donato and nodded. He smiled. He then said, "I can't believe I'm sitting in front of you in Ptown again. It's so surreal."

Donato blushed. The light from the sun reflected off the water and illuminated Luca's face. His blue eyes glistened, and his cute, round face was endearing. Donato reached his hand across the table and caressed the side of Luca's jaw. "I like that I can be affectionate with you here."

"Hmm. Yes, it's amazing."

"And, again, my father is on a short leash. We shouldn't have any trouble with him back in Rome."

"Are you sure? He seems like he could still be a problem."

"I assure you; he wouldn't dare. He stands to lose too much. But let's talk about us."

Luca's heart skipped a beat. The idea that Donato was talking about an 'us' and a 'we' was everything he wanted to hear, but now feared he would be the one to throw a wrench into things. He looked out across the water.

Donato noticed Luca's reticence and asked, "What's wrong?"

"Nothing," Luca said, already thinking he might not have the nerve to tell Donato. "By the way, how did your internships go? Will your estrangement from your dad jeopardize jobs in the future?"

The shift of topics surprised Donato. He said with little emotion, "The summer was good. I learned a lot and made some good connections."

"What will happen when you go back to Rome? Will you stay with your parents?"

"I don't think so. I'm going to look for an apartment. It's time I have more independence."

Luca nodded. Wheels were already turning in his head about looking for an apartment with Donato. But every time he tried to imagine that in his mind, his heart fluttered, realizing he had to get over this last hurdle.

"And your mother? Will she stay with your dad?"

"I think so. They've been through worse. I think my dad will need my mother's support. He comes off like a tyrant, but he's very insecure."

"Hmm," Luca murmured, realizing how often insecure people sought to control others.

"And your dads are okay now? I'm sorry my father did what he did. It's horrible."

"They're working things out. And you don't think your dad will repeat similar things in the future?"

"He stands to lose a lot if I expose him."

"And you would do that?"

"Probably not. I'd lose a lot, too. I hope he doesn't call my bluff."

"Me, either. But your father is very influential. He could make life difficult for my father."

"He could, but for the time being, he won't."

The server brought them their meals. They raised their glasses and said, "Cheers."

Luca consumed his salad with abandon, nervous to continue the conversation and grateful for a distraction. Donato glanced up from time to time and noticed how evasive Luca's eyes were and how preoccupied he seemed.

"Are you having second thoughts?" Donato finally interjected, as he placed his fork on the table and gazed intensely at Luca.

"No, no, no," Luca exclaimed. He reached over and placed his hand on top of Donato's and rubbed it affectionately. "This is fantastic," he said, although with less emotion.

Donato sensed Luca's restraint, his hesitation, but could extract nothing from him.

They finished their meals, paid the tab, and walked through town. Luca hoped a casual walk might relax him and help him broach the topic. They passed a psychic shop, and Luca thought it might be a casual way to introduce the subject. He asked, "Should we get our cards read?"

Donato paused and glanced at the young woman sitting behind a small table surrounded by dark blue drapes. She looked up and smiled at him. Donato shook his head, as if responding to the implicit invitation of the reader. "I'm not into that," he said matter-of-factly.

"I don't know. I think there's something to it."

"Well, go ahead if you like," Donato said to Luca.

"No. That's okay. I just thought it would be fun to have someone do a reading. You know, to see if there was some destiny involved in our meeting."

Donato's heart skipped a beat. With everything that had transpired during the summer, he wondered the same. But, in practice, he didn't give credence to psychic stuff, to notions of destiny or providence. And he certainly didn't want to share his thoughts with Luca, who seemed so smart, rational, and cool. He couldn't imagine someone like Luca dabbling in the esoteric.

"I'm just enjoying our walk."

"Me, too," Luca said, now certifiably reluctant to come out to Donato.

They walked east, past the town pier and through a ramble of old shops - some that had been renovated and others a reminder of the edgier side of historic Ptown.

Luca held Donato's hand. It felt warm. He didn't like to do readings of people without their consent, but he couldn't resist his mounting curiosity. Donato was calm and confident. He was embracing his identity and embarking on his own path. Luca sensed affection and joy. He glanced over at Donato, who seemed mesmerized by the comings and goings on Commercial Street.

Luca took a deep breath and said, "It's been a big summer for you. You've come out and challenged your father."

Donato turned toward Luca and smiled. "I couldn't have done it without you."

"I was just a catalyst."

"No. You were and are so much more. Don't be frightened, but I love you so much."

"But how do you know? You haven't dated," Luca noted, testing Donato's resolve.

"What about you?" Donato replied.

Luca realized both of them were inexperienced in terms of relationships. But he knew there was another connection, one from at least a life before. Donato's question would have been a perfect segue to say something about past lives, but he held back. "I have a good feeling about you. I did from the moment I first saw you. Nothing has proven me wrong. I love you, too."

Donato's heart melted. He was happy that he had showed valor and fortitude to Luca and hoped that the hesitancy he was picking up from Luca was just Luca's concern about Donato's parents. They continued to walk east. Luca took Donato into several galleries, and they visited the one where Francesco and Taylor had shown their drawings. They retraced their steps and returned to the West End, where Rita and Anna had just come home with Laura after lunch and shopping.

Everyone gathered in the family room. Giancarlo prepared some light snacks and poured everyone a drink.

"Did you guys have a nice lunch?" Oliver asked, his eyes slightly widened to imply a deeper question.

"We did," Donato said. "Luca's such a great guide. We walked through the gallery district. By the way, Francesco, your drawings are incredible."

"Thanks," Francesco said, glancing at Luca for more elaboration.

Luca picked up on the implied question and said, "It's been

encouraging to hear about Donato's coming out. Such a big step he's taken this summer."

"We're all taking big steps," Giancarlo said, staring at Luca.

"Some are bigger than others. It's amazing what Donato has accomplished," Luca noted. He then stared back at Giancarlo and made an almost imperceptible nod no. He hoped his father read the signal and backed off his interrogation.

Luca glanced over at Francesco, who nodded. He knew Luca had not come out to Donato about being a wizard. He wanted to make Luca feel okay with himself and said, "It's been a momentous summer for everyone. And it's not over yet."

Luca took a deep breath. He needed more time.

They continued to visit, sharing more information about Ptown with Laura, who continued to be amazed at the art, history, and vibe of the village.

Around five, Francesco asked, "Is anyone going to Tea this afternoon? Taylor and I are going."

Giancarlo and Oliver looked at each other and nodded.

Donato glanced up at Luca, who took an evasive sip of his drink. He shrugged his shoulders as if to say, "What the heck?"

Anna and Rita looked at Laura. Rita placed her hand on top of Laura's hand and said, "Tea is a big gathering of people on a deck overlooking the water. Everyone is drinking, dancing, and flirting with each other."

"Sounds marvelous," Laura said, chuckling.

Luca wasn't sure she would react well to the crowd of mostly buff gay men who left little to the imagination in terms of dress and intentions. He glared at Rita.

Rita glared back defiantly. "Come, Laura. I have some things you can wear to Tea. We'll go out to dinner afterwards."

Laura smiled, giddy at her new best friend.

Luca gazed at Donato and shook his head no. Donato raised his hands in a gesture of 'nothing I can do,' and stood up. "I'll go back to the inn to change."

"I have things upstairs, if you want," Luca interjected. Donato smiled, nodded, and they both went upstairs.

"You think it's a good idea for my mother to go to Tea?" Donato began.

"She seems to be taking it all in quite enthusiastically."

"I know. But Tea? What if it is too much? That would not be good."

Luca's heart raced. Donato's remark only reminded him of the limits he felt he had to respect in Donato's capacity to face new information.

Luca found a pair of shorts and tossed them to Donato, who dropped his jeans and slid them on. "And here's a shirt for you. The color goes well with your golden tan!"

Donato blushed. He unbuttoned his shirt, took it off, and stretched the pullover over his head. Luca observed his taut chest and walked up to Donato, licking his pecs.

"Do I get to dress you?" Donato asked.

"What about undressing me?" Luca asked playfully.

Donato nodded. He grabbed the tail of Luca's shirt and pulled it over Luca's head. He ran his hands over his chest and gave him a moist kiss. "I think you need a whole new outfit — pants, too!" He unbuttoned Luca's jeans and let them drop to the floor.

Donato approached Luca and massaged his side, running his hands over the back of his buttocks. Luca loved Donato's warm touch, but he continued to be uneasy. He tensed up, and Donato noticed. He turned toward the dresser and began rummaging through Luca's clothes. He pulled out a trim pair of shorts and a tight-fitting pullover. "These will be perfect."

Luca turned red. "I can't wear those," he objected.

"Why not?"

"They are too tight," he noted.

"I want everyone to see what they're missing," Donato said, winking.

"I don't think you do."

"I totally trust you."

"I'm glad. But these aren't appropriate," Luca noted. He turned and searched for an alternative outfit, pulling out a larger pair of shorts and a loser fitting pullover. "These," he said, holding them up.

Donato stuck his lips out in a pout.

Luca stepped into the shorts and pulled on the pullover. He walked out of the door into the bathroom, freshened up, and returned to find Donato holding up a photo and staring at it.

"That was one Halloween when we came to the Cape."

"You're Harry Potter, right?"

Luca gulped and nodded.

"Cute. I don't know much about the books or the movies, but I recognize the costume."

"Do you ever dress up for Halloween?" Luca asked, hoping to steer the conversation away from Harry Potter.

"No. My parents weren't into it."

"I'll have to bring you back here for Halloween sometime. It's a blast."

Donato took hold of Luca's shoulders and gave him a scrutinizing look. "I like this outfit. You're definitely a hottie! *Andiamo?*"

"Yes. Let's go." Luca grabbed Donato's hand and led him downstairs.

Oliver and Giancarlo were standing on the front steps. Laura, Anna, and Rita were coming out of Anna's and Rita's bedroom. Laura had on a casual pair of jeans and a blouse. She looked so American. Francesco had already gone to pick up Taylor.

244 of MICHAEL HARTWIG

"*Andiamo?*" Luca said to them all, his body trembling with nervous energy.

The Boatslip was packed. It was a beautiful late afternoon in August. Sunlight reflected off the moored boats in the harbor, loud disco music was wafting from the dance area out onto the deck, and long lines formed at the bars. Laura's mouth was agape at the gathering of handsome men. Fortunately, some of Anna's and Rita's women friends were there, so they joined them.

Francesco walked in with Taylor. They pushed their way to a bar, grabbed some drinks, and then searched for the others. They found Giancarlo and Oliver staring out over the water and approached.

"Taylor," Giancarlo said as they arrived. "You're looking particularly striking today!"

Taylor blushed. Taylor wore a tight-fitting pair of jeans and a long-sleeve white Oxford shirt. Oliver chuckled to himself as the outfit reinforced Taylor's gender fluidity.

"Thank you, Giancarlo. Do you guys want to dance?" Taylor asked.

Giancarlo and Oliver looked at each other and nodded no. "Why don't you both head to the dance floor? We'll join later."

Taylor took Francesco's hand and led him toward the dance area set under the second-floor overhang of the hotel. Donato and Luca were inside, standing at the edge of the dance area, nursing drinks. Francesco and Taylor walked onto the floor and began to dance. Although the dance area was full, both stood out and garnered exceptional attention. The women were fascinated with Taylor and couldn't keep their eyes off them. The men pushed their way toward Francesco, whose curly dark hair, sensuous mouth and luscious nose had them drooling.

"They're quite the pair," Donato exclaimed, pointing to Francesco and Taylor.

"Hmm, yes. I have to say, they look really sexy together. I never thought about it before, but Francesco has a kind of androgynous look to him, too. People sometimes compared him to Donatello's 'David' in Florence. I never really bought it, but as I see the two of them together, their gender fluidity is more evident and incredibly sensual."

Donato looked at Luca with some alarm. It was one thing to come out gay. It was another to adopt gender non-conforming dress and mannerisms. He liked Luca who could easily pass as an athletic straight man. He wasn't sure he could warm up to someone who was more gender fluid.

Luca looked at Donato and nodded. "You want to dance?"

Donato set his drink down and followed Luca onto the dance floor. They were both good dancers and quickly settled into a nice flow with the music. It was warm, and Luca took off his pullover. His skin glistened with light perspiration. Donato's eyes widened with excitement. Luca was the hottest guy on the floor, and he was with him!

Luca pivoted and, to his alarm, noticed Ben dancing in the far corner of the floor. He was dancing with a friend, not a date or boyfriend. He hadn't noticed Luca yet, but Ben slowly turned, and out of the corner of his eye, noticed Luca.

Ben placed his hand on his friend's shoulder and whispered in his ear. His friend pivoted, glancing at Luca. He nodded.

Ben lost all sense of time and space. He no longer heard music. Despite the crowd, the vision of Luca was unfiltered and unmediated, an Adonis standing amongst mortals. His friend grabbed his hand and led him out onto the deck.

Luca, in turn, felt faint. All day he had worried about disclosing his identity to Donato. Now the only guy who had gotten him, someone who could probably embrace him as a wizard right away, was standing only feet away.

Donato noticed Luca's face grow pale. He whispered in his ear, "Are you okay?"

Luca nodded. But Donato sensed something wasn't right, took his hand, and led him back to the edge of the dance area where they retrieved their drinks. "What's up?"

"Nothing," Luca said emphatically. "I'm fine. Let's go get some air."

Luca led Donato to the open deck and breathed in the fresh salty air and let the gentle breeze caress his face. He didn't want to look back at the crowd of guys, fearing he would see Ben again and have to strike up a conversation.

Francesco had noticed Ben and Luca spot each other. He knew his brother had to be struggling with the juxtaposition of Ben and Donato. He grabbed Taylor, led them out onto the deck, and searched for Luca. When he found him, he walked up to him and whispered in his ear, "Ben's not the one. Donato is. You have to come out to Donato."

Luca peered into his brother's eyes. He was his little brother, but he was his guide, his muse, the one who kept him on track. He was struck by Francesco's confident and emphatic message; one he wasn't sure he shared. What if Donato wasn't the one? What if he ended up alienating and losing them both?

Luca hesitated, gave his brother an embrace, and then turned to Donato. He now realized he just had to do it. The longer he hesitated, the more daunting it would become. He blurted out, "I have an idea."

Donato peered into his eyes, not sure what to expect.

"I'm not sure I'm up for the crowd this afternoon. You just arrived, and I want to spend time alone with you."

Donato was surprised by Luca's interest in leaving. They had just arrived, and everyone was there. "But my mom and your grand-mothers are here."

"They'll be fine. They're over there with a group of friends," he said, nodding toward a cluster of women near the pool sipping drinks and laughing.

Donato noticed his mother was having a good time. He wondered if perhaps she had found her tribe and might finally break free from her abusive husband. He smiled.

Luca took Donato's hand possessively and said, "Let's take a walk and go out to dinner. Just the two of us."

Donato glanced around the deck at all the handsome men and wondered if Luca was becoming possessive and jealous. It wasn't like him, but they were in unfamiliar territory.

"Your mom will go out with my grandmothers. Francesco and Taylor are going out with Taylor's friends. My dads need some time alone. I want to be with you. Alone."

Donato nodded reluctantly. "Where?"

"I know a nice romantic place. It's right on the water."

"Okay," Donato said, still perplexed. "Let me tell my mom. Will you tell your dads?" he asked, pointing to them near one of the bars.

Donato approached his mother and explained he and Luca were going out. He glanced toward Giancarlo and Oliver, who were talking with Luca. He walked toward them, weaving his way through the crowd. Halfway across the deck, he bumped into Ben. They recognized each other, and Ben held out his hand. "I'm Ben. I think we met once."

"Yes. I'm Donato."

"You're here with Luca, right?"

Donato nodded, blushing. He picked up on Ben's prickliness, and realized that Luca had probably seen him earlier, thus their rushed departure. He scratched his chin and said, "Nice to see you again."

Ben just nodded.

Donato walked toward Luca and his dads. He took hold of his hand, and Luca could sense Donato's consternation. Luca was alarmed. He said, "Ready to go?"

"Sure. Although I'm not sure what the rush is," Donato said, knowing full well that Luca was trying to avoid Ben.

"Yeah. I know. But I need some air and quiet."

They walked outside onto Commercial Street. Luca led them to one of his favorite restaurants and asked for a table at the edge of the deck overlooking the harbor. The afternoon light reflected off the wharf and fishing boats, creating a kaleidoscope of brilliant colors. The maître d' knew him, winked, and gave him a nice, quiet, out-of-the way table. The server came, took their drink orders, and returned promptly with glasses of red wine. Luca was restless, fussing with his napkin. He raised his glass to Donato, and they both said, "Cheers."

"By the way, I saw your friend at Tea today. Ben's his name, right?"

Luca felt his legs grow weak. "Really? Sorry I missed him."

Donato detected Luca's insincerity and furrowed his brow. Luca wrung his hands. "There's something I have to tell you."

"Oh, no," Donato said. He wondered if there wasn't something going on between Luca and Ben. He then said, "You're with someone. *Cazzo.* I messed up. I came back too late, didn't I?"

"No, no, no," Luca assured him. He reached his hand across the table and took Donato's. Donato took a deep breath.

"Do you remember the day we went on the tour with my father?" Luca asked.

"How could I forget it? It was my first gay kiss, our first kiss."

"Hmm. Yes."

"I was so apprehensive," Donato said.

"Why?"

"I felt like I was being drawn into a vortex. You were so alluring. I couldn't take my eyes off you. I memorized every detail of your face and of your body. I knew then, once and for all, that I was gay."

"Any regrets?"

"Only that I wish I had met you sooner."

Luca smiled, but he continued to shake nervously.

"Do you recall anything particularly unique about the day?"

"Well, let's see. I remember the tour with your father, the ride to San Felice Circeo, the swim, the kiss, and dinner. It was all incredible."

Luca squirmed in his chair, not sure how to segue into the next topic.

"Anything special about the tour?"

Donato tilted his head quizzically. There had been something, but he had almost forgotten it. Luca's question prompted his recall. He wasn't sure he wanted to share what he had seen. It had been spooky, almost frightening.

"What about you? Is there something you're thinking about?" Donato asked, hoping to avoid having to disclose anything himself.

"Well. Yes," Luca said, nervously.

"What?"

"When we were underground, walking through the structure," he began timidly.

"Yes, it felt odd," Donato interjected, before Luca could finish. He recalled that as they had walked through the structure, it felt oddly familiar, a place he could easily picture himself inhabiting.

"How so?" Luca asked, hoping Donato might help him out.

"I don't know. It didn't seem so foreign or ancient."

"Hmm," Luca said. "Yes. If I recall, we both remarked we could see ourselves in it."

"Were you frightened when we were underground?" Luca asked. It was really a question he was asking himself.

Donato nodded no. But he sensed Luca was hinting at something he had experienced too – an odd sensation when he had glanced at his new chum during the tour. The worry and consternation on Luca's face now was obvious. Luca continued to quiver as he tried to formulate words. Donato could feel Luca's legs shaking under the table. He reached over and held Luca's hand firmly.

The stress on Luca's face was unnerving. His eyes became

increasingly sullen. Both stared at each other without saying anything. Donato could feel Luca's hands become cold, and his face lost color.

Luca's heart began to pound inside his chest. Donato continued to feel Luca's anxiousness, and his own pulse accelerated.

They continued to peer at each other. Both lost all sense of time and place. Trancelike, they both began to murmur. Both slowly formulated words, the same words, "I saw you."

Luca's eyes widened in surprise. "What?"

"Yes, I saw you. I was staring at your face in the half-light of the underground space. It was you but a different you – perhaps from another time. There were eyes in your eyes gazing at me. It was terrifying," Donato said.

"Why didn't you say something?" Luca inquired.

"It was too strange. So, you had the same experience, too? What do you think happened?"

Luca trembled. He was about to name his truth. It was more overwhelming than coming out gay. "Do you ever have odd experiences? Premonitions? Sensations? Even a sense that you are in another time and place?"

Donato nodded no. Sure, he occasionally sensed familiarity with a place or person and, from time to time, he knew something was about to happen. But he didn't think anything was remarkable. The only odd thing was seeing Luca in the excavation and the uncanny sensations he had felt around the sarcophagus.

"Any *déjà vus* or things of that sort?"

"Not really," Donato said, raising a brow. "Do you?"

Luca looked off evasively and then turned back to Donato. "I do all the time," Luca said.

Donato's eyes widened.

"Remember when we first saw each other at the Vatican Museums?" Luca asked.

Donato nodded.

"It felt as if we knew each other. It seemed as if the sarcophagus – one in particular – was familiar, right?" Luca pressed.

"Hmm," Donato murmured, unnerved by what Luca might say regarding the tomb.

"Donato. I have to tell you something. Since I was young, I have had a lot of experiences, psychic ones. I have premonitions. I imagine and visualize things, and they happen. I pick up on all sorts of things when we are strolling through Rome – historic things, as well as what people are thinking and feeling around me. To make a long story short, we discovered that I inherited a gift, or gifts. That I am connected to a grimoire, a book of magic, and am a wizard."

"A wizard?" Donato asked, his eyes wide.

Luca nodded.

"Like Harry Potter?"

"It's a little more complicated than that. But yes, like Harry Potter."

"Thus, the wand," Donato murmured.

"What wand?"

"On the sarcophagus. Jesus is holding a wand as he performs miracles."

"You noticed? When?"

"I went back to the museum the other day. I had felt such a powerful sensation there, and I wanted to make sense of it."

"And?"

"Well, you might think this is strange."

"Probably not," Luca assured him, almost chuckling.

"It was as if the images of the couple on the front of the sarcophagus were familiar. Even though I'm not a believer, after the experience of seeing you in the excavations, I asked if perhaps there was some past life connection with the marble piece. Weird, right?"

"No. Keep going," Luca said, surprised that Donato would refer to past life phenomena.

"I noticed the wand in Jesus's hand. It seemed odd. I never thought of Jesus as a magician. There was one particular image of Jesus where he is blessing and distributing loaves of bread. He's facing outward. His eyes were piercing, haunting. They were looking straight at me, into me."

"And?"

"I ran. Or, rather, I walked briskly out of the museum."

"I'm sorry. This may be too much," Luca said apologetically.

"No. I've given it more thought. I had a lot of time to think on the flight over."

Luca stared at him, inviting him to continue.

"I never really gave much thought to the notion of past lives. I had a curious encounter with a guy in Rome. You'll have to meet him. Marcello. He helped me think about my experience in front of the sarcophagus."

"Marcello?" Luca asked worriedly.

"Don't worry, he's no one important. The important thing is that maybe there is something to past life experiences. Maybe we are connected."

Luca nodded, relaxing a bit.

"I'm still not sure what it all means. I've been trying to make sense of it," Donato said.

"So, you said the image of the couple on the front of the sarcophagus seemed familiar?"

Donato nodded.

"Who?"

"I'm not sure. At first, I wondered if they were my parents. But that seemed too predictable and not that compelling."

"Who else could they be?"

Donato hesitated. He wasn't sure he wanted to say what was to follow, but he took a deep breath and blurted out, "Maybe they are your parents – Oliver and Giancarlo."

Luca furrowed his brow.

"Yes, your dads. Let me explain. When I stood in front of the sarcophagus and felt the unsettling stare of Jesus, I realized it was laden with an implicit question or invitation."

"Go on," Luca said, intrigued.

"The more I stood there and looked, the more unsettled I became. It was as if Jesus was inviting me to something I wasn't prepared to undertake or embrace. I asked myself what I was afraid of, and the immediate answer was my sexuality."

"Do you think you may have been gay in another life, in an ancient Roman one?"

"Perhaps. But I don't get the sense that was the issue – if the notion of past lives is even real."

"Go on," Luca said.

"If you think about it, Christianity was a whole new paradigm or worldview that emerged in the 3rd and 4th centuries. It became a wedge between families and friends – those who embraced it and those who clung to the Roman traditions."

Luca smiled. He realized where Donato was going. He nodded for him to continue.

"If there is such a thing as past lives, then what if you and I were separated by the new religion? I'm not sure which side each of us was on, but we could have been friends or lovers – perhaps two male lovers or a man and a woman. Regardless, one of us, probably me, was reluctant to embrace the new religion, and we lost each other."

Luca could feel sadness in his heart as Donato shared his theory.

"The eyes of Jesus looking at me in the museum seemed alive. I felt as if I was being invited again to embrace something new. But I'm already a Christian. The fact that Jesus is holding a wand seemed peculiar to me. I've been trying to make sense of it for days."

254 ~ MICHAEL HARTWIG

"I'm sorry to add to your stress. This must be bizarre."

"What you've just shared with me makes sense, and oddly, puts me at ease."

"How?"

"You and your family represent a whole new paradigm for society, one that is more inclusive of sexual diversity and gender diversity. I know I am being invited to embrace that in myself and claim it proudly, even in the face of condemnation from my father."

"You've taken some amazing steps!"

"If the idea of past lives is true, then we must have been separated in a past life over my inability to embrace a new paradigm."

Luca nodded pensively.

"Over the past couple of weeks, I have had an odd sensation of sadness. When I am with you, I am inspired, but I also feel sadness, as if I let you down. I'm sure some of it stems from the realization that I have let my father come between us, and I lament that. But now I sense the sadness comes from another time and place."

"You're quickly becoming a very intriguing man, Donato!" Luca said, his eyes glistening with excitement.

Donato blushed. "Maybe a deeper healing needs to take place, and if it means embracing you as a wizard, I am willing to do it. I don't want to lose you again." Donato paused, chuckled, and then continued, "I can't believe I'm saying that."

Luca's eyes turned red. Tears streaked down his cheek. He had always imagined sitting across from a lover and talking about being gay and what that might mean in terms of family life. Never in his wildest imagination did he visualize a hot sexy guy sitting across from him and casually using the word wizard in reference to him. He realized he had probably internalized shame about his identity, and this was a defining moment of self-love. He gazed into Donato's alluring hazel-green eyes, and his heart melted.

Luca said, "You don't know how reassuring that is."

"I thought it was difficult coming out as gay, but I can't imagine what you've had to deal with if you are both gay and a wizard."

"Since I grew up in a gay family and I came to learn of my magical abilities early in life, I never thought about it. But now that I am older and looking for someone to share life with, the identities are scarier and fraught with peril."

"So, what's it like?"

"Being a wizard?"

Donato nodded.

"Well, I hide a broom in my closet and sneak down to the basement for demonic rituals," Luca said with as straight a face as possible.

Donato's eyes widened in disbelief.

Luca broke out laughing. "*Scherzo*! Kidding!"

Donato took a deep breath, and his shoulders relaxed.

"In all seriousness, the images of Jesus using a wand on the sarcophagi are terribly reassuring. I've studied this, so excuse the academic mini lecture to follow. I believe Jesus came to help us tap into the divine side of our humanity. Jesus wasn't human and divine in an exceptional way. He was human and divine in an exemplary way. He came to teach us what it is like to have a divine side to us. We all have it."

Donato held his hand up to his mouth in a fake yawn and chuckled.

Luca stared him down and continued, "If you think about it, God imagined the world into being. Imagination is basically what magic is all about. It is creation. We have a thought or image in our mind, and we seek to manifest it or realize it in the world. The world is the place where our imagination takes shape and form. That's all magic is. And if God created us in God's image and likeness, then why isn't imagination or magic one of the fundamental gifts of human nature, of our godlikeness?"

"That makes sense. In fact, that doesn't seem so odd."

"In one sense, it's not. We are all witches and wizards – sorcerers. Spells and incantations are just ways we take imagination and give it emotional support. If I visualize or imagine something and trust that it will come to be, it will. Jesus said, if you have faith, you can move mountains. Faith is another way of referring to imagination and belief in intentions."

"So why is magic shamed and marginalized?" Donato asked.

"Gender and power," Luca said without hesitation or elaboration. Donato furrowed his brow.

"Women have learned to be intuitive and resourceful. Their bodies have subtle changes each month, and they have learned to trust their intuition. They also have had to be resourceful since they were usually excluded from the spheres of economic and political power. The shaming of sorcery or magic was basically about controlling women and monopolizing spiritual power in organized religion."

"My dad's going to love this!" Donato said.

"Hmm, yes," Luca said with concern.

"So, your dads and brother?" Donato asked.

"We're a small coven," Luca said, chuckling. He took a breath and continued, "In all seriousness, they've struggled with this as much as I. We've all learned to be more intuitive. And while we believe everyone can tap into spiritual and magical abilities, I seem to be particularly gifted. Perhaps it's something one learns and perfects over many lives."

Donato glanced off into the distance. Luca noticed concern on his face. He asked, "Is this too much?"

Donato turned back to Luca and stared into his eyes. "I'm nervous, apprehensive, and afraid. But I'm not sure if it is about magic or about love."

Luca reached over and took Donato's hand. He rubbed the inside of his palm and felt warmth. "Aren't they the same?" Luca proposed thoughtfully.

Donato returned a quizzical look.

"In both, we are expressing our soul. We are reaching into the deepest parts of ourselves and casting something out into the world – our hearts, our dreams, our hopes. We wrap them with excitement and optimism. Then we wait for them to become manifest, to become real."

Donato furrowed his brow, as if confused.

"Love and magic aren't certain. We can't force someone to love us. Nor can any spell guarantee a magical outcome. Love is vulnerable. Magic is vulnerable."

"But if you are a wizard, aren't you able to make things happen?"

"Yes, and no. If you have a powerful imagination and trust your vision, things will happen. But the universe comprises many complex and competing forces. Ultimately, magic requires a strong and clear intention and a commitment to what you want. But there's a level of vulnerability in magic, as we never know how our intentions will unfold."

"Like love?" Donato asked pensively.

"Yes, like love," Luca murmured.

"So, did you cast a spell on me?" Donato asked half-jokingly, half-seriously.

"I think it was the other way around," Luca said, peering into Donato's seductive eyes.

Their server returned and took dinner orders. Both Donato and Luca had lost all sense of place and time over the course of their conversation. Luca was relieved to have come out to Donato, but still wanted more confirmation. When the server left the table, Luca asked, "So, this doesn't freak you out too much?"

Donato nodded no. He rubbed the top of Luca's hands, nestled in his. "For the past several weeks, my heart has been restless, and my stomach tied in knots. For the first time in a while, I feel calm. I feel like I'm in the right place and with the right person."

Luca felt his pulse race with excitement.

Donato continued, "Actually, it's kind of cool - you being a wizard and all. It doesn't frighten me. How many people can say their boyfriend is a wizard?"

"Not many."

"How do I introduce you?"

"Merlin, my boyfriend," Luca said, chuckling.

Donato stared at him and smiled warmly.

Luca added, "You don't know how relieved I am."

"Will you teach me?" Donato inquired in a low but thought-ful voice.

"About what? Magic?"

"About love and magic."

"Why don't we teach each other?" Luca suggested.

"That sounds like a wonderful plan."

Luca gazed into Donato's hazel eyes and felt warmth and joy. He turned slightly and glanced out over the harbor where the bright August sun glistened on the water. He had contemplated the same setting countless times before as a young boy and, later, as a teenager. There were luminous threads dancing about in his head – threads that tied Boston and Provincetown and Rome. He felt ribbons of love swirling about his grandmothers, his fathers, his brother, and his *madrina*, people who had blazed trails before him and supported his own unique journey. He smiled as he thought of his old mentor, Etienne, who bequeathed him the grimoire, and Rahel, who helped him decode it. He sensed he was the beneficiary of a rich legacy, one that had been carefully guarded and passed on from one generation to the next.

As he felt Donato's hand in his, he realized he was connecting with another thread, one that was both familiar and novel. As much as he was skeptical of the term soul mates, he realized he and Donato resonated with each other on a deep level, that they had been connected before, and were now being given an opportunity to embark on new adventures together. He felt that his heart had found its companion and that together they would learn much.

A gentle breeze blew across the deck, and Luca breathed in the salty air. He gazed at the waves lapping against the yellow sand, bright and hot in the fiery afternoon sun. Countless times before, he had recited spells that evoked the four elements of air, water, earth, and fire. At this moment, he realized how they had all come together in such an unexpected and enchanting way.

Magic is real. It is but imagination cast in the world, a place where fundamental elements are shaped by hope and love. On the edge of the Atlantic, far from Rome, Luca and Donato marveled at how diverse worlds had been bridged and joined. The physical horizon that stretched out before them was but a mere representation of the horizon each felt within, both ready to love deeply and dream boldly.

The End

RO1235

Author

Michael Hartwig is a Boston and Provincetown-based author of LGBTQ fiction. Hartwig is an accomplished professor of religion and ethics as well as an established artist. His original oil paintings are represented by On Center Gallery in Provincetown.

Hartwig grew up in Dallas but spread his wings early on – living in Rome for five years, moving to New England later, and then working in the area of educational travel to the Middle East and Europe. His fiction weaves together his interest in LGBTQ studies, ethics, religion, art, languages, and travel. The books are set in international settings. They include rich local descriptions and are peppered with the local language. Characters grapple not only with their own gender and sexuality but with prevailing paradigms of sexuality and family in the world around them. Hartwig has a facility for fast-paced plots that transport readers to other worlds. They are romantic and steamy as well as thoughtful and engaging. Hartwig imagines rich characters who are at crossroads in their lives. In many instances, these crossroads mirror cultural ones. There's plenty of sexual tension to keep readers on the edge of their seats, but the stories are enriched by broader considerations – historical, cultural, and philosophical.

For more information on other books and those forthcoming, visit: www.michaelhartwigauthor.com

CPSIA information can be obtained
at www.ICGtesting.com
Printed in the USA
BVHW031808161222
654416BV00015B/323